LOVE YOU S'MORE

BOOK THREE OF THE CAMPFIRE SERIES

BETH MERLIN

FIREFLY HILL PRESS

Printed in the United States of America

Firefly Hill Press, LLC
4387 W. Swamp Rd #565
Doylestown, PA 18902
www.fireflyhillpress.com
info@fireflyhillpress.com

Print ISBN: 9781945495038
E-Book ISBN: 9781943858156

BOOKS IN THE CAMPFIRE SERIES

For M & H

CHAPTER ONE

D amn the United Kingdom and their bloody roundabouts! They were everywhere on almost every major road. I'd lived in England almost four months and still wasn't sure how to navigate them. It was even harder in the dark. During the day you could at least make eye contact with the other drivers and motion them to go ahead or wait their turn. At night, you were pretty much flying blind.

I let car after car go ahead of me and waited for a break in the traffic. Finally, when I saw one, I closed my eyes and gunned it. I made it all the way around and then turned off at the sign for Badgley Hall. I switched on my brights and steered off to the small cobblestone road that wound through miles of unspoiled woodlands eventually leading up to the house.

I'd made this same drive hundreds of times but still felt awestruck every time I pulled up to the front gates of the estate. Although Gideon insisted Badgley Hall was my home now too, I wasn't sure I would ever feel completely comfortable in such grandeur. Gideon came down the steps to greet me as I parked the car.

He glanced down at his watch. "Let me guess, you got stuck at the roundabout again?"

"I know those things are supposed to help with traffic flow, but, if you ask me, they just slow things down."

"That's because you let everyone go ahead of you."

"I like to make sure the coast is clear."

He shook his head with a chuckle. "We'll practice again this weekend. Are you hungry?"

"A little. I didn't have time to grab anything before class."

"How was it tonight?"

I shrugged my shoulders. "Better. Less whispering."

His eyes widened. "Well, that's something, right?"

You had to hand it to Gideon, always the optimist. I hadn't graced the covers of any tabloid magazines in the last several weeks, but that didn't mean people didn't still recognize me as the woman caught "cheating" with Perry Gillman the night of the royal wedding. The story was so big and so sensational, sometimes it felt like the whole world knew who I was. The students in the design class I was teaching at Gloucestershire University certainly did. They spent most of my first lecture whispering and passing notes about me.

"I still feel like a fraud. I've had no formal training, and I'm teaching a class on the fundamentals of construction? What's that expression? Those who can, do. And those who can't, teach?"

Gideon kissed me on the forehead. "Sweetheart, you can do *and* you can teach. Besides, you're just filling in for a few weeks, right?" Gideon took my bag off my shoulder, carried it into the house, and set it down on the floor of the entryway.

I turned toward the kitchen, and then looked back at Gideon. "I'm gonna go make myself a sandwich or something. Do you want anything?"

"I have a surprise for you first. Come with me but keep your coat on." He took me by the hand.

I peeked around the corner. "My mother's not here, is she?"

"Nobody's here," Gideon said, laughing.

I followed him up several flights of stairs and into one of the bedrooms off the East Wing.

"Did you just find out that Mary Queen of Scots or a Habsburg once slept in here or something?"

Lately, Gideon had become almost obsessed with finding out new historical facts about Badgley Hall that could be included as part of the tour, making the estate even more of a tourist attraction. So far, the house historians unearthed that not only had Henry VIII and Anne Boleyn spent one of their honeymoon nights at Badgley Hall, but so had Queen Victoria and Prince Albert. Gideon was thrilled at the discovery. His new angle was to market Badgley Hall as a lovers' destination.

He shook his head and reached up to a rope tucked into the ceiling. He pulled it down along with a set of stairs.

I reached around him to get a better look. "Where do those lead?"

"Follow me and find out," he said.

He went first, leading the way, and I followed closely behind him. The stairs opened into an attic that was almost the entire length of the house. It was a massive space filled with everything from furniture to artwork.

I was amazed by the sheer number of artifacts.

"Antique Roadshow would have a field day up here. What *is* all this?" I asked.

"Believe it or not, every single thing up here is cataloged and accounted for by the house historians," Gideon answered.

"I believe it. It's incredible. Is this the surprise?"

"Not the surprise. Keep following me."

I followed Gideon deeper into the attic, until we came to a much smaller set of stairs leading to a door. Gideon motioned for me to go first.

"Hmm... curiouser and curiouser." I walked up the staircase and pushed open the door.

I turned back around to Gideon. "The roof?"

He nodded, rushed past me through the door, and held his arms wide open. "Welcome to my favorite spot in all of Badgley Hall."

Gideon had set up an elaborate picnic under the stars, complete with two portable space heaters. I did a full turn around in my spot. "What's all this?"

"I wanted to do something special to celebrate your new job and just how happy you being here these last few months has made me."

He walked over, pulled out a bottle of champagne, and popped it open. He handed me a flute and poured us each a glass.

"To us," he said.

"To us," I repeated, clinking my glass to his.

He motioned for me to sit on the carefully laid out blanket and passed over a tray of small hors d'oeuvres. I reached for a stuffed mushroom cap and placed it on my plate.

"This is beyond thoughtful, thank you." I leaned in and gave him a kiss.

Gideon served himself some starters and propped back on his elbows. "Perfect night for stargazing. Cold but clear."

I popped the mushroom cap into my mouth and stood up to get a better look at the view. I walked to the edge of the roof and Gideon came up behind me.

He took my arm and pointed it into the distance. "You see that spot right there, between the hedge maze and the stream? That flat piece of land? I thought that would be a perfect spot to put a tent up for our wedding reception."

I turned around to face him.

"Unless you want to get married at your parents' house in the Hamptons or a hotel in New York City. We don't have to have it here. I just always thought it'd be a really special place for a wedding. And now that we know Victoria and Albert spent a honeymoon night here... "

"It is a special place. A fairy tale, really," I answered.

He narrowed his eyes. "But?"

"There's no but. I'm just not sure what I want yet."

"It's been four months since I proposed, Gigi. At some point, we need to make a decision. I was thinking we could do it here this summer, but we'd need to give your side of the family and friends some proper notice, so they could make their plans."

"What friends?" I asked, looking down.

Gideon tilted my chin up. "Jamie will come around."

"Well, what about your parents?"

"I don't know how many times I have to tell you that my father likes you very much, and my mother... well, she'll come to love you as much as I do, once she gets to know you a bit better."

"She barely acknowledges I exist, let alone that I live in her house."

"She's very friendly with Margaret Ellicott. They went to Mayfield together. I suppose she's holding a grudge on her behalf. But, she'll have to accept you when you're my wife and next in line for her title."

I shook my head. "The Countess of Harronsby. I can't imagine ever getting used to that."

"You'd be surprised. Anyway, your personal stationary can say whatever you want. The title's more for the Register and newspapers anyway."

The newspapers. The last thing I wanted was my name back in the press. Over the last few months, I'd had to deal with headline after headline about me and my alleged secret relationship with Perry Gillman. Every time I thought they couldn't possibly come up with another angle for the story, the tabloids managed to dig up one more person to interview.

I wasn't at all surprised when Alicia told me about the exclusive interview in *US Weekly* with Tara Mann, my former Chinooka CIT, where she dished any gossip she could remember from when Perry and I were Head Counselors together. I wondered if they paid her for the story, or if the notoriety and fifteen minutes of fame was enough of an incentive to get her to talk.

South Gloucestershire provided some insulation from the rest of the world, but not much. All I had to do was take a quick scroll through Twitter or walk through the aisles of the local market to see I was still the subject of speculation and innuendo. But, Gideon had stuck by my side through all of it, even if at times it'd resulted in his own name being dragged through the mud along with mine.

Last month, there was a preposterous article in *The Sun* purporting that back when we were counselors at Camp Chinooka, Perry and I'd hatched a plan to infiltrate the upper crust of British society. The story suggested we each had purposefully sought out well-to-do members of the aristocracy for different gains, while still secretly dating each other. That particular article stuck with me because of the incredibly unflattering picture of Gideon they published along with the story. When I reluctantly showed it to him, he simply laughed and tossed it into our bedroom fireplace. He loved me. I didn't have to question it or doubt it. All I had to do was accept it and agree to set a date.

I turned back around to face him. "Show me again where you'd want to set up the tent."

He pointed out to the field. "Right there, just past the hedge maze."

I leaned over the railing. "I always thought that small clearing there would make a better spot for a wedding reception. It gives you the best views of the property, the house, and the gardens."

His eyes brightened. "Yes, that spot would be perfect. What do you say? May? June?"

"How about July? Maybe over July 4th? It may kill my mother

not to be able to throw her annual Independence Day shindig, but I think she'll understand it gives my side the benefit of a few extra days off to travel. Plus, we know the weather should cooperate that time of year."

Gideon took out his phone and scrolled through the calendar. "July 4th is a Thursday this year, so that's perfect. We can start the wedding events that day and carry them through the weekend." He leaned over and whispered in my ear, "Hey, Georgica, am I crazy or did we just set a wedding date?"

I threw my arms around his neck. "Not crazy. Not crazy at all."

CHAPTER TWO

The next morning, I grabbed a cup of coffee and hurried out to the gift shop before anyone else was up. Other than asking me to pass the milk or sugar, Gideon's mother barely ever spoke more than two words to me over breakfast. Gideon's father and I exchanged normal pleasantries, but not much more than that. After several awkward attempts at conversation, I realized it was far simpler to snatch a scone from the pantry and avoid the encounter altogether. This morning, I told Gideon I had to take inventory before some new shipments arrived. He kissed me, rolled over, and mumbled something about seeing me around lunchtime.

When I first agreed to move to Badgley Hall, I assumed I'd continue designing, just from there instead of our New York studio. Jamie wasn't speaking to me, but I was certain it would blow over, and in short order, G. Malone would be back on track. In the weeks and months leading up to the royal wedding, more and more investors were coming to the table, ready and eager to help our brand go public. But, following the story that claimed Perry and I had been involved in an ongoing affair right under the royal family's nose, most of those same investors pulled their support. As Jordana once warned me, "Nobody wants to get in bed with a scandal."

Right now, G. Malone was on life support. Jordana and the few investors left in play felt it'd be best if I took a step back for the time being and let her and Jamie see if they could resuscitate our business. For all intents and purposes, I was on the outs.

I spent my first and most of the second month at Badgley Hall in a daze and the third month exploring life on an old English estate, trying to familiarize myself with the home's history and importance to the village. By the fourth month, I was itching for any way to make myself useful and stumbled into the property's gift shop.

The Badgley Hall gift shop was located in a small, converted cottage where the land agent once lived. It was quaint and charming, filled with local teas and books about the house's history, but all in all, not a huge moneymaker for the estate. Gideon told me the same local woman from South Gloucestershire had been running the gift shop for as long as he could remember, and before she retired, his parents had left all the decisions about ordering and inventory to her. After looking over the financials, I asked if he'd be willing to give me a shot at managing the store and changing around some of the merchandise. At this point, he was in favor of anything that might turn the shop around so that it was operating in the green. He gave me free rein to do whatever I thought might breathe some new life into the store.

I started by going to some of my favorite spots, The Old Spitsfield Market and Portobello Road, and convincing some vendors to allow me to carry a few of their one-of-a-kind accessories and handbags. Then, I reached out to some local designers I'd been keeping an eye on and made an exclusive deal to sell some of their pieces out of our store. I mixed in some estate-related merchandise, like canvas totes and tea sets carrying the newly updated and much more modern Badgley Hall logo, and got rid of the items that looked like they'd been sitting there since the 1970s.

Within a few weeks, the gift shop turned the first profit the shop had seen in years. I made some other changes, and over the last few months, the store became a destination in its own right, even earning a write-up in some prominent travel and fashion magazines. Tourists and locals were coming in droves to check out the unique merchandise and have lunch or tea in the ultra-chic teahouse I redesigned in the property's carriage house.

I fell into an easy routine, running the store and teahouse during the day and teaching a design class two nights a week. There were some days it was hard to even remember my life before Badgley Hall. But then, there were the other days, when a visitor would recognize me from the wedding scandal, and suddenly, all my accomplishments would be summed up by one single, regrettable moment with Perry Gillman.

Perry tried to reach out to me after the news broke, but I didn't take his calls. If this story was ever going to die, I needed to put as much distance between us as possible. Besides, he was off in New York being lauded by critics and audiences alike. His concerns that *Elizabeth* wouldn't resonate with American theatergoers were for naught. The show was an unparalleled success and sold out for at least the next year and a half, the length of Perry's contract. Getting a ticket was virtually impossible, and hundreds of fans were showing up hours before the show in the hope they might win one of the twenty seats raffled off via lottery every night.

From the little I'd heard, Perry and Annabelle reconciled for a few months following the wedding, but finally called it quits when he moved to New York. His success and notoriety pushed his fame into the outer stratosphere, and it seemed he was being linked to a different starlet each week. At this point, I knew better than to believe everything I read, but even still, there was no denying Perry Gillman was just as hot a commodity as a ticket to see *Elizabeth.*

Gideon knocked softly on the gift shop door. I finished hanging up a dress, handed it to a customer in the dressing room, and went to greet him. I glanced down at my watch.

"Lunchtime already?"

"Not quite, just passing through on my way into town to pick up a few things for later and wanted to check to see if there was anything special Alicia asked for?"

I shook my head. "She said she's bringing everything she needs for Sloan."

"You must be excited to see her?"

"I am. It'll be nice to have a friend here."

Gideon bent down and kissed me on my forehead. "I'm your friend—you know that, right?"

"You're my lover *and* employer. Actually, is there someone I should speak to in HR about that? It feels like a conflict of interest."

"Unfortunately, that's me also."

"Ahh, I see," I said, leaning into his chest. "Are we ready for this weekend?"

"As ready as we'll ever be," he answered.

For the last several months, Gideon had been readying Badgley Hall to host large events like weddings or parties. It was the way many of these old country estates managed to turn a profit and stay operational. This weekend, Gideon had invited friends and family to come for a trial run of his new business endeavor. He wanted to ensure everything was running smoothly when he opened the house up to the public in a few weeks.

He encouraged me to ask friends from back home to join us, so I asked Alicia if she wanted to come with Asher and Sloan. I was thrilled when she accepted my invitation and had looked forward to her visit for weeks.

"I have a car picking them up from the airport later," he said. "And I set them up with a suite in the East Wing."

"I thought the East Wing was haunted?"

"Nah, it's just a line we use for guests that have overstayed their welcome."

I shook my head. "I still have so much to learn."

I sat on the front steps and waited for Alicia's car to come down the long, winding road to the house. When I finally spied the black Escalade appear through the clearing, I ran down to greet it. Once they pulled up, Alicia opened the door, lifted Sloan out of the car, and set her on the driveway. A tiny, blonde mini version of Alicia bounded over to me. I picked her up off the ground.

"She couldn't possibly remember me," I said, walking toward the car with Sloan in my arms.

"After an eight-hour flight and another two and a half hours in the car, I think she's excited to see anyone other than me and her dad. Besides, I kept telling her we were going to visit Mommy's friend—the one who sends her all the good presents."

"She's in luck. I have a few more inside," I said, passing Sloan back to Alicia.

"You're too much. Speaking of too much, was that a moat we crossed?" she asked, looking back toward the bridge.

I nodded my head as Asher made his way around the car to greet me.

"Tell me, where *does* Gideon keep all the dragons?" he asked.

"Don't tell me you're obsessed with *Game of Thrones* too?" I asked.

"We both are. Asher even read all the books," Alicia answered.

I shook my head. "So did Gideon."

Gideon came down the front steps to greet our guests. "What'd I do?"

"Read all the *Game of Thrones* books," I answered.

"Ahh, yes, guilty as charged but well worth the effort." Gideon extended his hand to Asher's. "Nice to see you again, mate."

Gideon met Alicia and Asher several months ago, when we all had dinner together in New York. As expected, Gideon got a big thumbs-up from them both. Alicia thought Gideon's easy, sweet nature was a good complement to my personality, and unsurprisingly, Gideon and Asher hit it off like gangbusters. Asher ran his family's real estate holding firm and found a lot of parallels between his role and some of Gideon's responsibilities at Badgley Hall. They talked nonstop through dinner, and Gideon often emailed or called Asher when he was looking for some business advice.

"Most of the staff doesn't arrive until tomorrow, so we may have to make more than one trip," Gideon said, picking up a few pieces of luggage.

Asher handed Alicia the diaper bag. "Why don't you head inside with Gigi and get Sloan settled? I'll bring in the rest of the bags with Gideon."

I took the bag from her shoulder and motioned for her to follow me up the front stairs. I pushed open the dark oak doors with the large bronze lion door knockers and led her into the foyer. She stopped in her tracks and stared straight up at the glass dome.

"Holy shit, Gigi, this isn't a house, it's a museum."

"The first time I came here, Gideon told me not to freak out, that the house gets less impressive the farther in you go. That's not true, though. The whole place is pretty spectacular."

Alicia shook her head in amazement and followed me up the stairs toward the East Wing. As we walked, I pointed out some of the house's artifacts and art work. Alicia fired off questions like she was on a tour of one of the galleries at the Metropolitan Museum of Art. I did my best to answer but told her one of the house docents could likely provide better insight. Gideon asked a few to be around over the weekend, to provide the guests with a better experience.

We turned a corner and came to the end of the long hallway and the set of rooms Gideon readied for Alicia's visit. Alicia put Sloan down and let her walk into the bedroom first.

I opened up the light blue taffeta drapes to let some sun into the room. "Gideon thought you'd be the most comfortable here. All the bathrooms have been updated, and I thought the adjoining sitting room would be perfect for Sloan's Pack 'n Play."

Alicia placed her bags down on the canopy bed. "It's a beautiful room. Probably too nice for us these days. I'll try to keep Sloan from destroying anything extremely valuable."

"I baby-proofed earlier and moved the Fabergé eggs and Vermeers down to the library."

"Seriously?"

"No," I said with a laugh. "Don't worry, anything super valuable has a velvet rope in front of it. Everything in here is fair game." I opened up the dresser. "There's even a Smart TV if Asher wants to watch some *Game of Thrones* on HBO on Demand."

Alicia sat down on the edge of the bed. "So it's really been converted from a house to a hotel, then? Does that bother Gideon?"

"Not Gideon. He's excited about all the changes. I think it's harder on his parents. Definitely his mother. But I understand her feelings. This is her home. Of course, she'd feel protective of it."

Asher walked in carrying some of the luggage, followed by Gideon, who was dragging in the rest.

"So, what's on the agenda for this evening?" Alicia asked.

"My parents offered to keep an eye on Sloan so we can go into town for dinner," Gideon said.

"We couldn't possibly take them up on that," Alicia protested.

"Of course you can. They've been looking forward to it all week," Gideon answered.

Asher crossed the room to Alicia. "Sweetheart, Sloan's exhausted from traveling. She'll be fast asleep before we even leave."

Alicia glanced over to where Sloan was playing with her new baby doll. "If you're really sure they won't mind?"

"They won't mind. Mum in particular is salivating at the idea of becoming a grandmother. She'll take a baby any way she can get one," Gideon said glancing over at me.

I shifted uncomfortably. It's not that I didn't want children. I did, very much. But, I was beginning to get the feeling Amelia and George would be expecting an heir to the family title much sooner than later.

"It's settled then. The Earl and Countess of Harronsby will watch the little princess, and we'll go out on the town," Asher said.

"It's South Gloucestershire—you may want to temper your expectations," Gideon joked.

We left Alicia and Asher so they could get ready and retreated to our suite of rooms to do the same.

Gideon stepped out of the shower while I finished applying the last of my makeup. He towel-dried his hair and sat down on the corner of my vanity.

"It's nice to have people staying in the house again and that Sloan, what a doll."

I leaned forward for some better light. Badgley Hall was very beautiful but also very dark.

"What'd Alicia say when you told her we set a date for the wedding?" he asked.

I swung around to face Gideon. "I haven't told her yet."

He averted his eyes to the ground. "Any reason?"

"I just haven't had the opportunity." I stood up and dabbed on some perfume. "I'll tell her tomorrow, or we can do it together tonight, if you prefer?"

"I just want to make sure you haven't changed your mind."

"The only thing I've changed my mind about is going into town tonight. The last time we went to the pub, it felt like everyone in the place was talking about us."

"That was right after the wedding story broke. Tonight, we'll just be two couples getting pissed at a bar."

"I hope so."

Gideon handed me my coat. "I know so."

CHAPTER THREE

I rolled over and ran my hand over the empty side of the bed, lifted my head, and looked at the clock. Jumping up, I grabbed my pajama pants and balled-up T-shirt from off the floor and hurried downstairs. Alicia, Asher, Gideon, and Sloan were already dressed and seated around the table, having breakfast with Gideon's parents.

Gideon's father lifted his head up from the morning paper. "Morning, Georgica. We left a chair open for you."

Amelia barely glanced up from her half of a grapefruit.

I slid into the seat next to Gideon, unfolded the napkin into my lap, and whispered to him, "Why didn't you wake me up?"

"I tried. You were out cold and snoring like a drunken sailor." He passed me the pot of coffee.

Alicia was freshly showered, wearing the perfect Ralph Lauren maroon blazer, crisp white button-down, and dark jeans. She'd even taken the time to curl her hair. I fastened the top two buttons of my pajamas. "What time did you guys get up this morning?"

"Sloan woke us around 5:00. Probably the jet lag. Asher went for a run while I unpacked," she said.

"The property is massive. I ran a couple of miles and don't think I hit the end," Asher said.

"I'll give you a proper tour today," Gideon chimed in. Gideon's mother turned to Alicia. "If you want to go with them, I don't mind keeping an eye on Sloan again. She was an absolute angel. I'll take her down to the stables to feed the horses. She'll love that. We even have a new pony, Napoleon Cheshire."

My head shot up. "Napoleon Cheshire?"

Gideon turned and winked at me. "Mum let me name him." He leaned into me and whispered, "I couldn't resist."

Alicia refilled her coffee cup. "I couldn't impose, Amelia."

Gideon's mother smiled warmly. "It's no imposition."

"We have to be back at the house in the early afternoon to greet the weekend guests, so we won't be gone long anyway," Gideon added.

Alicia thanked Gideon's mother and passed me the tray of croissants and muffins. I scanned the table for something greasier. A baked good wasn't going to do a thing to help my pounding headache. Tomorrow, Gideon would be serving our guests a traditional English breakfast of sausages, bacon, black pudding, fried spam, cooked tomatoes, beans, and hash browns. This morning, the kitchen kept it simple. I'd have to make do with ibuprofen and sunglasses to combat my massive hangover.

"I'd love to see the yew hedge maze and Gigi's store," Alicia said.

"Absolutely. Let's split up. Gigi, you can take Alicia on a tour, and I'll show Asher around," Gideon said.

"Gigi might want a few minutes to freshen up first," Gideon's mother said between sips of tea.

I leaned toward Gideon. "I don't know why I've been worried about your mom meeting mine when they have *so* much in common."

He practically spat out his tea.

After breakfast ended, I excused myself and headed back upstairs to get ready. Gideon followed closely behind.

"Alicia can tag along with me and Asher, if you want to take it easy today," he said.

"I'm fine. Nothing a few gallons of water and some Advil can't fix."

Gideon reached for my shoulder, and I came down two steps to meet him. He brushed my cheek with his hand. "You can't keep letting complete strangers get to you like that," he said.

I tilted my head to the side. "You were at the pub. You saw that table of women pointing and whispering about us."

He took my hands into his own. "Did it ever occur to you they were pointing and whispering because you and Alicia just happened to be seated next to the two best-looking gents in the place?"

I softened my stance. "I'm sorry, Gid. I shouldn't have had so much to drink."

"You don't have to apologize to me. Now, that woman you flipped off on your way to the loo, *she* might be looking for an apology."

"I flipped off a woman on my way to the bathroom? Great, I can already see the headline in tomorrow's tabloids, *The Future Countess of Harronsby Comes Unhinged.*"

"You didn't come unhinged. Well, not completely anyway."

I leaned down and kissed him on the cheek. "I'll try to do better."

"That's all I ask."

Gideon and Asher took off for the stables, while Alicia and I made our way over to the gift shop and teahouse. Fiona and Sally, two local girls I'd recently hired as sales clerks, were inside restocking shelves and tidying up the merchandise. I introduced them to Alicia, who was already distracted by the hand-studded, bright-colored leather handbags on display on the front table of the store. She picked two bags off the table and modeled each one against her side in front of the mirror.

"I think I need at least one in each color. These are fantastic," she said.

"Aren't they incredible? The designer's a local woman."

Alicia looked down at the tag. "At this price, I *will* take one in each color."

"I know. I keep telling her Harrods or Bergdorfs would charge three times what she does."

Alicia put a bright orange and hunter green bag by the register and turned to the racks of clothing. "Where are the Georgica originals? I'll start there."

I glanced up from the inventory sheet. "Oh, none of the pieces over there are my designs."

Alicia popped up on her tiptoes and scanned the store for my section.

"I haven't been designing. Not since Victoria and Alexander's wedding anyway."

Alicia nodded her head and turned back to flipping through the clothes. She pulled a few hangers off the rack and carried them into the dressing room. Almost an hour later she'd accumulated a large collection of clothes, jewelry, and accessories she piled up by the register.

Fiona wrote up a receipt and announced her total after applying the friends and family discount. Alicia handed over her Amex.

I shook my head in amazement. "You hate shopping."

"I don't hate shopping. I just can't put clothes together the way you can. I don't have that kind of eye. That's why this boutique is so great. You took all the guesswork out of it."

Sally offered to bring her shopping bags up to the house later, and we set out for the hedge maze. As we walked, I pointed out some of the property's best features, like the hunting grounds, chalk streams, archery fields, and riding trails.

"Past the hedge maze and down that hill is one of the best fly-fishing streams in all of England," I said, pointing toward the clearing.

Alicia laughed. "This place reminds me a lot of Camp Chinooka. The archery fields and riding trails. All that's missing is Gordy."

"Can you imagine his blaring voice coming over a loudspeaker, waking up all the guests? Gooood morning, Badgley Hall!"

"You know what, I actually can. Good old Gordy."

"Good old Gordy," I repeated.

We continued walking until we found ourselves at the entrance to the hedge maze.

"Is there a map or brochure or something we should take in with us so we don't get lost?" Alicia asked.

"Nah, we'll use our instinct and intuition."

Alicia looked at me like I was crazy.

"I know the maze like the back of my hand, don't worry."

Alicia relaxed her shoulders and followed me into the labyrinth as I explained the maze's rich history at Badgley Hall.

"Mazes played an active role in royal courts and aristocratic households. They were commissioned so secret matters of the family or state could be discussed away from prying eyes and ears. The first Earl of Harronsby had this one built so he could carry on a relationship with one of the scullery maids. They'd arrange for secret meetings in the center of the maze."

"Couldn't have been that well-kept a secret if we're talking about them now," Alicia teased.

"This particular maid went on to have several of the earl's illegitimate children so, as you can imagine, word got around quick."

"The first Earl of Harronsby sounds like quite a cad."

"No, the local historian said he was in love with the maid. Would have married her if his position allowed it. His marriage to the countess was one of obligation, probably even arranged."

"Well, let's be thankful that the future Earl of Harronsby lives in a different time."

"I know. Gideon'd never have been allowed to consider marrying a commoner like me. I have a feeling his mother wishes some of those customs were still in practice."

We finally reached the center of the maze, marked by the beautiful white marble fountain in the middle of the clearing.

"So, Gideon and I settled on a date for the wedding. It'll be this summer. July 4th weekend. We figured it will give my side the benefit of the long weekend to get over here."

"The wedding's going to be here at Badgley Hall?"

"When Gideon proposed it, of course I said yes. I mean look around, who wouldn't want to get married here?"

Alicia stood up and walked over to examine the large marble statue that stood in the middle of the fountain. She ran her hand over its two faces, each one looking toward a passage that might lead out from the center of the maze.

I came up behind her. "That's the Roman god Janus. They say the younger face is looking toward the past and the older face, toward the future," I said and sat back down on the fountain's edge.

Alicia turned to me. "If these mazes were commissioned so secret matters of the family could be discussed away from prying eyes and ears, think it's safe enough for us to finally talk about something?"

I took off my shoe and shook a rock out from inside it. "Sure. What's up?"

"Gigi, I have to ask. What really happened with you and Perry that night in the hotel?"

I shook my head. "Nothing. Nothing happened."

"I know it's nothing like the papers implied, but why was he in your hotel room in the first place?"

I slipped my shoe back on. "He wanted to talk."

She narrowed her eyes. "Talk about what?"

"You have to promise whatever I say stays here."

She crossed her heart. "I promise."

"Perry proposed. Although, technically, I guess he re-proposed."

Alicia's eyes got huge. "He proposed?"

"I don't know whether it was part of his original plan or not, but he got down on one knee and told me he never stopped loving me, and he'd spend the rest of my life trying to make things right between us."

Alicia suddenly whipped around to face me. "Didn't you learn anything from what happened with Joshua? You were in love with him for years. *Years.* If you'd only told him."

"Then what? He would have chosen me? You and Joshua were far better for each other."

"So much better that I ended up marrying somebody else. Was Perry better off with Annabelle?"

"Maybe. Perry and I seem to bring out the worst in each other."

"The worst? When you were with Perry, you built G. Malone. You were named CFDA's Women's Wear Designer of the Year. Perry wrote *Elizabeth* and graced the cover of *Rolling Stone* magazine for Christ's sake. You're just afraid. It's why you ran away to Chinooka then. It's why you're running away to Badgley Hall now."

"I'm not running away. I'm building a life with my fiancé."

"What life? You've stopped designing. You and Jamie aren't talking. You've pretty much walked away from G. Malone."

"I'm letting the dust settle. I'm figuring things out. You were in the pub last night. You saw all those people pointing and whispering about me."

"You're going to hide out in this maze forever? Is that the plan?"

Tears sprang to my eyes. "You have no idea what it was like to go to bed on top of the world and wake up the most hated woman in England—maybe even the whole world. Gideon believed me when nobody else did. He stuck by me through all of it, despite what his mother thinks, despite what every tabloid tried to dredge up about me."

Alicia stepped forward and wiped the tears from my cheeks. "You're my best friend. I want to see you happy, that's all. You know I like Gideon very much, but you don't owe him the rest of your life just because he stuck by you. All I'm saying is that I hope in the end this is all enough for you. I can't help but think it may not be."

"Look around. I got the fairy tale, complete with a castle, prince, even a moat. Of course, I'm happy. Of course, it's enough."

She put her arm around me. "If you say so, I'll never bring it up again."

"I say so."

I peeked up at Janus, and for just a moment, I could swear, both his faces were looking at me—like they didn't believe a single word I'd just said.

CHAPTER FOUR

L ater that afternoon, the weekend guests, a mix of Gideon's parents' friends and Gideon's friends from boarding school and university, started arriving at Badgley Hall. Alicia headed back to her room with Asher to put Sloan down for a nap and get cleaned up for dinner, while Gideon organized the staff and assigned them to their posts. Gideon asked me if I'd mind greeting visitors as they arrived to ensure everything ran smoothly at the reservation desk.

I stationed myself at the front gate, armed with weekend itineraries and glasses of champagne. I recognized some of the first arrivals, friends of Gideon's parents I'd been introduced to at dinner parties and other social events. Most made polite chitchat with me before following the bellhop and their luggage into the house. When I saw Linney's silver Mercedes coming up the gravel driveway, I rushed over to say hello.

Over the last few months, Gideon's sister, Linney, and I had become good friends. She was every bit as thoughtful and considerate as her big brother and made a point of checking in on me at least once a week. She'd recently started dating an American journalism student finishing up a graduate program in

International Diplomacy at the London School of Economics. Spencer had dreams of becoming a foreign correspondent and was working part-time for one of the news desks at the BBC, while also going to school. He and Linney met at one of the few pubs in London that regularly showed American football games. Linney was practically dragged there by a friend, but immediately hit it off with Spencer, who later admitted he was both captivated and intimidated by her posh accent and bright red hair.

They were a great couple, but I couldn't help but be jealous of how much Gideon's parents liked Spencer. It completely discounted my argument that Gideon's mother disliked me because I was an American. My nationality apparently had little to do with it. No, the current Countess of Harronsby was firmly convinced I'd betrayed not only her son, but her future queen, and in all these months, I hadn't been able to convince her otherwise.

Spencer popped the trunk and walked around to retrieve their bags. Linney greeted me with her signature European double kiss and then reached over to snatch an itinerary from my clipboard.

"Shooting, fishing, and riding—all the usual fun and games," she said, handing the paper back to me.

"Gideon has a few surprises up his sleeve, don't worry."

Spencer came around the car with their luggage. "Which way are we headed? Or are we staying in Linney's old room?"

"Not this weekend. We upgraded you guys to one of the refurbished suites," I said, handing him his room key. "You're staying next door to my friend Alicia and her husband."

"Oh, that's right, I completely forgot your friend Alicia was coming. I can't wait to finally meet her," Linney said.

"Annaliese. Annaliese," a high-pitched woman's voice called from behind us. We all turned to look. Who had invited Margaret and Henry Ellicott for the weekend? All the blood drained from my face and into my feet.

"Margaret Ellicott is the literally the only person besides my 87-year-old grandmother who calls me Annaliese," Linney whispered in my ear before forcing a smile. "Margaret, what a nice surprise seeing you here."

"We haven't been out to Badgley Hall in forever, so when Amelia asked us to come for the weekend, we couldn't say no. Oh, hello, Gigi. I didn't see you standing there."

"Hello, Mrs. Ellicott," I squeaked out.

"Is our room ready? It was a long drive, and we'd like to freshen up."

I scanned the guest list and didn't see the Ellicotts' names anywhere on it. "I don't see your reservation. Let me run inside and find Gideon. Apparently, there's been some sort of mix-up."

"Apparently," Margaret replied coolly.

I left the Ellicotts with Linney and Spencer and hurried into the house to find Gideon. I checked the kitchen and salon first. He wasn't there. One of the servers told me he thought he last saw him in the library. I rushed over and found Alicia and Asher having a drink by the fire. Sloan was sitting on the rug beside them, playing with the baby doll I'd given her.

"Gigi," Alicia called to me, "come have a drink with us."

I walked toward the fireplace. "I'm looking for Gideon. Have you seen him?"

Alicia scanned the space. "He was just in here. What's the matter?"

I pulled Alicia over to a corner of the room and lowered my voice. "The Ellicotts are here."

Alicia's eyes got huge. "Victoria and Annabelle's parents?"

I nodded my head. "Amelia invited them. I had no idea they were coming."

"Maybe check the music room? I heard Gideon say something about wanting to make sure the sconces in there were lit for the concert later?"

I left Alicia and turned down the long hallway leading to the music room. As I got closer, I heard raised voices from inside. When I got to the doorway, I could hear Gideon having a full-blown argument with his mother.

"Christ, Mum, you didn't think you should tell me you invited the Ellicotts for the weekend?"

"If Gigi is really as innocent in all this as you believe her to be, why should it make any difference?" Gideon's mother asked, her voice firm with conviction.

"Because their presence is going to make my fiancée incredibly uncomfortable."

"I suppose I should be grateful she's still just your fiancée and not your wife. That's something," Amelia mumbled.

"Mother, we set a date. We're getting married this July. Georgica will be my wife and the future Countess of Harronsby."

"There's more to the title than just signing your name in an official register, Gideon. Look around this house. There's over five hundred years of history, *our* family's history."

"You think I don't know that? I've dedicated the rest of my life to preserving that history."

"Has she? Does she really understand what she's signing up for?"

"She isn't designing. She gave up her business. She seems content enough teaching and running the shop."

"For now. Be careful, Gideon. Maybe you're right and she didn't sleep with Perry Gillman that night, but she certainly concealed their past from everyone that mattered. A woman who does that is certainly capable of concealing her true feelings."

"She didn't conceal it from me. I knew about her and Perry all along," he admitted.

"Then you are more of a fool than I thought."

"I have to go find some sort of accommodations for the Ellicotts and try to salvage this weekend, which, let me remind you, may mean the difference between us keeping Badgley Hall or seeing it sold to the highest bidder. Now, if you'll excuse me."

I heard the doorknob start to turn and hurried back down the hall and out of view. I grabbed some Badgley Hall pamphlets out of Gideon's office and pretended to arrange them on the large mahogany table in the foyer. Gideon came down the hallway and noticed me.

"What's all this?" he asked, forcing a smile back on his face.

"I thought it might be nice to have some brochures laid out for people when they came inside."

Gideon took the remaining papers from my hands and placed them on the table. "I have to tell you something, and I don't want you getting upset. Margaret and Henry Ellicott are here. My mother just informed me she invited them for the weekend."

"I know. I was outside when they arrived."

"I had no idea they were coming. I swear."

"It's okay. I understand."

He looked around the foyer. "No, really. I don't even have a room to give them."

"What about our room?"

His eyes widened. "Really?"

"The last thing I want is to give them any more of a reason not to enjoy this weekend. They're longtime friends of your family, and it's important they have a good time. Ours is the only refurbished room left in the house. The question is, where should we move to? We can't exactly go to a hotel in town since we need to be here to oversee things. Linney's old bedroom is free?"

"It's not actually. I'm using it as an extra storage room until we figure out a better system for housing all the towels and toiletries. I might have a solution. There's a small apartment over the carriage house. It hasn't been renovated since the 1970s, when the last groundskeeper moved out, but it's clean, comfortable, and has a working bathroom. That is more than I can say for the bedrooms on the top floors of the house."

"Yeah, I think I'd rather steer clear of a chamber pot situation," I teased.

"I figured. The apartment will be fine for a few days. When I was a kid, I'd tell my parents I was running away and go hide out in the apartment for a few hours. Of course, they knew where I was the whole time, but still let me think I was getting away with something."

I smiled. "I'll go clear out our things and let housekeeping know they should make up our room for guests."

Gideon leaned in and kissed me on the forehead. "I don't deserve you."

"I'm the reason you're even in this mess with the Ellicotts. It's the least I can do."

I went upstairs, packed a suitcase to take to the apartment, and then emptied out the closet. I moved the rest of our clothes to a wardrobe in one of the empty rooms on the fourth floor and grabbed all our toiletries out of the bathroom. After I finished tucking away the last of our things, I dragged the suitcase out into the hall. Linney and Spencer spotted me on the way to their suite.

"Where are you running off to?" Linney asked.

"We're giving our room to the Ellicotts and moving to the apartment above the carriage house for the rest of the weekend."

"You know that used to be Gideon's secret hideaway. I wonder if the groundskeeper's old *Playboy* magazines are still under the bed," Linney joked.

"Is it bad I'm happy to discover there are at least a *few* skeletons in Gid's closet?"

"More than a few. Wait 'til you meet some of his friends from Eton this weekend. They'll fill you in on some of Gideon's boarding school antics."

I raised my eyebrows.

"Make sure to have them tell you about the time he got caught making out with the headmaster's daughter *in* the headmaster's office."

A few hours later, Gideon and I met up in the apartment to change for dinner. He was right, the space looked like a time capsule from the 1970s, complete with shag carpets, lacquer furniture, and popcorn ceilings. I knelt down and peeked under the bed, half expecting to find a *Playboy* magazine with Farrah Fawcett on the cover.

Gideon smoothed down the bed skirt and gave me a wink. "The groundskeeper took all the issues with him when he left."

I stood back up. "You must've been disappointed," I teased.

"Nah, I found my father's stash not too long after."

I covered my hand with my mouth. "Not the Earl of Harronsby?"

"If you think the first Earl of Harronsby was a cad... he doesn't hold a candle to the seventh."

"Apple doesn't fall far from the tree? I heard *you* once got caught making out with the headmaster's daughter in his own office."

Gideon narrowed his eyes. "Who told you about that? Alistair? Freddy?"

"No, I haven't had the pleasure of meeting the boys from Eton yet. Linney let me in on your sordid past."

"I don't know if it was necessarily sordid," he said, leaning into me. "It was basically all my girlfriend's idea. I just went along with it."

"Kicking and screaming, *I'm sure.*" I held up two hangers. "Which one do you think will offend your mother less?"

His eyes darted back and forth between the two evening dresses. "The one on the right."

I hung the losing dress back in the closet and laid the other one on the bed so it wouldn't get wrinkled.

"Honestly, wear whatever you want, Gigi. It doesn't matter what my mother thinks."

"No, the last thing I want is to provide any more ammunition to her and Margaret Ellicott."

Gideon unzipped his garment bag and pulled out his tuxedo. "You're being silly. The fact the Ellicotts came here should show you they're over what happened."

"I guess we'll see tonight. Speaking of which, is everything set at the house?"

"When I left, the staff was setting the formal dining room and library for dinner, and the musicians were unpacking their gear."

"Did you decide to stick to the authentic Renaissance menu?"

"A Tudor feast, a modern take on what the Second Earl of Harronsby would have laid out for Henry VIII and Anne Boleyn when they came here on their honeymoon tour. At tomorrow's dinner, we'll serve more contemporary fare. I thought we should showcase what the house is most famous for tonight."

"It's sort of ironic, isn't it?"

Gideon walked to the mirror to tie his bow tie. "What is?"

"Didn't you tell me half the country turned on the Second Earl of Harronsby for welcoming the adulteress Anne Boleyn into his home?" Gideon turned back around to face me as I walked over to straighten his tie. "As far as your mother's concerned, I might as well be Anne Boleyn."

Gideon cocked his head to the side. "She'll come around, Gigi."

"You've been saying that for months. It's bigger than what happened with Perry. She doesn't think I'm good enough for you, or her title." I sat down on the bed. "What did you mean when you said I was content enough teaching and working at the shop?"

He sat down on the bed. "You heard us talking?"

"I'm sorry, I wasn't trying to eavesdrop. I was coming to let you know the Ellicotts had arrived."

"She's worried you won't feel satisfied living here, making Badgley Hall your first priority."

"I'm taking a break from designing. But you know, I'm not giving it up forever, right?"

"I know that. I thought maybe we could even turn this apartment into a studio for you. You can design pieces for the store."

"Gideon, at some point, I have to go back to G. Malone. It's my company. Jamie and I built it from nothing, and now it's an international brand. I can't just walk away from my responsibilities."

"You did walk away, though. Four months ago, you walked away and came to live here."

"Temporarily. I *temporarily* walked away because it was what was best for the business."

"That's the only reason you came? Because it was good for your business?"

"Of course not, Gid. How could you even think—"

Gideon looked down at his watch. "Is it okay if we finish this later? I have to get back to the house."

I nodded. "Yes, of course. Go."

Gideon leaned down and kissed me on the forehead. "You look beautiful. I'll see you at dinner?"

I forced a smile. "I'll see you in a bit."

CHAPTER FIVE

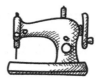

When I got to the house the guests were beginning to file into the Great Hall to check the seating chart for dinner. I found Alicia and Asher standing together in the far corner of the room and joined them.

"You look gorgeous," Alicia said.

"So do you," I said, kissing her on the cheek.

"What a great idea having Fiona watch Sloan tonight. I was able to actually shower and put on makeup, like a real person."

"Sloan took to her?"

"Right away. It might be the accent. She seems to think everyone in this house is a character from *Peppa Pig*."

"*Peppa Pig?*"

"A cartoon about a British family of pigs. Sloan's pretty obsessed with it," Asher chimed in. "So where are we sitting for dinner?"

I walked over to the seating chart and ran my finger down it. "Looks like you're both at a table in the library. I'm in the main dining room."

A few minutes later, Gideon stepped into the center of the room and announced that dinner was served. Asher took Alica's arm and escorted her to their chairs as I made my way into the dining room and took my place. I was relieved to see the Ellicotts seated well on the opposite side of the room. Linney took the seat beside me.

"How's your room? Are you both comfortable?" I turned to ask her.

"I'm not going to lie, it's a little strange to have your own home feel more like a hotel. After growing up in this drafty castle, though, I'm not going to complain about a heated towel rack in the bathroom. You've done a brilliant job with the renovation."

Gideon entered the room and came to his seat. He picked up his glass and clinked his fork against it a few times to call for everyone's attention.

"As most of you know, a few months ago, I set out to turn Badgley Hall from my family home into a real visitors' destination. I thank you all for joining me this weekend and for being willing guinea pigs in this little experiment of mine."

Everyone at the table was politely laughing at Gideon's joke.

"Tonight, please enjoy a modern take on the feast served to King Henry VIII and Anne Boleyn when they stayed at Badgley Hall on their honeymoon tour. As the ledger books in our library show, no expense was spared in celebration of the Tudor king and his new bride. We've done our best to provide you with an equally spectacular experience."

Gideon clapped his hands and an army of servers appeared carrying trays of steaming soup.

"This is a Crème Ninon, or French Green Pea Soup," the server said, placing the bowl down in front of me. "It's the chef's take on a traditional pottage or soup of meat and vegetables."

Gideon leaned over to me. "What do you think?"

I took a few spoonfuls. Creamy, rich, and layered with complex flavors. "It's wonderful," I answered.

"The chef's a local kid I hired right out of culinary school.

His technique completely blew me away. Mark my words, in the next few years, Badgley Hall will have a Michelin-starred restaurant," Gideon said, his eyes gleaming.

The servers brought out the rest of the courses, each better than the one that came before it. Meatballs in a honey mustard glaze sprinkled with saffron, roast duck stewed in wine fruit and spices, bacon-wrapped cod with frisée.

I picked up my fork and Gideon nudged my side.

"You know, you should hold your fork in your left hand and your knife in your right," he said.

"But I'm a righty," I whispered back.

"It doesn't matter, it's a formality thing."

I set my knife down and switched the fork into my left hand.

"And you should never set the knife down during the meal," Gideon mumbled.

I turned to him. "Even if I'm not currently cutting something?"

"The knife stays in your right hand like this," he said, gesturing his hand toward me.

I exhaled and picked my knife back up. "You should've left me a primer, I would've studied up before dinner."

"It's not *such* a big deal when it's just us, but when we attend dinners with our guests they'll be certain protocols expected of the Earl and Countess of Harronsby. Don't worry, I'll see if my mother has some time to go over some basic etiquette with you."

"Basic etiquette? You know I grew up on the Upper East Side of New York City and not a barn right?" I teased.

"You should pick it up quite easily then," he said, ignoring my comment.

After the last of the ports were served, Gideon announced the evening concert was going to start shortly in the music room. As the room slowly cleared out, I stayed behind to see if Gideon needed me to do anything.

"I'm going to run down to the kitchen and make sure the

staff has everything under control. If you can make sure the musicians are all set, that'd be a help," he answered.

"Of course. On it, Boss." I gave him a mock salute and turned on my heels.

"Hey, Gigi," he said.

I turned back around.

"This is going to work, I just know it," Gideon said, grinning from ear to ear.

Guests were milling about in the Great Hall and rooms adjacent to the music room while the musicians finished setting up. I spotted Linney in the doorway to the salon, chatting with a small group of people who looked to be around our age.

"Georgica, over here." Linney waved me over. "I wanted to introduce you to some of Gideon's mates from Eton."

I made my way through the crowded room and over to where they were huddled.

Linney took my arm. "Gigi, this is Alistair Eades and Caroline Barker. Alistair went to school with Gideon and I've known Caroline practically forever. And this is Freddy Munson another friend of Gideon's from Eton and his wife, Laurel."

"Nice to meet you. I've heard a lot about you all," I said.

Caroline turned to Laurel. "Us too," she muttered under her breath, just loudly enough so I could hear her.

I cleared my throat. "Freddy, you were Gideon's roommate at Eton?"

"Just the last few years. We were in the same house throughout, though. Alistair too."

"You'll have to forgive me. I'm new to the world of boarding and preparatory schools."

"You grew up in New York City though, right? They have their share of prep schools, don't they?" Alistair asked.

"They do, but my father believes very strongly in the New York public school systems, so I didn't attend one."

Freddy leaned in to me. "They're not all they are cracked up to be. A lot of pomp and circumstance, not to mention royals."

"That's right. I forgot you all also went to school with Prince Alexander," I said.

"I went to Mayfield with Victoria and Annabelle," Caroline said through pursed lips. "Annabelle was my roommate. I'm surprised you don't recognize me from the wedding. I *certainly* recognize you."

My cheeks went crimson. "If you'll excuse me, I should probably go check on the musicians."

Caroline gave me a little wave. "Catch you later, Gigi."

I left Linney and stumbled over to where the musicians were tuning up. I tapped the harpist on the shoulder and asked if I could get her or any of the musicians anything before the start of the concert and then took a seat beside Alicia in the audience.

"Are you okay? Your hands are shaking. Did Mrs. Ellicott say something to you?" she asked.

"Linney invited a friend for the weekend who also went to school with Victoria and Annabelle. She made no secret of the fact she recognized me from the royal wedding."

Alicia put her arm around me, and a few minutes later, Gideon joined us in the music room, along with the rest of the guests who had been mingling in the hallways. He stepped to the middle of the floor, and the room quickly quieted.

"In keeping with tonight's theme, celebrating the wedding of Henry VIII to Anne Boleyn, I'm pleased to welcome tonight's performers, The Tudors, a musical ensemble specializing in Medieval and Renaissance music, as well as traditional and contemporary classical music. Please enjoy."

Gideon took the seat beside me and took hold of my hand. He leaned into my ear. "How do you think everything's going?"

There was a fire roaring in the hearth. The overhead lights

were dimmed in favor of the candle sconces around the perimeter of the room, creating the most vibrant orange glow against the dark mahogany paneled walls. The dark blue velvet curtains were drawn, making the vast room feel intimate and cozy. It was picture-perfect, and the guests were completely entranced by the music and atmosphere, just as Gideon hoped they'd be.

"You better hire more staff. I think we're about to be the hottest spot in South Gloucestershire," I answered.

"Forget South Gloucestershire, between the restaurant, accommodations, and your shop, I'm aiming for all of Europe." Gideon glanced down at my lap. "Gigi, your clutch is vibrating."

I pulled my phone out of my bag and studied the screen. "I don't recognize the number," I said, pointing to the door. "I'm going to step outside for one second and see who it is."

Gideon nodded, and I ducked out of the room and into the hallway.

"This is Georgica Goldstein," I said, answering.

"Hi, Gigi, it's Jordana."

"Jordana, hi, I didn't recognize your number. Did you change it?"

"Jamie and I both changed ours a couple of months ago, when we got tired of fielding calls from the press. How are you? How's life in the English countryside?"

"Quiet, but good."

"And Gideon? Did you two set a date for the wedding yet?"

"We're thinking July 4th weekend. I'd love it if you could come. You and Jamie both."

"I can't speak for him, but of course, I'll be there."

I checked my watch. It was close to 2:00 a.m. in New York. I asked Jordana if everything was okay.

"You know me, chronic insomniac. Am I catching you at a good time?" she asked.

"We have some people staying at the estate for the weekend.

Alicia's actually here visiting. But it's fine. I was able to step away."

"Good. I'm calling because I heard from the *Top Designer* production team last week. They wanted to talk to me about your appearance on the finale show."

"The finale show?"

"Remember our agreement with them was for you to guest judge on a two-episode arc, the *Code Wed* episode *and* the final runway show?"

"They couldn't possibly still want me for that? I'm persona non-grata in the fashion world. Did they want to talk about letting me out of the contract?"

"Quite the opposite. They *really* want you for the finale show. Think about it. You went from designing the most celebrated gown in the world to almost obscurity in a matter of twenty-four hours. Nobody's really seen or heard from you since the story broke. Having you as a guest judge would be a huge ratings draw."

I drew a breath and let her words sink in. The last thing I wanted was to be thrust back into a spotlight as white-hot as *Top Designer*. I'd turned down interviews with every major news and entertainment outlet in the word, some who were offering mind-boggling paydays for my side of the story. There was no way I was walking back into the lion's den now.

"You'll have to get me out of it," I said firmly.

"It's a contract, Gigi. I can't get you out of it. We could break the agreement, but that might bankrupt G. Malone. Just do the appearance, and then you can go right back to playing princess in South Gloucestershire," she said.

I moistened my lips. "Can you send me the contract?"

"I did. Days ago. Check your email. I assumed you'd want your father to read it over? Our attorney's already reviewed it though, and it's iron-clad. We committed you to the finale show, and they want you. They realize they've got the golden ticket, your first public appearance since the scandal broke. They aren't going to budge," she said, before adding, "Maybe it's the push you need to come back to the land of the living?"

"Can I get back to you after I have my father take a look?"

"Of course. Give Gideon my best. Night, Gigi."

I hung up the phone and slipped it back into my clutch. I tiptoed back into the room and over to my seat. I immediately recognized the music the ensemble was playing as the overture to *Elizabeth*. I could swear all the eyes in the room were on me, waiting for my reaction to the song. Margret Ellicott was whispering into her husband's ear, while Caroline and Laurel were laughing about something in the opposite corner of the room.

Gideon squeezed my hand and whispered, "Is everything all right?" He obviously didn't recognize that the music was from *Elizabeth*.

I looked up at him. "What do you mean?"

"The phone call?"

Before I could answer, one of the kitchen staff tapped Gideon on the shoulder to ask him to come approve the setup of the dessert and coffee stations.

"I'll be right back," he said and followed the server out to the Great Hall.

I sat in a daze the rest of the concert. When it ended, the guests in the room stood up to applaud the musicians. Alicia called my name.

"Coffee, dessert, and brandy are being served in the library. Join us for a nightcap?" she said.

"A nightcap sounds good," I answered.

As we turned toward the door, Caroline and Laurel cut in front of us.

"What a wonderful concert. We thoroughly enjoyed it," Laurel said.

"I especially enjoyed the tribute to *Elizabeth*. Gigi, was that a special request of yours?" Caroline asked.

"Excuse me, I don't think we've been introduced. You are?" Alicia said, jutting out in front of me like a protective mama bear.

"Caroline Barker," she said, extending her hand. "I'm sorry, I didn't catch your name."

"Alicia Scheinman-Reiss."

She scanned Alicia's face. "Alicia Scheinman? Why does that sound so familiar? Have we met before?"

"Possibly. I lived in London for a few months a couple of years ago. I did a training program—"

"With Annabelle Ellicott, that's right!" she said, speaking over Alicia. "How are you, darling?" She leaned in to give her a kiss on the cheek. "You look wonderful. What are you doing here?"

"Gigi invited me," Alicia answered. "She's my oldest and dearest friend."

Caroline eyed me up and down. "Oh, small world. We'll have to catch up later. It was absolutely lovely to see you. Excuse me, Georgica," she said, pushing past me and out the door.

"She's a piece of work," Alicia said as soon as Caroline and Laurel were out of earshot.

"Is she? Or was she rightfully being a bitch to the woman she's thinks betrayed her friend?"

"No. She's a piece of work. I remember her now. Back then, Caroline Barker's only goal in life was to marry a man with a title and a large bank account. She's probably just jealous *you're* the one with Gideon." Alicia looked down at her watch. "I should go relieve Fiona. Are you going to be okay if I leave you and head up to bed?"

"Oh sure. I mean, now that I know for certain everyone in this room despises me, it'll be a lot easier to navigate," I teased.

Alicia cocked her head to the side. "There's only one person in this room you have to worry about, and from what I've seen, Gideon adores you."

After Alicia and Asher headed upstairs, I went to find Gideon. He was in the library by the fireplace, chatting with the Ellicotts. After a few seconds he looked up, and our eyes met. I gave him a small smile before he broke from my gaze and went right back to his conversation.

CHAPTER SIX

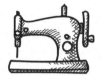

That night, Gideon never came back to the apartment. In the morning, I discovered his side of the bed completely untouched and his black leather toiletry case still sitting on top of the bathroom counter in the same spot he'd left it in the night before. I took a quick shower and hurried to the house for breakfast. When I walked into the dining room, the staff was laying out silver buffet trays and tureens, with Gideon overseeing the whole operation. He spotted me in the doorway and rushed over.

"I hope you're not angry with me? By the time I got everyone settled into their rooms and did a run-through with the kitchen staff of today's menus, it was easier to just grab a few hours of sleep in one of the vacant rooms on the third floor. I figured when everyone's eating I can run back over to the apartment to freshen up."

"I'm not angry, just worried about you. You've been running around nonstop. Is this pace sustainable?" I asked.

"I've actually never felt better. It's invigorating to steer your own ship and be your own boss. It's hard to understand unless you've done it."

I chewed my bottom lip. "I *have* done it."

"How stupid of me. Of course, you'd understand from your time at G. Malone."

I searched his eyes. "My time at G. Malone?"

"I'm just saying I get now how incredible it must have been to run your own design house."

I furrowed my brow. "Why do you keep talking in the past tense? I still own fifty percent of the company."

One of the servers tapped Gideon on the shoulder. "Mr. Cooper, can you come check the linens? I want to make sure we have the right ones laid out for the table."

"I'll be there in a minute," he said, before taking hold of my hands. "Look, Gigi, I've told you a million times, you can design, teach, run the shop, or become an acrobat for all I care. Do whatever makes you happy. You just need to be somewhat realistic about what it would mean to go back to running G. Malone. We're getting married, and hopefully in the not-too-distant future, we'll have children. I thought you wanted to make a life here, with me? None of this works without you."

Gideon's words hung in the air as the guests made their way into the dining room for breakfast. Sloan came tearing in ahead of Alicia and Asher, almost knocking an entire tray of blood sausages to the floor. Luckily, I was there to catch it before it slid off the table.

Gideon leaned in to me and whispered, "See, none of it works," before kissing my cheek and heading back to the kitchen.

"Good thing I ran those extra few miles around the property this morning," Asher said, scooping heaping piles of food onto his plate.

Alicia rolled her eyes at Asher and turned to me. "Where should we sit?"

I held my arms out. "Anywhere you want. Open seating for breakfast."

"It's okay for us common folk to mix with the lords and ladies?" she teased.

"Haven't you heard? It's our most progressive meal of the day."

Alicia laughed and grabbed a plate off the pile. "What's on today's schedule?"

"Gideon arranged for some country sports, if Asher wants to try his hand at fly-fishing or skeet shooting? I organized a small luncheon and fashion show featuring some local designers and clothes from the shop in the teahouse for the ladies. It should be a great show."

We set our plates down at the main table. Alicia portioned out some eggs and hash browns onto a smaller plate for Sloan before turning to me. "Don't you miss it?"

I looked up from my breakfast. "Miss what?"

"G. Malone? Don't you miss designing your own pieces?"

"It's no different than when you changed jobs after having Sloan."

"I cut down on my hours a bit, so I'd have more time with her. I didn't give up my career altogether. I love working in finance. I couldn't imagine walking away from it completely."

"I'm not walking away completely. I'm just taking a break."

"So you *are* planning on going back to New York?"

"I haven't had a chance to mention this to Gideon yet, but Jordana called last night. I have to fulfill my contract with *Top Designer* to judge the finale show. I'll be back in New York in a couple of weeks. I don't see any way out of it, so I'll go for the show and then come straight back for Badgley Hall's official opening. Gideon will need all hands-on deck."

A server came over carrying hot coffees and a glass of milk for Sloan. He set them down on the table and cleared away the empty plates.

"Gideon has to be pleased. Everything's been running seamlessly so far," Alicia said.

"Truth be told, I've never seen him happier."

Alicia lowered her voice. "Quick, don't look behind you. Incoming, twelve o'clock."

I didn't need to turn around. I could hear Caroline's shrill laughter behind me. It was unmistakable.

Caroline, Laurel, Alistair, and Freddy took seats beside us at the table. They chatted with one another, barely acknowledging the fact we were sitting right beside them.

"How was everyone's night? I hope the rooms were comfortable?" I asked, trying to break the obvious tension between us.

"Quite comfortable," Freddy answered. "Gideon did a great job with the renovations. I remember coming here for a few days of our winter holiday back when we were at Eton. Gid put me in a room without a bathroom. When I asked where I should take a piss, he tossed a seventeenth-century chamber pot at me. Now, you have proper toilets *and* heated towel racks. I'd say it's a big step up."

"I'd hope so," I said, smiling.

Caroline turned to Alicia. "So, last night, I was racking my brain to try to figure out why your name was familiar to me."

Alicia set her coffee cup down on the table. "I told you, we met back when I was doing that training program with Annabelle."

"But you and Annabelle stayed in touch afterward, right?"

Alicia shifted uncomfortably in her seat. "For a while we exchanged emails and cards. She stayed with me a couple of times when she visited New York."

"I knew it! She stayed with you right after you broke off your engagement, right?" Caroline asked.

My stomach dropped. All the color drained from Alicia's face. We both knew exactly where Caroline was heading with her line of questioning.

"Yeah, I think that's right," Alicia answered politely.

"I remember she came home and told me all about you. How you'd just found out your fiancé had been secretly seeing your *oldest and dearest* friend." Caroline turned to face me. "That would be you? Right, Gigi?"

The fork dropped out of my hand and onto the plate with a huge clang that echoed through the room.

Alicia cleared her throat. "That's not exactly the whole story."

"No? It has been a few years, so I may not remember all the details, but I distinctly recall Annabelle telling me how you broke off your engagement when you found out your closest friend had been sleeping with your fiancé. She felt so terrible for you. She couldn't believe any friend could break girl code like that, let alone a *best friend*."

I went to speak, but no words came out.

"It's more complicated than that. You don't know the first thing about it," Alicia spat.

"Oh, I think I know enough," Caroline answered. "What's that expression? Once a cheater, always a cheater?"

I glanced over at Freddy, Alistair, and Laurel, who were pretending not to listen. I started to rise from my seat when Gideon came up behind us.

"Good, you're all sitting together. It was so crazy last night, I didn't have a chance to do proper introductions. Gigi, this is Freddy Muson and his wife, Laurel, and this is Alistair Eades and Caroline Barker. You won't meet four nicer people or better mates. Everyone, this is the love of my life and future bride, Georgica Goldstein."

"We've met, actually," Caroline said tossing her hair back and away from her face.

I cleared my throat. "That's right. We met last night, and as it turns out, Caroline knows Alicia too, through Annabelle Ellicott."

"Funny. What a small world," Gideon said.

"I'd say it is." Caroline snorted.

"So small, in fact, that Caroline knows all about my past secret relationship with Alicia's ex-fiancé."

"Your what? I'm completely lost," Gideon said, shaking his head.

"My torrid affair with Joshua Baume. It happened about six years ago. Alicia broke up with Joshua before she left for a training program in London, and he and I started seeing each other. When she returned, they got back together, and I stepped aside and went to Camp Chinooka for the summer to get away from the situation. And yes, that's the very same camp where I met Perry Gillman, who incidentally, I DID NOT SLEEP WITH THE NIGHT OF VICTORIA AND ALEXANDER'S WEDDING!" I shouted.

Gideon placed his hand on my shoulder. "Might we have a word outside—NOW."

I followed Gideon outside to the front of the house. When we were a good several yards away from any guests or staff, he spoke.

"Gigi, do you want to tell me what the hell is going on?"

"I've had enough. I'm so tired of having everyone look at me like I'm damaged goods, someone who isn't anywhere near good enough for you. And maybe I'm not, but it isn't because of a few seconds caught by a paparazzi's lens that fateful night four months ago."

"Where is all this coming from? I know you've been upset, but the way you blew up in there, I don't know how I'm going to explain that."

I took a few steps toward him. "I don't want you to explain it. I don't want you to have to keep defending me and our relationship to all the people that matter to you."

"*You* matter to me. You're going to be my wife. Of course I'll keep defending you."

I searched his eyes. "Aren't you tired of all this? The whispering? The stares? The innuendos?"

He took hold of my hands. "No, are you?"

I nodded and pulled away. "I am tired. Tired of walking on eggshells. Tired of pretending not to notice people talking about me behind my back because now, it's not even behind my back anymore. They're letting me know how they feel about me straight to my face. And let me tell you, Gid, the reviews ain't good."

Gideon laughed and pulled me into his arms.

I looked into his eyes. "It's not funny."

"I know. What can I do?"

"When you proposed, you promised to keep the world away, with your bare hands, even."

"I haven't done a very good job at that. I'm sorry."

"No, it wasn't ever a fair promise to hold you to." I held my arms out. "This place, these people, it's who you are and how you grew up. I can't expect you to shield me from the reality of what that all means, but if you want out just say so."

He shook his head and took my hands into his own. "Maybe you just need to take a few days for yourself. Go to London. Do some shopping. Make some new contacts for the store."

"I have to be in New York in a couple of weeks to judge the *Top Designer* finale. Hey, I have an idea. Why don't you come with me? We could both use a break from Badgley Hall. We'll get Chinese food at Wo-Hop and hide out in museums and theaters. Besides, Alicia said that ever since New York City's mayor got caught sexting with underage girls, people have more or less lost interest in my sordid tale."

"A few weeks from now is right around the time of our official opening. I can't go. Is there any way you can get out of the show? We'll get egg rolls another time?"

"The agreement is for me to appear on the finale show. It shoots in three weeks."

"But, this is your last G. Malone obligation, right?"

"My last G. Malone obligation?"

"It's the last official event on the books, right? After that you're done?"

I couldn't get a read on what he meant by "done." It seemed with each conversation we had, Gideon was more firmly convinced I was putting designing on the backburner, so I could commit myself to Badgley Hall completely. If part of our arrangement was to be that I would never design for my company again, I didn't remember signing on the dotted line.

Gideon leaned in and kissed me on the forehead. "Go. Do what you need to do. We'll manage. Just hurry home. This place feels empty without you here."

I turned to head back to the house. "What about your friends? I should go back inside and apologize for my outburst."

"Don't worry. I'll take care of it."

"Gid—"

"I'll take care of it, Gigi. Just tell me one thing, are there any other skeletons in your closet I need to be made aware of."

"Not a one."

He raised his eyebrows.

"I got caught cheating on a math test in grammar school. I was never very good at division."

"Yeah, neither was I," he said, before heading back inside.

CHAPTER SEVEN

A few hours later Fiona and I were putting the finishing touches on the table settings for the teahouse luncheon. Instead of traditional linen tablecloths, we laid out colorful patterned fabrics I'd found at a small market in Dursley. I filled old-fashioned tins with bright pink teacup roses and scattered them throughout the room, while Fiona lit small votive candles and strategically placed them on different tables to create a warm and intimate setting.

I'd spent the last few months sourcing vintage floral china place settings from different antique shops and websites. When I instructed the staff to mix the different settings together, they looked at me like I was crazy. But when they finished, the interior was exactly as I imagined, bohemian and eclectic. Very different from the formality usually found at these sorts of luncheons. Fiona and I stood back to appreciate our work.

"You never told me, do you want to do open seating or place cards?" Fiona asked.

"Let's assign seats," I answered, trying to work out how to best organize the 30 plus guest while simultaneously keeping

Margaret Ellicott, Amelia, Laurel, and Caroline as far away from me as possible.

A few minutes later, Alicia walked into the carriage house with Sloan at her hip.

"Oh my God, Gigi, this looks amazing," she said, setting Sloan down on a chair.

"When Gideon told me he wanted to use the carriage house as an event space, he gave me carte blanche to do whatever I thought would help make it look less like, well... a stable. I whitewashed the walls and added those reclaimed wood beams to the ceiling to make the room warmer." I pointed to the back of the space. "I blew out that back wall and replaced it with the floor-to-ceiling glass, so guests could see straight out and to the hedge maze."

I walked to the center of the room and pointed up. "The final touch was the seventeenth-century chandelier. I may have fudged its historical significance a little bit to get Gideon to agree to spend the money on it, but we just had to have it. It pulls the look of the whole room together."

Alicia laughed. "What'd you tell him?"

"That it *may* have been commissioned for King Louis XIV for the Palace of Versailles. The antiques dealer didn't know a lot about its history. I just have to convince Gideon not to include that tidbit in the brochures."

"So not an out-and-out lie. It *may* have been commissioned for him. We'll never know. Either way, it's incredibly chic. Jamie would lose his mind over it."

Since Alicia invoked Jamie's name first, I didn't think I'd be putting her in a compromising position if I asked how he was doing. "Have you seen much of Jamie lately?"

Alicia took a seat and emptied some toys out of her bag onto the table for Sloan. "Yeah. He and Thom had a housewarming party just a few weeks ago."

"They finally found a new apartment?"

"It's gorgeous. Right off Central Park West. Plenty of room for the kids."

"I'm glad. And he's adjusting to fatherhood?"

"Like a pro."

I smiled. "I knew he would."

"He did ask about you. Wanted to know how you are. If we'd been in touch."

"What did you tell him?"

"That you were doing well." She shrugged her shoulders. "I didn't know what you'd want me to say."

"I've left him dozens of messages. I've sent countless emails. Nothing."

"He's hurt and angry. His name got dragged through the mud right along with yours. All his work, everything he put into G. Malone, was jeopardized because of what happened."

"But nothing happened with Perry. Didn't I deserve at least the benefit of the doubt?"

Alicia raised her eyebrows. No, I guess I didn't deserve the benefit of the doubt. Although I didn't cheat with Perry that night in the hotel, by agreeing to conceal our past relationship from Victoria and Annabelle, I'd put G. Malone on this collision course. Jamie had tried to warn me all along, but I hadn't listened. I was so sure the ends would justify the means that I didn't stop to consider what would happen if the truth ever came out.

"Maybe you two just need to talk in person, face-to-face? You said you may be in New York in a couple of weeks, right? These things take time. Remember what it was like for us? Our friendship didn't just snap back into place. We had to work at it," Alicia said.

"But at least you were *willing* to work at it. He's shut me out completely."

"He's hurt. People deal with hurt in different ways. For example, *some people* I know shout at their fiancé's oldest friends in a crowded dining room," she teased.

I sat down next to Sloan. "Caroline knew exactly what buttons she was pushing."

"And you let her push them. You know I'd never want you to change who you are, but you're going to have to rein in your emotions a little bit if you're gonna make it through the weekend, let alone the rest of your life. I get the feeling, scandal or not, some of these people still wouldn't think you were good enough for Viscount Satterley."

The directness of her statement stopped me in my tracks. Was she right? Even after the last of the wedding scandal smoke cleared would I still be fighting to prove I belonged on the arm of the Earl of Harronsby?

"I have to go check on the models for the show. They're getting ready over at the shop."

Alicia looked around the room. "Anything I can do to help here 'til you get back?"

"You can give Fiona a hand with the seating chart."

"But I don't know who anybody is?"

"It's easy. Seat like titles together, countesses with other countesses. Baronesses with other baronesses. That sort of thing. You'll get the hang of it in no time. Just be sure to keep Caroline as far away from me as you can, somewhere in the hedge maze would be most preferable," I said with a wink.

The gift shop was a flurry of last-minute activity as the local models finished getting ready for the fashion show. The local designers were helping the girls into their outfits, instructing the hair and makeup team on how to complete the overall looks they were each trying to achieve. I walked around making small adjustments to hems, collars, and accessories. I felt like Trini Bower before a *Top Designer* runway show, making sure each designer was putting his or her best foot forward. All of them were hanging on my every word and instruction, and for just a moment, I caught a glimpse of my old self in the floor-length mirror.

Sally tapped me on the shoulder and let me know she was going to begin moving the clothing racks to the backstage area behind the teahouse. I picked up my clipboard and lined the models up for the show, giving each a final once-over before sending them over to the tent.

When I was finished, I spotted Amelia watching me from the doorway. I had no idea just how long she'd been standing there. She made her way into the room as it slowly cleared. The last model walked out, leaving just the two of us surrounded by Badgley Hall commemorative plates and tote bags.

I set the clipboard down on the counter. "Amelia, hi, can I help you with something?"

"I came by to tell you the teahouse looks lovely. You did a wonderful job with its transformation."

I blinked hard. It was the single kindest thing she'd said to me since I came to live at Badgley Hall. "Thank you. I'm so glad you like it."

She surveyed the gift shop. "In fact, just about everything you've touched since you've been here is much improved. This store was an afterthought before you took it over. Now look at it, the gift shop is one of the biggest draws of the entire estate."

"Wow, that means a lot coming from you."

Amelia smiled and took a seat on the small pink settee in the corner of the room. "I heard about what happened in the dining room this morning."

I moistened my lips. "I'm very sorry about that. It's not easy to have people believe something about you that just isn't true. I think it finally got the better of me. I offered to apologize, but Gideon told me he wanted to take care of it. The very least I can do is apologize to you for any embarrassment I may have caused in your home."

"You know, this is going to be *your* home someday. When you commit to Gideon, you're committing to this whole way of life. Don't misunderstand me, this isn't *Downton Abbey,* titles and position don't mean quite what they used to, but Gideon is going to do everything in his power to see that we hold on to our home and legacy."

"I know all of that."

"I hope you do. It's not easy to sacrifice one's own dreams, passions, and talents for somebody else's. You think you won't resent them, and you don't at first. The resentment comes later. But by then, there are children and obligations, and it's far too late to change course."

I flashed back to the conversation my mother and I had on a rowboat at Camp Chinooka several years ago, where she confided in me about her own missteps and regrets. Her biggest fear was that I'd make the same mistake she did, following someone else's path instead of my own. It was strange hearing Amelia echo such similar sentiments.

"You're very talented. Whatever your harshest critics choose to say about your role in the royal wedding, don't let it overshadow your accomplishments."

"Thank you, Amelia."

"I mean it, Georgica. Think long and hard about what you'll be giving up to become the Countess of Harronsby. Throwing little tea parties and local fashion shows is perfectly fine for now, but is it really how you want to spend the rest of your life?"

After the way Amelia behaved toward me these last few months, it was hard to know if she was being genuine, or if her words were merely a ploy to get me to reconsider the engagement. The overall narrative would work far better for the family if I were the one to walk away. But there was something in her voice, a thickness that made me think perhaps she was, for the first time in our relationship, being sincere.

I cleared my throat. "I really appreciate you stopping by."

She nodded and stood up from the seat. "If you'll excuse me, I should be getting back to our guests."

After she left, I hurried over to the back of the teahouse where Fiona was waiting for me with a microphone and stack of index cards with information about the different designers. I shuffled through the pile and practiced pronouncing all the designers' names. Gideon walked into the tent as I flipped to the last card.

"Tea service just started. The servers are bringing in the trays of finger sandwiches and scones as we speak," he said.

I tucked the cards into my pocket. "Great. I'll be out to start the show in a few minutes."

"The space looks unreal, Gigi. King Louis XIV made a *huge* mistake when he decided not to hang that chandelier in Versailles," he said with a wink.

"Are you mad?"

"The chandelier's perfect. Even Caroline can't stop gushing about your taste and how fantastic the room looks."

"Speaking of Caroline, what'd she say when you apologized?"

"Caroline's not so bad. You two just got off on the wrong foot. You'd like her if you gave her half a chance."

"If I gave *her* half a chance? Her guns were locked and loaded before she even walked in the door."

"Look, all those girls, even Linney, their social circle's very small, very tight-knit. They give every outsider a hard time."

I raised my eyebrows. "Outsider?"

"You know what I mean. Anyone who didn't go to Mayfield or Eton. Who didn't summer in Saint Tropez and winter in Saint Moritz."

"You realize you're using *summer* and *winter* as verbs instead of nouns. And by the way, I have been to Saint Tropez. I springed there, once. Well, more like ran out of money there when I visited over spring break during my college semester abroad."

Gideon smiled and shook his head. "Not the same thing."

"Yeah, I didn't think so."

CHAPTER EIGHT

Following the fashion show, I arranged for the docents to meet the guests to give the full historical guided tour of the property. The women from the luncheon separated into smaller groups and made their way over to the front steps of the house. Alicia finally caught up to me in the foyer after she put Sloan down for a nap.

"Hey, do you have a second?" she asked.

I looked around the hall. The guests were paired up with guides and getting ready to set off on their tours. "Sure, what's going on?"

Alicia took my hand and pulled me toward the library. We stepped inside, and she closed the large oak doors behind us.

I settled down on the plush green velvet couch. Alicia took the seat beside me. She crossed her legs underneath her body and scanned the room for people.

I looked into her worried eyes and a wave of anxiety pooled in my stomach. "The docents are starting with the kitchen and old servants' quarters, so we should have this room to ourselves for a few minutes. Everything okay?"

Alicia swallowed hard. "I finally met Linney over lunch. I

know you've wanted us to get to know each other, so I put her at my table when I was helping with the place settings."

"Oh good, I've been meaning to get the two of you together all weekend."

"Linney walked in late. The fashion show was already underway, so she and I were never properly introduced."

I shifted in my seat. "Okay? Is there something I'm missing?"

Alicia averted her eyes down and away from me.

"Alicia, what is it?"

"After the show ended, Linney and the other ladies were finishing their tea and chatting. Your name came up."

My stomach lurched. "My name?"

"At first the comments were flattering. They loved the show and your flower choices. Then, the conversation turned more critical."

"Critical how? They weren't feeling my mismatched place settings or something?"

Alicia exhaled. "One of the women asked Linney how she felt about you taking her mother's place as the future Countess of Harronsby. Linney laughed it off and said it'll never happen. That there was no way Gideon will ever *really* marry you."

"*Linney?* Linney said all that?"

"She also called you a social climber and opportunist, along with some other choice names I won't repeat."

"Are you absolutely sure it was her?"

"Bright red hair? Looks just like her brother?"

I sank down into the couch, tears welling up in the corners of my eyes.

Alicia put her arm around my shoulder. "I shouldn't have told you. Asher thought I should just leave it alone, but I thought it was better you know. I'm so sorry, Gi."

"I thought Linney was my friend. She was my only ally in this family besides Gideon, and she thinks I'm an opportunist?"

"Maybe she was showing off? People are always saying things they don't mean, especially in a crowd like that one."

"No, she means it. They all mean it." I wiped my eyes with the back of my hand, rose up from the couch, and smoothed out my dress.

"Let's have a drink. There must be a priceless bottle of Chateau Margaux around here somewhere we can snag."

"I should make sure the tours are running smoothly, and then I have to check on the dinner service."

"Gigi, let's talk about this. Please don't shut me out. I can see how hurt you are."

I pulled out the tour schedules. "If you hurry, you can catch up to Group Two. The docent should be leading them into the drawing room any minute."

Alicia stood up and squeezed my shoulder. "If you need me *or* that drink, you know where to find me. I'll see you at dinner, okay?"

I shook my head, and Alicia left the library to join the tour. I took a few deep breaths and walked into the vast hallway.

Gideon called my name from down the corridor. I composed myself and waited for him to catch up to me.

"Did the groups get off okay?" he asked.

"The docents just set off for their tours."

He clapped his hands together. "The fashion show was a huge success. When I caught up with them, Caroline, Laurel and Linney were heading straight over to the store to do some shopping and you know what snobs *they* can be."

I looked down to the ground. "That's wonderful, I'm so glad."

Gideon tipped my chin up. "What's the matter?"

"Did you know?"

He searched my face. "Know what?"

"How Linney *really* felt about me?"

He closed his eyes.

"You knew. You let me sit at lunches and teas with her? She calls me at least once a week. Why?"

"I asked her to. I wasn't making much headway with my mother and I thought you needed to feel you had at least one ally in the family."

"But you knew it was a lie."

"She doesn't dislike you as a person, Gigi."

"She just doesn't think I'm good enough for you or her mother's title."

He moistened his lips and put his hand on my shoulder. His silence spoke volumes.

"I can't be fighting about this with everyone *and* you too," he finally said.

"What does *that* mean?"

"Your little outburst this morning didn't win you any more allies, quite the opposite in fact."

A lump rose from the center of my chest and settled into the base of my throat. "I told you Gid, if you want out all you have to do is say the word."

"Of course that's not what I want, but maybe this trip to New York is coming at a good time for us. Get away from Badgley Hall for a few days. When you come back the house will be open to the public and I'll need your head back in the game."

"I didn't realize it was ever out of the game."

He looked at his watch. "I should go check on the stateroom tours. I want to make sure the docents are highlighting all the art work in their talking points."

"I'll see you back at the apartment to change for dinner then?"

"I brought my clothes to the house. I won't have time to get back before dinner." His grey green eyes narrowed in on me. "I love you. You know that, right?"

I nodded. "I do and I love you too."

"We'll figure this all out, I promise," he said before hurrying down the hall to join up with the group headed into the library.

A few seconds later I found myself being drawn up the stairs to the bedroom where Henry VIII and Anne Boleyn spent their honeymoon night. Nobody besides the house historians were ever supposed to be in there. It was off-limits to even Gideon. I wasn't sure if it was the spirits that supposedly haunted these halls, but something or someone was beckoning me into the room. I peeked around to make sure the coast was clear and then stepped over the red velvet cord and sat down on the bench at the end of the large canopy bed. Hanging above me, the portrait of Anne Boleyn said to have been painted right around the time of her marriage to King Henry.

I lifted the ends of my hair so it was eye-level with the painting for comparison. Alan, the actor from the Renaissance festival circuit I'd met back at Camp Chinooka, had been right; with my dark features, we did resemble one another. I felt a sudden and very real kinship with the disputed queen, who, in her short life, was the constant subject of court gossip, rumor, and insinuation.

A few minutes later I heard the voice of the docent come thundering down the hallway, along with the footsteps of the tour group trailing behind her. I ducked behind the far curtain so they wouldn't see me in there.

"Accused of having affairs with numerous men, historians generally agree the charges against Anne Boleyn were shams, sparked by rivalries and jealousies in the court." The docent stopped in front of the doorway, so everyone could take a peek into the room before continuing. "It's likely Anne didn't even know how far in over her head she really was...until it was chopped off just sixteen months after becoming Henry VIII's wife."

"Gigi should take a few cues from Ms. Boleyn. A couple more outbursts like the one this morning and Countess Satterley will be calling for *her* head," I heard Caroline say to the group, who laughed at her joke.

"She's not so bad, is she?" another voice asked.

"I'll just say this, Gideon can do *a lot* better," Caroline replied.

"Come on, ladies, let's pick up the pace, or we won't get out to the gardens before dark," the guide chided.

After the docent and group were safely out of earshot, I dug into my purse and pulled out my phone. I closed my eyes and hit the callback button. Jordana picked up on the second ring.

"Hi, Jord, it's Gigi. I don't need to have my father look over the contract. I'll do the *Top Designer* appearance."

"That's great. I'll send over the final details as soon as I have them, so you can make your arrangements." Jordana softened her tone. "If I haven't said it already, it'll be nice to have you in New York for a few days."

I looked back up at the portrait of Anne Boleyn, her sad eyes staring down at me. "Yeah, it'll be nice to be home."

CHAPTER NINE

The flight attendant woke me as the plane reached its final approach into JFK. For the first time in as long as I could remember, I slept for the entire flight to New York. Stretching my arms up over my head, I lifted the window shade and peeked outside. The sun was just pushing up over the clouds, lighting up the gray morning sky. I adjusted my seat to its upright position and dug around my bag for my bottle of water.

"Whatever you took, I'm having my doctor prescribe some for me for the next time I fly."

I looked up. The woman next to me was reapplying her lipstick using a handheld compact. "You were out cold before we even left the gate at Heathrow."

"I didn't take anything," I answered.

"Really?" Her eyes were practically bulging out of her head. "You must've been exhausted." She slipped the lipstick back into her purse.

I was. The trial run weekend at Badgley Hall had gone mostly well, but Gideon and I did identify several issues that needed resolving. Maybe it was the guilt over having to leave for the *Top Designer* finale show, but I'd been burning the candle at both ends, working day and night to make sure everything was absolutely perfect for the first major event we were hosting at the estate. While he appreciated everything I'd been doing, deep down, I knew he was still disappointed I was going to miss the grand opening.

The woman adjusted her seat and slid her mules back on her feet. "Your accent? American? Headed home?"

"Sort of," I answered. "My fiancé's British, so I'll be moving to the UK permanently. I have a few work obligations I needed to take care of in New York, though."

"I'm meeting my daughter for a mother-daughter weekend. She's been in New York since January doing an internship with Conde Nast."

I nodded politely. "That's great."

"I know, she managed *somehow* to get us tickets for *Elizabeth*. Have you seen it?"

"I have, actually. Last year, in London."

She turned to me, her eyes wide open, expecting the usual accolades and high praise that typically gets rattled off after someone says they've seen *Elizabeth*.

"And?" she asked.

"And it was wonderful. As good as people say. Better."

She settled back into her seat. "Yeah, that's what I've heard. I tried to get tickets in London, but that proved impossible. Truthfully, though, this worked out even better because now we'll get to see it with Perry Gillman playing Dudley since he moved over to the Broadway production. He's quite the dish. I hope he's half as handsome in person."

The flight attendant came down the aisles handing out customs declaration forms. The woman reached into her bag for her passport, spilling out several magazines on the floor. I reached down and handed them back to her.

She glanced down and passed the magazine back to me. "Is that you?"

I took the magazine from her hands and slowly brought it up to eye-level. There I was, on the cover of *OK! Magazine* with the headline, *Out of Hiding, Georgica Goldstein Returns Home to Judge Top Designer Finale.*

The woman looked down at the magazine and then up again at my face. I swallowed so hard I could swear she heard the gulp.

"It's me," I said, handing the magazine back to her.

The woman nodded uncomfortably and tucked it back into her tote. I reached into mine for a pen to fill out the form but couldn't find one.

"Excuse me, do you have a pen I can borrow?" I asked.

I watched the woman take the pen she'd just been using to fill out her own customs form and slide it back into her planner.

"Sorry, no," she answered curtly, before turning away from me.

A few minutes later we touched down in New York. The flight attendant got on the intercom and announced our gate and luggage carousel. I stood up to retrieve my bag from the overhead bin.

I handed the woman her carry-on. "You know, you shouldn't believe everything you read."

"Have a lovely time in New York," she said coolly.

"Thanks, you too."

I made my way off the plane and was weaving in and out of the crowd trying to get to customs when I was hit with the overwhelming feeling of déjà vu. I looked over to the airport newsstand and, just as I feared, my face was splashed across almost every tabloid and newspaper, just like when it was leaked that G. Malone was picked to design Victoria Ellicott's wedding gown. News of my impending return had obviously made its way across the pond, and the press wasn't wasting any time exploiting that fact. I slipped on my sunglasses, raced across the terminal to the store, and scanned the stand and headlines. I picked up *People* off the shelf and was flipping through it when my phone started to vibrate. I dug it out of my tote and answered.

"Gid, I'm so sorry. I was going to call you as soon as I got through with customs," I said.

"How was the flight?"

I set the magazine back down. "If you can believe it, I slept the whole way here."

"I believe it. You've been working nonstop these last few weeks. Tell me, how does it feel to be back?"

"Strange. I'm currently staring at my own face on about a dozen or so magazine covers."

"Just *your* face?"

I glanced over at the shelf. Perry's picture and name was beside mine on almost every publication. Headline after headline suggesting my trip back to New York was merely a ploy to see him again.

"You know Perry Gillman's just as tied to this story as I am."

Gideon sighed into the phone. "Georgica, do I need to be worried about anything?"

"Of course not. How could you even ask me that?"

"I don't know. Ignore me. I must be half-delirious, it's almost 2:00 a.m. here."

"You don't have anything to worry about. I'll fulfill my obligation and that'll be that. I'll be back before you even have a chance to miss me."

"Too late for that."

I smiled and said, "I miss you too. Now, get some sleep, and I'll call you tomorrow, okay?"

I hung up quickly before Gideon could bring up selling my New York apartment again. Between dealing with a revolving door of subletters and constantly battling the building's strict co-op board, holding on to my New York place had become a bit of a headache. For months, Gideon had been pushing me to put it on the market, but I couldn't bring myself to do it.

Years ago, my father had generously offered to lend me the down payment for the apartment, but I refused to take him up on it. I wanted to make my own way. I was able to use most of my *Top Designer* runner-up winnings to purchase the place instead. I also set up G. Malone's first office. In those six hundred square feet, Jamie and I built our business out of nothing, and every time I slipped my key into the lock, I was reminded how far our little brand had come. I wasn't ready to let go just yet.

After making it through customs I went to collect my luggage. I pushed my sunglasses on top of my head and scanning the room for the driver Jordana arranged to meet me, I saw an older gentleman holding a sign that said "Reid Codswild." I breathed a sigh of relief, grateful Jordana had taken a page from Gemma Landry's playbook and used my royal wedding pseudonym to try to keep the press at bay. I walked over to greet him.

"Are these all your bags, Ms. Codswild?" he asked.

I nodded and started to follow him out to the car. As soon as the automatic door closed behind me, we were hit with a barrage of flashes and people calling my name. I ducked down behind the driver.

"Are you one of those Kardashians?" he asked. "I thought you looked familiar. Don't worry, I've driven for Lady Gaga a few times. I got this," he said, taking my hand and pulling me toward the car.

Once we were outside, the driver grabbed my luggage and tossed it into the back of the black SUV. He swung open the front door and catapulted me inside before running around to the driver's side of the car. He jumped in, tossed me a hat from the floor, and adjusted his rearview and side mirrors. "Don't worry, Miss, I'll lose 'em before the 59th Street Bridge," he said before slamming on the gas.

I slunk down in my seat. This was crazy. The story about me broke months ago. Of course, I expected a certain level of interest in my return, but nothing like what had just been waiting for me outside the airport.

Once we were finally a safe distance from the trailing paparazzi, I pulled out my phone to let my mother know I'd landed and find out where she wanted to meet for lunch. I typed in my passcode, and a news alert immediately popped up onto the screen.

Baby Makes 3. The Duke and Duchess of Sussex Announce They're Expecting Their First Child.

I took a deep breath and clicked on the headline and into the CNN article and continued reading:

The couple has reportedly agreed to sit down with the BBC in a few months for their first televised interview since getting married. The pair are said to be prepared to share details of their life as husband and wife, excitement over becoming first-time parents, and finally address some of the rumors surrounding their wedding.

I leaned back in the seat. Well, that explained the media's intense renewed interest in me. Victoria and Alexander were having a baby and back in the headlines, and so, by default, I was too. The timing of the *Top Designer* finale show could not have been any worse for me, or any better for their ratings. I slipped the phone back into my bag and leaned my head up against the glass.

The driver tapped me on the shoulder. "Miss, mind if we swing up to Ninth Avenue and then head down to avoid some of the midtown traffic?"

"Whatever you think is best. After the way you managed to dodge all those paparazzi vans, I trust you implicitly."

We cut through the city on 59th Street and over to the West Side before heading farther downtown. The driver turned down 44th Street. I peeked out the window and saw a huge crowd of people lined up across most of the block.

I sat up. "Do you know what that line's for?"

"They're waiting for the *Elizabeth* ticket lottery."

"*All* those people are trying to win a ticket? Don't they only raffle off like twenty a show?"

"Most of 'em know they won't win, but the cast does a small show every day for all the people waiting in line. The local press started calling it *Screams for the Queen.* Hundreds come out every day just to watch that. Closest they'll ever get to seeing the real thing."

We drove a bit farther down the street. The car stopped at a red light right in front of the St. James Theater and *Elizabeth* marquee.

The driver turned his head to the billboard. "I'm not big into Broadway musicals, but my girlfriend turned me on to this show. The soundtrack is killer. Not your typical showtunes. I got it right here, hold on," he said, synching his phone to the car's Bluetooth.

The driver turned up the volume. "I love this beginning rap, where Dudley explains how Elizabeth rose to take the throne. Did you know Elizabeth's mom was Anne Boleyn? That really messed with my head. Which side of the street is your building on?"

I opened my wallet to pull out some money for a tip. "Up here on the right is great. Thanks." I dug around my bag. "Shoot, all I have are pounds. I didn't exchange any money at the airport. Can you take a credit card?"

"Don't worry, your publicist took care of all that when she ordered the car. Can I ask now? You *are* one of those Kardashians, right?"

He looked so sure, I didn't have the heart to disappoint him. I nodded yes.

"I knew it!"

The driver pulled over at my building, and the doorman came outside to meet the car and help with my luggage.

He opened my door. "Welcome home, Ms. Goldstein."

"Thank you, Albert. How's everything been?"

"I can't complain. It's almost spring. Yankee opening day is right around the corner."

I patted him on the back. "Eternal optimist, huh?"

"We have some good prospects," he said, pulling my suitcase into the building's lobby. "Is Mr. Cooper in town as well?"

While I was working on Victoria's dress, Gideon probably made half a dozen trips to New York to see me, becoming a familiar fixture in the building. Albert got a kick out of trying to explain American baseball to Gideon and, by his last trip to New York, Albert managed to successfully convert him into a Yankees fan.

I dug around my bag for my keys. "Not this trip, unfortunately."

Albert nodded and went into the small mailroom behind his desk. He returned with a large stack of magazines and mail.

"Is all that really for me? I had my mail forwarded to the UK."

"Sometimes it takes a couple of weeks for the post office to make the change, especially if it's international. These are from a few months ago. I've been holding on to them until you got back."

I stuffed the large pile into my tote.

"You in town long, Ms. Goldstein?"

"About a week. I have a couple of work obligations, then I'll be heading back to London."

"Well, if you're thinking about selling the apartment, my sister-in-law just got her broker's license," he said, handing me her card.

I tucked it into my pocket. "Thanks. I'll keep that in mind."

I squeezed onto the elevator with my bags and rode up to the eleventh floor. Dragging my bags behind me, I walked down the long, narrow hallway to my door. At least half a dozen takeout menus were scattered around my welcome mat. I tucked them under my arm and pushed the door open to go inside.

I flipped on the lights and did a quick scan of the room. Relieved the last subletter left everything tidy and in order, I opened some windows to air out the apartment before kicking off my shoes and sinking into the couch. I pulled the stack out of my tote, set it on my lap, and sorted the mail into bills, cards, and magazines.

Tackling the bills first, I carefully opened each one to make sure I hadn't accidentally missed any payments these last few months. Next, I ripped open the cards. Most, were thoughtful notes sent from other designers and magazine editors months ago to wish G. Malone success with the upcoming royal wedding. Finally, I turned my attention to the magazines. *People, US Weekly, In Touch, OK! Magazine*—the issues from the days and weeks following the royal wedding. The front pages I'd been avoiding since the morning the world came crashing down around me. My hands shaking, I had just pulled the stack up to my chest when my phone began vibrating in my back pocket. I reached around, pulled it out, and answered.

"Oh good, you're alive. Of course, I know you're alive. I just saw a picture of you leaving the airport on Twitter, but I'm glad for the confirmation."

I set the magazines down on the cushion beside me. "Hi, Mom. Sorry, I meant to call you when I got into the car, but, as you saw, I was busy dodging paparazzi cameras."

"How was the flight?"

"Great. I slept the entire way."

"Hmm…what'd you take?" she said, her voice going up an octave.

I stood up from the couch and rolled my suitcase into the bedroom. "Nothing. I guess I was just tired. Where'd you want to meet for lunch?"

"There's this place on Twentieth and Seventh, I've been wanting to try."

"Really?" I was in shock. My mother hardly ever crossed town to the West Side, unless it was to see a show or visit my apartment. She only dipped below Fourteenth Street once a year to visit her gynecologist's office in SoHo.

"I'm expanding my horizons. Should I make the reservation for just us two?"

"I told you, Gideon had to stay in South Gloucestershire for the estate's grand opening."

She sighed into the phone. "That's too bad."

As soon as my mother learned of Gideon's pedigree and the fact his marriage proposal came complete with a Countess title for her only daughter, she became Team Gideon all the way.

"I just walked in and have a few things to do, so let me hang up," I said.

"Is one of those things a haircut? You know all I'd have to do is call Frankie and he'd squeeze you in for a cut and color."

"Bye, Mom. I'll see you later."

CHAPTER TEN

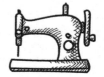

"Mom, this is not a restaurant." I slid out of the cab and onto the sidewalk right in front of the famed Kleinfeld Bridal Boutique.

"I knew you'd never agree to go wedding dress shopping with me."

"Unless what? You blindsided me?"

She waved her hand in the air. "Don't be so dramatic. Your wedding is in less than six months. You need a dress, and *this* is a store with dresses. Don't turn this into more than it is."

"I was thinking I'd just look for a dress at some of my favorite vintage shops while I'm in town."

Her face crumpled. "Yes, but then I don't get to be a part of it."

I softened my stance. "Is that what this is about?"

"My mother bought my wedding dress at Kleinfeld, well back when the store was in Brooklyn. I've always imagined the day I'd get to come here with my daughter to help her choose her dress." She took hold of my hands. "You don't have to say yes to a dress today, but may I have the small pleasure of going to this appointment and getting to see my only daughter try on some wedding gowns?"

When I was a girl, every single shopping trip with my mother ended with me in tears after her telling me the clothes I was trying on would look a *tad* bit better if I lost some weight. At around twelve years old, I stopped shopping with her and started making my own clothes. It was my line in the sand, a way of finally standing up and letting my mother know I might never fit into the perfect mold she envisioned for me.

Unfortunately, she viewed my designing as an act of rebellion, and our relationship never quite recovered. In the beginning, she stopped asking me to join her on shopping trips, and then, over time, she just assumed I didn't want to take part in any of the things she liked to do. What my mother never knew was how much I wanted to be like her. In so many ways, she was responsible for my career. Her impeccable taste and distinctive style was the lens through which I viewed and created fashion. She was chic and one-of-a-kind, from her signature chignons to her unmistakable cherry-red Chanel lips.

I smiled warmly. "Sure, yes. I'd love to try on dresses with you, Mom."

She pulled me in for an uncharacteristic hug before mumbling, "Vintage store? Are you crazy? My daughter is not wearing someone else's old curtains to her wedding."

I pulled away, laughed, and held the door open for her. The lobby was swarming with brides and their large entourages scattered across every couch, waiting to enter the main floor of the boutique. My mother pushed her way to the front of the line of women checking in for their appointment.

"Reid Codswild," she said, and then turned to me. "I used your pseudonym so the press wouldn't get wind of the appointment."

I raised my eyebrows. "Good thinking."

The receptionist rose from behind her desk and passed my

mother a clipboard. "Wonderful. If you could take a seat and fill this out, your bridal consultant will be out shortly."

My mother passed me the clipboard as we found an empty couch in the corner.

"Georgica, you can take off your sunglasses. I told you, I used a pseudonym, so nobody here knows who you are."

Just as she finished her thought, a woman wearing a headset and holding a clipboard approached us.

"Hi, Gigi Goldstein, right? I'm Maryanne Cox. I work for a reality show we film right here in the salon. You may have seen it? We follow brides as they choose their wedding gown."

I leaned close to my mother and whispered, "So much for the pseudonym." I turned back to Maryanne and pushed my sunglasses on top of my head. "Sorry, yes, of course I've seen it. I've spent many Friday nights binge-watching the show in my pajamas."

"Great! I just love hearing that. We would be thrilled to have you sign on for a future episode. Can you imagine, the most famous wedding gown designer in the world purchasing her *own* wedding gown. How fabulous would that episode be?"

"Totally fabulous," my mother chirped.

"It wouldn't require too much from you. We'd film a couple of talking head segments, just you giving us some background on your fiancé and the wedding. Then, we'll take some footage of you trying on dresses and, ideally, choosing one. What do you think?" Maryanne asked.

"While I am flattered you'd want to include me, I think I want to shop for my wedding gown privately."

Maryanne took a seat next to me. "Are you sure? I can't tell you how many brides wish they had the moment they found their perfect dress documented forever."

My mother chimed in. "She makes a good point. Gideon's mother and sister are over in London. It might be nice for them to be able to watch this and feel like they were a part of the experience."

"I can assure you, they will be perfectly fine not being a part of this particular experience."

Maryanne leaned in close. "Your fiancé is British? What's he like?"

"He's great. Kind and funny. Dependable and romantic."

Maryanne jumped up. "See, that right there is all we'd need for the talking head segment. Not such a big deal, right?"

"What's not a big deal?" Alicia asked, approaching us.

I stood up to greet Alicia. "Hi. What are you doing here?"

"Your mother invited me. What's not a big deal?"

Maryanne pushed through to introduce herself to Alicia. "I'm Maryanne Cox. I work on a reality show we tape here—"

"Oh my God. I love that show!" Alicia squealed. "Is Gigi one of the brides you're profiling?"

"We're trying to get her to agree," Maryanne said.

Alicia snorted. "Good luck with that."

I shot Alicia a look. "Maryanne, I really appreciate the interest in me, but I think I'm going to have to pass. I've been in the headlines a lot this year, and I want to keep everything about this wedding as low-key as possible."

She couldn't hide the disappointment in her face. "In case you change your mind," she said, handing me the media release forms.

A few minutes later, a woman who looked slightly older than my mother came out to greet us. She was wearing a chic fitted black suit and a killer pair of Louboutins. She extended her hand. "Georgica, hello, I'm Francesca. I'll be working with you this afternoon. Whom do you have with you today?"

"This is my mother, Kathryn, and my friend, Alicia. Both of them former Kleinfeld brides."

She clasped her hands together. "Wonderful. I have to admit, I'm a little bit nervous. How do you dress the woman who designed the most iconic dress of this century? Have you given any thought to how you want to look on your wedding day?"

I glanced over at my mother and Alicia. Their eyes were firmly fixed on me, awaiting my response.

"Not so much, actually. I've been busy with other things."

"That's okay. Sometimes getting a sense of the venue helps me with a direction. Where's the wedding going to take place?"

"At my fiancé's home."

Alicia chimed in. "It's not a home. It's a freakin' castle. It even has a moat."

"So, we'd be looking for something grand? A ballgown, maybe?" Francesca asked.

"Yes!" Alicia screeched. "I'd love to see her in a ballgown."

"Oh, me too." My mother grabbed Alicia's hand excitedly.

"I'm not so sure I want *such* a big dress."

Francesca strummed her fingers against her chin. "How about something to show off your figure but with a dramatic bottom? More of that mermaid style."

"No, no, that silhouette won't work on Georgica. Too form-fitting," my mother said, shaking her head.

Francesca put her arm around my waist. "How 'bout this, why don't you and I take a walk through the stock room and see if anything catches your eye? You two can have a seat out on the floor," she said, directing Alicia and my mother to a pair of couches.

Francesca led me into the back room, where there were literally hundreds of dresses on racks that stretched across the full length of the room and ceiling.

"That section over there," she said pointing to a large area of the stockroom, "Are all the dresses most similar to Victoria Ellicott's gown. For the last few months it seems like every bride who walks in here wants to look exactly like Victoria on her wedding day."

I glanced over. "Really?"

"Honey, that dress was on another level. We do our best to find them *something* that evokes a similar feeling, but you should see how their faces fall when we explain that those were real Cartier jewels affixed to the gown." She turned to me. "You don't have to answer this, but can I ask why you aren't designing your own wedding dress?"

"I'm taking a small hiatus from designing."

"I've been a fan since your season of *Top Designer*. I remember well how you slayed the *Code Wed* challenge. We showcased your winning gown in our window. I can't tell you the kind of foot traffic and interest the store received from that."

I'd almost forgotten my prize for winning the challenge was having my toilet paper wedding dress displayed at Kleinfeld. It was a huge moment for me as a designer, and the first time I remember feeling like I had any business being in that competition.

Francesca motioned to the back of the stockroom. "Here's a question, what do you think your fiancé would like to see you in? Sometimes that's a good place to start."

"Gideon? I guess something simple and classic. He's from a very prominent and old family, so nothing too flashy or trendy."

"I have a few things in mind. One dress in particular," she said, pulling hangers off the rack.

I followed Francesca into one of the larger dressing rooms, where she hung the gowns for me to view. I immediately honed in on one of the grouping.

"I think I'd like to try that one first," I said, pointing to a lace sheath dress.

A smile crept across Francesca's face. "I knew it!"

Francesca slipped it off the hanger and over my head. It slid down my body, hugging all the right curves without being too clingy. It was a beautiful and intricate Duchesse Needlepoint Lace that had been hand-dyed in a pale gold rinse to create the most incredible iridescent quality.

The dress was constructed with a cap sleeve, high neckline, and featured a corseted bodice with draping to the front and a heart-shaped detail at the back. The organza and tulle underskirt was perfectly layered to enable the most sublime floor-sweeping princess-y movements.

"Wow," I said, taking it in from all angles.

"I agree. Wow. Should we go show them?"

I nodded. "Let's show them."

I followed Francesca out to the floor and onto the large pedestal in front of a set of floor-length mirrors.

Before I even turned around, I could hear my mother sniffling behind me.

"What does everyone think?" Francesca asked.

Alicia covered her mouth with both hands. "With no disrespect to any of your designs, Gigi, that is one of the most beautiful dresses I've ever seen."

"Mom, what about you? What do you think?"

She covered her heart with her hand. "I love it. It's perfection on you."

I don't think in all my life I'd ever heard her use words like those in association with anything I was wearing. "Really? It *is* a more fitted dress."

She dabbed the corners of her eyes. "Really."

"Let me get the matching veil, so you can see the whole effect," Francesca said.

A few seconds later she returned with a cathedral-length veil made of the same Duchesse lace. She slipped the comb into my hair and let the veil cascade like a waterfall down my back.

Alicia took two steps toward me. "You look like a princess. No, a countess. You're going to be a countess, right?"

"Viscountess until Gideon becomes Earl of Harronsby," my mother said with what I could swear was a slight British accent.

Francesca raised her eyebrows. "What does everyone think? Should we keep going?"

"I can't imagine anything being more perfect for you, Gigi," Alicia said.

Francesca bent down to straighten the bustle. "I'll go get one of our fitters to measure you. We should get the dress ordered as soon as possible. You said your wedding's in less than six months, right? As it is, we'll need to put a rush on it." Francesca stood up. "I'll leave you to talk it over with everyone."

I took another glimpse at myself in the floor-length mirror. The back of the dress was simple. Plain, really. Jamie was of the firm opinion the back of a wedding gown should be at least as spectacular as the front, if not more so. After all, the bride spends most of the ceremony with her back to the guests.

Alicia came up behind me. "Is this the one?"

"It doesn't feel right to make this big a fashion decision without getting Jamie's blessing."

"This isn't about what Jamie thinks. Or me or your mother. What do *you* think?"

An outbreak of cheers erupted on the other side of the salon. Alicia and I both turned to see what was happening. A cameraman was circling a bride standing on a pedestal, tears streaming down her face.

The bride fanned her face as she continued to gush, "I love this dress so much. I can picture walking down the aisle to meet Andrew, and his face when he first sees me in it."

"Jennifer, are you saying yes to the dress?" her consultant asked.

"Yes!" she screamed, and her entourage went crazy.

The consultant handed Jennifer a box of tissues, and she blotted her cheeks.

"It's everything I ever dreamed of," she said, and then turned to the couch where her friends and family were sitting and screeched, "I'm getting married to the love of my life!"

I turned back to the mirror as Francesca walked over with the fitter, who pulled a tape measure out of her apron. "Let's get you measured."

"You know what?" I said stepping down from the pedestal, "I'm gonna think on it. It's a beautiful dress. Gorgeous—puts my own designs to shame—but I don't think I can say yes today."

"With the time frame, you know your window to order something is closing," Francesca said.

"I know," I answered.

Alicia stood up to join us. "Are you positive, Gigi? I can't imagine anything more perfect, can you?"

I looked back over at the bride across the salon. The look on her face said it all—no doubts, no second-guessing she was ready to be Andrew's wife.

"I'm not positive."

Alicia leaned in close. "About the dress or Gideon?" she whispered.

I took one last look at myself in the mirror, and my heart sank when I realized I wasn't sure how to answer her question.

CHAPTER ELEVEN

I took a seat at the bar while we waited for my father to arrive at the popular midtown restaurant and checked my phone. He had texted to say he was running late from a deposition but was on his way. I looked over to the hostess stand, where my mother was having a full-on argument with the maître d'. The bartender set a menu and bowl of spiced olives in front of me.

"What'll you have?" he asked.

"Just a seltzer would be great."

"You sure? I make a fantastic dry martini," the bartender said.

I caught a glimpse of my messy bun in the mirror behind him. I could already hear my mother's voice asking me why I couldn't have taken five minutes to have at least brushed my hair before dinner.

"You know what, I'll take you up on that martini," I said.

"Coming right up."

Pausing, he asked, "Do you want me to close the tab?"

I nodded and handed him my credit card.

"Georgie, put that away," a voice said from behind me.

I swiveled around on the stool. "Dad, I can buy my own drink."

"My city, my treat," he said, handing over a twenty.

I stood up to give him a hug.

"Where's Mom?" he asked.

"Arguing with the maître d'. I think he lost our reservation. You know, we could always blow this joint and just head downtown to Wo-Hop? I've been craving egg rolls and hot-and-sour soup for months," I said.

"What? No decent Chinese food in South Gloucestershire? I'm shocked," he said with a devilish grin. "Actually, that place we went to in London wasn't half bad."

I smiled warmly. I'd never forget the way my father rushed to my side the morning after the story about the wedding broke. He held my hand firmly as we forced our way through the sea of photographers and paparazzi waiting to snap a photo of me outside The Savoy. We jumped in his car and headed off to a Chinese restaurant in Soho, as if there was nothing out of the ordinary happening. He was my rock that day.

My mother marched over to us. "Even though I called to tell them we were running late, the maître d' gave our table away. They have one table they can seat us at now, but it's close to the kitchen, which I know you hate, Mitchell."

"It's fine, Kate. Let's just sit at the table by the kitchen."

"We can wait for a better table, but they can't tell me how long it'll be."

My father shook his head. "I'll sit *by* the kitchen, *in* the kitchen, in the alley *behind* the kitchen. I haven't eaten a thing all day, so unless they can seat us in the next five minutes, I'm going with Georgie to Chinatown for dim sum."

My mother rolled her eyes. "You two are impossible. Let me go tell him we'll take the table."

My father passed me my martini off the bar. "You might need this."

I pulled my hair out of the bun and smoothed it down the best I could. "Bottoms up," I said, throwing back the drink.

We followed a hostess to the back-corner table right outside the kitchen's swinging doors. She handed us each a menu and let us know the waiter would be by shortly to take our orders.

"How was dress shopping?" my father asked.

My mother slipped on her reading glasses and perused the menu. "Gigi found a gorgeous gown but, surprise surprise, couldn't commit," she said without looking up. "She's apparently the only one who *isn't* concerned about the fact her wedding is in less than six months."

She took off her glasses and handed them to my father. He slid them on and picked up a menu. "Mitchell, when are you going to get your eyes checked?" she asked.

"I can see just fine." He looked up and over to the specials board. "Tonight's specials," he read, "Grilled prime rib rye served with roasted baby carrots and caramelized cipollini onions *or* crispy scale black bass and Maine lobster topped with Japanese cucumbers, baby leeks, sea grass, and basil oil. I think I'll get the prime rib special. What's everyone else having?"

My mother turned to me. "Distance. He can see distance just fine. It's everything else he needs glasses for." She looked over at my father. "And not the prime rib Mitchell, you're supposed to be keeping an eye on your cholesterol. Can you please order a piece of fish?"

"I can keep reading," he said ignoring my mother's comment about the fish. He looked back up to the board. "Hey, is that Joel Swensen?" he asked.

My mother turned to look before rising from the table. "Joel. Trish. Over here," she said, waving them over.

A couple who looked to be about my parents' age squeezed their way over to our table.

"Right by the kitchen, Mitchell? You couldn't get them to rustle up a better table than that?" Joel ribbed.

"Do you see this crowd? We were lucky to get any table at all. I had no idea this place was so popular," my mother said.

"Well, it's midtown, and walking distance to the theater district. Speaking of which, if we don't get seated soon, I'm having Joel get me a hot dog from one of those carts across the street. There is no way we are missing a single note of *Elizabeth*," Trish added.

"Not after what we paid for those tickets," Joel snorted. "They were being auctioned off by a charity we're involved with. I practically had to take a second mortgage out on our apartment to win them."

Trish threw her husband a disapproving look. "If it's even half as good as Kathryn said, it'll be well worth the money."

My head bolted up from the menu. "Mom, you saw *Elizabeth*?"

She patted my hand. "We'll talk about it later, Georgica."

"*This* is the famous daughter? Excuse us for being so rude. It's nice to finally meet you," Trish said.

"We're the ones being rude," my mother said. "Trish, Joel, this is our daughter, Georgica."

"Nice to meet you both," I said, smiling politely.

"Is there some sort of protocol? Aren't you marrying a duke or something?"

"An earl. He's not actually an earl yet. He's next in line. So, I'm nobody. The short answer is that there's no real protocol."

"We're *such* Americans. I've been boning up on my British history all week so I can follow *Elizabeth*," Trish said.

"It's wonderful. You won't have any problem," my father added.

I glanced over at my father, who quickly averted his eyes.

"Trish, the maître d' is waving at us. I think our table's ready," Joel said.

Trish turned to her husband. "You better know what you want to order before we sit. We have exactly fifty-one minutes before we need to be out of here. Lovely to see you, and wonderful to meet you, Georgica."

My mother folded her napkin back in her lap. "Now, who wants to share the Burrata with me?" she asked once Joel and Trish were out of earshot.

"Are you being serious?" I asked.

"Yes, I'm back on dairy. I'm completely off carbs, though."

"Not about the Burrata. Were you planning on telling me you saw *Elizabeth*? How did you even get tickets? You told me your broker couldn't get them. Please don't tell me you reached out to Perry?"

"We reached out to Perry," my father said matter-of-factly.

"You reached out to Perry! Have you both lost your minds? You couldn't wait a few months and buy a scalped pair of tickets like everyone else?"

My father slipped off his suit jacket and hung it behind his chair. "Georgie, he couldn't have been nicer. He gave us orchestra seats and a backstage tour."

"Oh my God, you saw him!? I mean, not just as Dudley, but you saw him, saw him? You guys *talked* to him?"

"He had us wait until after all the press left, and then gave us a guided tour of the sets and dressing rooms. He spent at least an hour with just the two of us after the show ended."

"You didn't think that was some sort of violation of the breakup code?"

My mother chimed in. "We treated him like a son for four years. I know you two didn't work out, but that relationship should count for something. We thought maybe he'd be able to scrounge up two tickets. We certainly didn't expect the VIP treatment we got from him but what can I say, once a gentleman always a gentleman."

I leaned back in my seat. "I mean, I guess I'm glad after everything that happened between us, he was so kind to you both."

"More than kind," my father said. "And I'll be honest, his real father couldn't have been any prouder than I was of him that night." My father handed my mother back her glasses. "He asked about you, you know."

I cleared my throat. "Yeah? What did he say?"

"He asked how you were you holding up since the story broke. Said he's been trying to reach out to you for months."

"I thought it was better to put some distance between us while our names were still in the headlines."

"He wished you well on your engagement, but I could tell he's still broken up about it all." My father placed his hand over my mother's. "We men know when we have a good thing. We also know when we've *royally* screwed up. No pun intended."

My mother shot my father a disapproving look. "Georgica, you never did see the second half of *Elizabeth*, right?"

"No, I left at intermission. Why?"

"If you ever get the opportunity, you should go."

"I know what happens. I saw all the rough cuts of the show."

"I believe he's made quite a few changes since then," she said. "So, the Burrata? What do you say?"

I folded my arms on the table and smiled. "Sure, Mom, whatever you want."

When we finished dinner, my parents offered to have their cab drop me off at my apartment. I thanked them but told them I was happy just to walk. I missed New York, the sounds, the smells, the crowds, and the energy. I appreciated the quiet and serene beauty of places like Camp Chinooka and South Gloucestershire, but for me, this city would always feel most like home.

Without even realizing, I found myself on West 44th Street and right in front of the St. James, where the last of the crowds were pushing their way into the theater for the evening performance of *Elizabeth*. After they were inside, I walked up to examine the posters of different scenes from the show, lining the walls outside the theater. I had to give him his due, Perry Gillman still looked good in a pair of breeches. I thought about what my mother said about the Second Act and pulled open the glass door and walked into the lobby of the theater. One ticket window was still open to customers.

"Can I help you, miss?" the person behind the window asked.

"I know this is probably a long shot, but do you have any tickets for this week?"

He started laughing. "This week?"

"I'm only in town for a few days. I just need the one, and I'll sit anywhere, or even stand. Any standing tickets available?"

"Honey, we're sold out through next year."

"So nothing at all?"

"You can try your hand at the lottery. We give away twenty tickets a performance. Other than that, my hands are tied, unless, of course, you know Perry Gillman," he said, laughing at what he thought was a joke.

I felt my phone ringing from inside my bag, dug it out, and stepped outside.

"Hey, Jordana," I said.

"Just wanted to make sure you're all set for tomorrow's finale show. I had the rough cut of the last *Top Designer* episode couriered over to your apartment a few hours ago. Please watch it before the runway show, so you can familiarize yourself with the two finalists."

"No problem. I'll watch it tonight before I go to bed. What time should I meet you at the tents?"

"It's really loud. Where are you? I can hardly hear you."

"I'm outside the St. James Theater. A bunch of high school age kids are already lining up by the *Elizabeth* stage door."

"Right, the Gillman Girls," she said.

"The what?"

"Perry has a following of teenage fans that dubbed themselves the Gillman Girls—get it, like the *Gilmore Girls*. They wait outside for him after every show. They scream and carry on. If they're lucky, they can snap a few photos of him, or better yet, with him."

"I had no idea."

"It's a thing. *New York Times* even had an article in the Arts and Leisure section about them last weekend. Between the period costumes, unrequited romance, modern music, female empowerment angle, and let's face it, Perry's brooding good looks, these tween girls are obsessed with him and the show. One girl they interviewed saw *Elizabeth* nineteen times in London and six times here. So, tomorrow, want me to pick you up at your apartment? We can cab over together?"

She was obviously still worried I was going to duck out on my *Top Designer* obligations. "Jordana, you live on 87th and 1st. That doesn't make any sense."

"I don't mind. I can swing down your way, then head back over to the West Side."

"Don't worry. I'm not skipping town. She's seen the show nineteen times? Really?"

She laughed. "See you in the morning, Gigi."

CHAPTER TWELVE

J ordana was waiting for me outside the *Top Designer* tent
at Lincoln Center. The finale show wasn't starting for
several more hours, but she thought it would be better
for me to arrive early and avoid the droves of press sure
to be waiting outside.

"Let's use the models' entrance in the back," she said, waving
me over to a side door.

Even though we were early, the backstage was a flurry of
activity. I'd spent the last twelve hours binge-watching the entire
season so I'd be caught up for today, and immediately recognized
the top two designer finalists.

Bryson Pratt was born and raised in Salt Lake City, Utah, and
grew up in a conservative Mormon family. He was home-
schooled, and by his own admission, was given little exposure to
pop culture or the world of fashion. For someone who'd grown
up on the fringe of mainstream America, his take on women's
fashion was not only cutting-edge, but totally unexpected. He
easily won the Code Wed challenge redux by managing to create
a gorgeous lace-like textile out of Charmin two-ply. His toilet
paper wedding gown was a work of art, and back when we guest

judged that episode, Jamie predicted he'd be one of the last contestants standing. He was right.

His main competition throughout the season was Carina Sandoval, a Cuban-American designer from Miami. Her designs were colorful, flirty, feminine, and beyond chic. Carina liked to use unique out-of-the-box embellishments, and in her most memorable look of the season, she covered an entire bodice with crushed sea shells, creating a brilliant texture that blew all the judges away.

Bryson and Carina were on separate sides of the tent, each surrounded by garment racks and half-naked models. Bryson was on the ground, hand-stitching a pant hem, while Carina was hunched over her sewing machine, both completely oblivious to the chaos happening all around them.

"Bringing back some fond memories?" a woman with a soft Scottish accent said from behind me.

I turned around and smiled. "More like PTSD. Hi, Trini."

Trini leaned in to give me a double kiss on the cheek. "Welcome home, Georgica. I'm so pleased we were able to convince you to come out of the witness protection program for a couple of days."

"I don't know if I had much of a choice. Anyway, I'm sorry I haven't been in touch. I keep meaning to pick up the phone, but life's been so crazy lately."

She laughed and put her arm around me. "Oh, I'm sure. Being the object of public ridicule can be quite the time-suck."

Jordana came over to where we were standing. "Production created a makeshift dressing room for you and the other judges over in that corner," she said, pointing to the far side of the tent. "Since we're here a bit early, they asked if you'd mind going first for hair and makeup."

"Sure, no problem." I turned back to face Trini. "I should probably get going, and I'm sure you have a thousand fires to extinguish."

"Let's be sure to talk after the show," she said.

"I'll just call you sometime this week, and we'll grab a coffee."

She tilted her head to the side. "It's important, promise me you won't leave 'til we've had a chance to chat."

I held my hand up. "I promise."

"Good."

A few hours later, the tent was packed almost wall to wall with people. Models scurrying back and forth between the hair and makeup stations, while dressers escorted finished girls over to the designers for final fittings. Camera crews from the show were scattered everywhere, doing interviews and capturing the chaotic behind-the-scenes fashion show footage audiences had come to expect from a *Top Designer* finale.

Jordana let me know the audience was starting to shuffle in, and after the last rows were seated, the judges would be announced to take our seats. I spotted Charlotte Cross across the tent getting mic'd by a production assistant, and the other judge, Marc Jacobs, getting his suit jacket steamed by the show's stylist.

One of the show's producers tapped me on the shoulder. "Excuse me, Georgica. Do you have a minute for a quick interview?"

I looked up to find a huge camera and floodlight in my face. "Umm, sure."

The producer quickly ushered me over to the far corner of the room, while the sound guy set up the boom microphone overhead. He counted down on his fingers, and then asked, "It's been six seasons since your finale show aired. What's it like to be back?"

"Hey, Jamie, we need you for a picture," a voice called out from behind us. My breath caught in my throat. Was Jamie here? I'd secretly been hoping he might show up and have no choice but to finally talk to me. I whipped my head around. A tall willowy model, not Jamie Malone, stepped in front of the *Top Designer* set to get her photograph taken.

My heart sank as I turned back to the camera. "Ummm, surreal?"

The producer switched the camera off and sighed. "We're going to need slightly longer answers to have something to work with in the editing room. Let's go again on three." He turned the camera and lights back on. "It's been six seasons since your finale show aired. What's it like to be back?"

"Surreal. In some ways, it feels like my finale show was a million years ago, and in other ways, it feels like no time has passed at all."

"What advice do you have for Bryson and Carina?"

"To try to enjoy the moment. I famously let the pressure of the finale get to me, but win or lose, the show is an amazing platform for new and up-and-coming designers."

"You arguably just designed the most important dress of this century. What's next for Georgica Goldstein and G. Malone?"

I closed my eyes and tried to recall the carefully worded soundbite Jordana had me practice should this or any similar type questions come up. My mind went totally blank.

A PA tapped the producer on the shoulder and whispered. "Mr. Malone just arrived. Should we try to get him on tape now in case he's too hard to pin down later?"

My eyes shot open. "Jamie Malone *is* here?"

The producer said, "Thanks, Gigi. We have all we need for now. We'll get the rest after the show."

"Sure, yeah, whatever you need."

Jordana came over to let me know the judges would be going to their seats in a few minutes.

"Jord, did you know Jamie was going to be here?"

"As a past contestant, he's invited every year. Same as you."

"Yeah, but he usually steers clear of anything having to do with *Top Designer.*"

Jordana shrugged her shoulders. "When we last talked, he wasn't coming. I don't know what changed his mind."

A PA came over to where we were standing. "They're ready for you in the tent, Ms. Goldstein."

I nodded and followed her and the other judges to the stage. The PA handed Charlotte Cross a microphone, and she came out from behind the curtain. I turned to watch the monitor.

"I want to welcome everyone to the Season Six *Top Designer* finale. Our designers have worked so hard to get here, and we can't wait to share their fabulous collections with all of you. Without further ado, let me introduce tonight's judges. First, the *always* stylish, Marc Jacobs. And you know her from Season One of *Top Designer* and as the co-creator of Victoria Ellicott's wedding gown and other winning looks, Georgica Goldstein."

Marc and I came out from the curtain, walked down the runway, and took our seats in the front row. I scanned the audience for Jamie, but the intense production lights were making it difficult to make out individual faces.

Charlotte Cross continued, "Now, to start our show, I'm pleased to introduce Ms. Carina Sandoval."

Carina walked to the center of the stage and introduced her collection. Inspired by the opera *Carmen*, she managed to combine the carefree, effortless gypsy sensibility with a more modern fit and aesthetic. The deep reds, royal blues, and emerald greens radiated off the stage, the overhead lights bringing out the richness of the hues. There wasn't a single look I wouldn't have happily worn straight off the runway. I peeked over at Charlotte's look book. She'd scribbled out the words *brave* and *bold* in the margins beside the photographs of the garments.

Bryson came out next to introduce his collection. He'd found his inspiration in the retro-futuristic works of H.G. Wells and Jules Verne. His garments managed to combine the femininity of the Victorian era, through his use of lace and silk, with the innovation of Steam Punk and the Industrial Age. His incorporation of metallic and unexpected embellishments like actual nuts and bolts made each piece more special than the one that came before.

After the show ended, Charlotte brought Carina and Bryson out for one more ovation before sending them back to the green room to wait while the judges deliberated. When I was a contestant on the first season of the show, I practically handed the grand prize to Kharen Chen. Fear of failure completely took over my entire being and I never fully recovered. How different would my life have been if I'd embraced my talent and instincts and executed a collection? I still may have lost, but I wouldn't have so badly lost my way. Some days it still felt like I was fumbling my way back to the starting line.

We reviewed the sketches and tapes of their best moments of the season. Then the models came out to exhibit the final looks. After some heated exchanges and debate, we declared Carina the runner-up and Bryson Pratt, Top Designer. I knew in my heart, he wouldn't waste the opportunity like I had done.

Trini found me backstage getting my hair and makeup touched up for the after-party. She pulled a chair up to the mirror. "Good, you're still here," she said.

"I'll make a quick appearance at the after-party, finish up a few interviews, and then I guess I'm officially off the hook."

Her face softened. "Was it really so terrible?"

I put my hand over hers. "No, no. I loved seeing the collections and meeting the designers. I know what a huge platform this is. This has *nothing* to do with *Top Designer*. I'll always be grateful for the opportunities the show's afforded me."

"What is it then? Still this business with the wedding and those stupid photographs?" Trini took my hands into her own. "Georgica, what happened?"

"I should've told Victoria about my relationship with Perry.

We were wrong to conceal our past. But, no, there was no ongoing affair, no night of passion at the Goring Hotel."

"No plan to infiltrate the British upper crust?" she teased.

"No, although that was my favorite of all the allegations."

She flashed a wicked smile. "Mine too."

I pulled my hands back and placed them in my lap. "What's that quote by Flaubert? 'There is no truth, only perception?' Trini, all my work, everything I poured into those designs, was forgotten in an instant. Now, all anyone remembers, all anyone cares about, are the screaming headlines that followed."

Trini leaned over her chair, pulled a magazine out of her tote, and handed it to me. "That's not quite true."

I looked up at her. "What is this?"

"I've been holding on to this for you. Just read."

I looked down at the *Women's Wear Daily* issue published one full week after the royal wedding. There was no mention of the Goring Hotel or Perry Gillman anywhere on the front cover. Instead, the headline read, *Designers on Top, How G. Malone Brought Timeless Elegance and Historical Significance to the Modern Age.*

I flipped through and landed on the article about G. Malone. Page after page was spent praising the different looks we'd created for all the wedding-related events, and the penultimate page focused on the ceremony gown. I skipped down a few paragraphs to read the review.

The gown was well received not merely because it was beautiful, but, this collaboration also marked a significant fashion moment because of the selection of its lesser-known designers, who not only rose to the enormity of the occasion but well surpassed it.

Scattered throughout the dress, six million dollars of Cartier jewels accented every element of the sublime design. It was a stroke of sheer brilliance for Georgica Goldstein to harken back to the designs of the Elizabethan Age for inspiration, incorporating England's rich history in every detail from the Leaver Lace to the hand-embroidered needlework completed at Hampton Court Palace.

The gown was not just technically unparalleled in its execution but channeled a new take on classicism for a modern-day bride who will one day be queen. Bravo!

Women's Wear Daily was an industry magazine people in fashion circles referred to as "the Bible." It was considered *the* authority on trends in the worlds of fashion, beauty, and retail, and by all accounts, they'd given me a rave review. I looked up, and Trini handed me a large stack of several more fashion-focused magazines full of articles praising my work as a designer, with not one mention of the scandal.

All these months in South Gloucestershire, I'd firmly convinced myself there was only one version of that night anyone cared about. Now, looking at the more than half a dozen articles in front of me, I had to acknowledge that simply wasn't true.

I wiped the tears from my cheeks and handed Trini back the magazines. "Thank you for sharing these with me."

"It wasn't entirely altruistic. Georgica, I have a proposition for you."

"If it's *Top Designer All-Stars*, I'm not sure I have that kind of stamina anymore."

She laughed. "No, not *Top Designer All-Stars*, although I'm sure the producers would be thrilled to have you. I'm here to help convince you to serve as honorary chair of the Met Gala."

The Met Gala, also known as the Met Ball, was an annual fundraising gala for the benefit of the Metropolitan Museum of Art's Costume Institute in New York City. The Gala was easily regarded as one of the most exclusive events of the year, with designers fighting to dress the high-profile celebrity attendees.

Trini continued, "This year's theme is *Fashion Queens, the Royal Influence on Style*. The magazine was blown away by what you created for the wedding, especially the subtle historical references. You're the absolute perfect choice to take this on."

My head was spinning. While it was a huge honor to have even been considered for this job, the gala was on the scale of the royal wedding. Covered by all the major international media outlets, the Met Ball was considered the biggest night of the year for anyone remotely interested in fashion.

"While it's so flattering that my name is even being considered, I just don't think—"

Trini put her hand up. "Georgica, you aren't being considered. You've been chosen. Anna Wintour wants you. The only queen that matters on this side of the pond just pardoned you—take the olive branch."

"The Met Ball's only a few months away. I wouldn't even know where to begin."

"The effort is mostly led by Jan Klaus, Director of the Costume Institute, but he's an art historian by nature. We want him to partner with someone who can provide a more current take on the theme. Someone who'd be able to make the fashion more accessible and relatable to current trends. After seeing how seamlessly you married the old and new in Victoria's dress, I know you're the perfect person for this. Your aesthetic is right on the money."

"Can I think about it?"

She stood up from the chair. "Think about it, but don't take too long. Opportunities like this don't come around too often in our industry."

"To chair the Met Ball?"

"To come back from the dead."

CHAPTER THIRTEEN

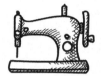

The after party at the Empire Hotel was overflowing with celebrities, designers, and former *Top Designer* contestants. Jordana gave our names at the door, and a large bouncer nodded us past the velvet rope. After we squeezed our way into the room, I sprang up on my toes and scanned the space for Jamie but couldn't make him out in the sea of heads. For all I knew he went home after the runway show and wasn't even there.

Jordana passed me a glass of champagne from a server's tray and pulled out her phone.

"There are a couple of things I need to wrap up. Are you going to be okay if I leave you for a few minutes?"

"If I'm not in this corner, I'll be over by the buffet table, stuffing my face with canapés," I teased.

"Production still needs to finish out your one-on-one interview, and then you'll shoot the finale promo spot with Charlotte and Marc on the roof." Jordana was still looking at me like she was sure I was about to bolt out the door at any moment.

"Go," I said, waving her off. "I'll be fine."

She nodded reluctantly before disappearing into the crowd. I polished off the champagne and had just set it down on a nearby high-top table along with my clutch when I felt it vibrate. I slid my phone out of my bag. It was Gideon calling.

"Hi, I can't hear you. Let me step outside and call you back," I said.

I hung up and pushed my way to the front door and outside, where a huge line was wrapped halfway around the block, waiting to get inside the party. I moved to a quieter spot in the corner and dialed Gideon back.

"What are you still doing awake?" I asked after he picked up.

"Just making sure the linens and silverware are laid out for tomorrow's breakfast," he said.

"I'm sorry I can't be there to help."

"We'll have other grand openings."

I chuckled. "No, we won't."

"No, I guess we won't," he said softly. "How was the finale show?"

"It always feels just a little bit strange to be seated on the *other side* of the judges' table."

"Bryson won, right? He's been killing it all season."

"Viscount Satterley, have you been secretly watching *Top Designer*?"

"What can I say, a certain contestant from Season One made me a lifelong fan."

I smiled. "I can't wait to see you in a few days."

"You won't have to wait that long. I booked a plane ticket to New York. I'll be there on Monday."

"Wait? Why? I'm coming back to London on Thursday."

"The opening's going well. Everything's running like clockwork. You're right, we can afford to take a few days to ourselves—hide out in museums and theaters. Eat all the Chinese food we can stuff ourselves with."

"I would absolutely love that."

"Good. That's what I was hoping you'd say."

"I should probably get back inside now, though, otherwise Jordana's sure to send out a search party for me any minute."

"I'll let you go, then. See you Monday."

"See you Monday." I hung up and cradled the phone in my hands for a few seconds, then heard my name being shouted from almost every direction, followed by a barrage of camera flashes.

I threw my hands up to block my face and flew back inside, practically knocking the three-hundred-pound bouncer off his feet. I mouthed, "I'm sorry," to him and took cover by the chocolate fountain.

"Gigi, there you are." Jordana bulldozed her way through to the buffet table. "What's wrong? Why do you look like that?"

"I stepped outside to take a call and was met by a wall of paparazzi. I can see the headline now, *Georgica Goldstein's Booty Call.*"

Jordana leaned in to me. "Was it a booty call?"

"God. No. It was Gideon."

Jordana was biting her lip while her eyes darted around the room. I nudged her arm. "What's wrong?"

"Jamie's here," she answered.

I scoured the room. "Where? Where is he?"

"Over by the bar," she answered.

"What do you think the chances are that he'll talk to me?"

She shrugged her shoulders. "He knew you'd be here. He'll never admit it. He'll say he wanted to support the show, but we both know he came to see you."

I nodded and went to find my friend.

I popped up on my tiptoes and whispered into Jamie's ear. "Watch out for those Mind Eraser shots. I know a girl who took too many, and then spilled the beans about designing Victoria Ellicott's wedding dress to the world."

Jamie slowly turned around from the bar. "Remind me, is this the same girl who uttered sweet nothings into her ex-fiancé's ear in the doorway of a hotel she knew was swarming with paparazzi?"

"The very same one."

"She sounds remarkably like my best friend. You might know her? Georgica Goldstein?"

"Hmm the name rings a bell," I answered.

The smallest hint of a smile registered on Jamie's face. "It's good to see you, Gigi. Should we go somewhere a little quieter to talk?"

I nodded and followed him out of the party and up to the rooftop. It was a cool night, but at least the space was quiet and paparazzi-free. I walked to the edge of the roof that looked out to Lincoln Center. I'd been imagining this moment for months. Now it was finally here, and I didn't have the first clue where to begin, so I said the first thing on my mind.

"When I lost *Top Designer* all those years ago, I walked off the runway so sure I'd never show in the tents again. Then, just three years later, G. Malone debuted its first collection. Remember how nervous we were?"

Jamie took two steps forward to stand beside me. "I remember. We stayed up all night until the first reviews came in, and then celebrated with mussels, French fries, and vodka shots at Schillers."

I turned to face him. "I've reached out to you at least a dozen times since the wedding. Left countless messages. Written apology note after apology note. What can I say or do to make things right between us?"

"The morning of Victoria's wedding, I got on that plane back to New York thinking every single one of my dreams was coming true. I was about to become a father. I'd just completed the most important work of my professional career. I was sure the wedding gown and collection was going to be the thing to take G. Malone public. All our sweat and blood and tears—all our years of struggle and sacrifice—was about to pay off. Then, in an instant, all of that was overshadowed by you and Perry. I needed some time to process the loss. But then, when I finally came to terms with it all, you were nowhere to be found. You were off living a totally new life in South Gloucestershire."

"I thought I should let the smoke clear. Jordana said the investors were getting skittish, and that it might be better for me to stay away."

Jamie slammed his fist on the railing. "Bullshit. That's what you do when things get tough, you run."

"That's, that's not true," I stammered.

He raised his eyebrows. "It isn't? Christ, Gigi, you've been running from yourself as long as I've known you. Self-sabotaging the *Top Designer* finale? Getting fired from Diane von Furstenberg? Running to that camp of yours to get out of that mess with Alicia and Joshua? Sending back the engagement ring to Perry? And now your new career as what, proprietor of Badgley Hall?"

"Talk to me when the world's called you a whore. A home-wrecker. A liar. An impostor, and a fraud," I spat.

"You know where Perry Gillman was the day after he was called all those very same names and worse? He was on stage at Her Majesty's Theater, performing in *Elizabeth*. Why? Because he knew none of those headlines were the truth. This doesn't have a thing to do with what happened at the Goring Hotel. You got scared by how big things were about to be for us, and it was easier to disappear to the English countryside. I'm not even angry anymore, but I can't keep believing in you *more* than you believe in you. It's too exhausting."

I searched his eyes. "What are you saying?"

"I want to dissolve G. Malone. I accepted an offer to take over for Jenna Lyons as Creative Director for J. Crew."

Tears were streaming down my face. "Is that why you came here tonight? To tell me you want to walk away from our partnership? *You* came to *me*. You were the one that stayed at Chinooka helping to finish the costumes for *Fiddler* and begged me to take a chance on us. Don't you remember?"

He titled up my chin and brushed away the tears. "Of course, I remember and we did great, kiddo. We took this thing way farther than I ever thought possible. But, it's time to cut our losses. Without a new collection to show, G. Malone's going to continue to bleed money. If we dissolve now, we each walk away with our initial investment, plus a healthy profit even *after* paying back the investors." He pulled an envelope from the inside jacket pocket of his blazer and handed it to me. "These are the dissolution documents, including the current valuation of the company. Feel free to have your father look them over."

I quickly scanned the paper and my mouth almost hit the floor. "That's a lot of money, Jamie."

"Like I told you, we did great, kiddo."

"What about Jordana? Her whole life is G. Malone."

"Jordana's not even twenty-five years old and helped build and run a global brand. We gave her a golden ticket. She'll be able get a job with any fashion house she wants. The question is, what are *you* going to do?"

I thought of Scarlett O'Hara's famous line from *Gone with the Wind*, Jamie's favorite movie, and, in my best Southern accent, said, "I can't think about that right now. If I do, I'll go crazy. I'll think about that tomorrow."

A knowing grin tiptoed across Jamie's face. "After all, tomorrow is another day."

He held his arms open, and I flew into his chest. "I'm so sorry, Jamie. I never meant to hurt you."

"I know," he whispered as he stroked my hair.

I looked up at him. "Where do we go from here?"

He let go and stepped back. "If I thought dissolving G. Malone meant you would never design again, I'd gladly go down with the ship. Strike out on your own. You've been dancing around it for years. It's time, Gigi. Take the money from G. Malone and finish that amazing collection you started a few years ago."

About six years ago, when I was still a designer for Diane von Furstenberg, I'd begun working on my very own collection. I set up a studio in my living room and lined the walls with bolts of unusual and colorful fabrics. Within a few months I'd created some of the best pieces of my entire career. A few were even featured in *Vogue*, along with an accompanying article entitled, *Avant Un-Guarded.* I was approached by several investors about mounting a show in the tents and starting my own line, but I let myself get derailed. My relationship with Joshua deteriorated along with my confidence, and I eventually abandoned the entire venture.

"There you two are. I was about to call search and rescue." Jordana bounded toward us. "Charlotte, Marc, and Trini are on their way up with the production crew."

"I should get going," Jamie said. "Thom's been on duty all night. When do you go back to London?"

"Not until Thursday."

"We'd love for you to finally meet Clara and Oliver. I don't start my new job for a few months. I decided to take a little time to be at home with the twins. Why don't you come by this week?"

"I'd like that. Very much," I said.

He leaned down and kissed my forehead. "Think about everything I said. I'll call you tomorrow."

"Is that what I think it was? Did you and Jamie just reconcile?" Jordana asked once Jamie was out of earshot.

"I hope so. I've really missed him. I don't think I even realized how much until tonight."

"Don't let his cool exterior fool you. He's been a mess for months," she said.

The producer from earlier came up behind her and asked, "Gigi, we have a few minutes while the crew sets up for the shot, can we pick up the interview from where we left off before?"

"Go," Jordana said, waving me off. "Then all you have left are the cast photos, and you're done."

We moved to a quieter corner of the roof. The cameraman lifted up the boom mic and switched on the camera. The producer turned to me and said, "Let's take it from the last question on three." He counted down with his fingers and said, "You arguably just designed the most important dress of this century. What's next for Georgica Goldstein and G. Malone?"

I took a deep breath. "I've been asked to chair this year's Met Ball, so that'll keep me busy these next few months."

"We can expect great things from Georgica Goldstein?"

"I think maybe you can."

I looked up. Trini had overhead my interview and was grinning from ear to ear.

CHAPTER FOURTEEN

Gideon arrived early Monday morning. I did a quick check in the mirror to smooth down some bedhead and opened the front door to wait for the familiar ping of the elevator chime.

"Do I smell bagels and lox?" Gideon asked, coming down the hallway.

"A delivery man from Russ and Daughters *may* have been here already this morning?" I called back.

He pulled his suitcase around the corner and up to my front door. "I've been fantasizing about this," he said, leaning in for a kiss. "And smoked salmon all morning."

"Well, at least I got top billing over the fish," I teased.

He came inside, set his bags down on the floor, and lifted me up for another kiss. "I missed you," he whispered.

"I've only been gone a few days."

"What can I say, it felt longer." He set me down and stood back to survey the kitchen table. "You outdid yourself."

"Hand-sliced Gaspe Nova smoked salmon, smoked sable, scallion cream cheese, hand-rolled bagels and bialys—everything and onion, and a chocolate babka for dessert. Sit, let me get you some coffee, or would you prefer tea?"

"Coffee, strongest you have. I didn't sleep much on the plane."

I poured Gideon a cup and took the seat next to him at the table. "So, tell me everything about the grand opening. I've been on pins and needles waiting to hear."

He took a few sips of the coffee and set the mug back down on the table. "It went really well. The staff executed everything flawlessly, and the guests couldn't stop gushing about the food and teahouse." Gideon sliced a bagel and smothered it in cream cheese, lox, and chives. "We're completely booked up through the fall."

"Wow, that's amazing."

"And that's just based on word of mouth. Wait until Badgley Hall hits all the travel books and websites. The Realis and Chateaux people have already reached out to do a tour of the property." He set his bagel down on the plate. "Enough shoptalk. What's on the agenda today?"

"I have a surprise planned for later this evening, but the rest of the day is wide open for whatever you feel like doing."

"As long as egg rolls and fried rice at Wo-Hop are somewhere in my future, I'm a happy man."

Gideon held his arms open to me, and I climbed onto his lap. He wrapped his arms around me and said, "Can I be honest about something?"

I swiveled around to face him. "Sure?"

"This trip wasn't entirely just to see you. It was the main reason, of course, but not the only one. Asher helped set up some meetings with some potential investors. Between the write-up on the shop and the feedback we've been getting on the chef and property updates, I think we can expand on the idea of Badgley Hall as a true visitor's destination. But, we need the additional financial backing to finish the improvements."

"How much would you need?"

"A few hundred thousand pounds."

I raised my eyebrows. "That's a lot of money, Gid."

"With the sale of this apartment and getting one or two investors on board, we should come pretty close."

I stood up and took a few steps away from the table. Gideon rose, came up behind me, and put his hands on my shoulders.

"What's the matter?" he asked.

I turned around to face him. "I need to be honest with you about something also. I was offered the opportunity to serve as honorary chair of the Met Ball. It's the biggest fashion event of the year, and I've been asked to curate it." I swallowed hard and continued, "I accepted the position."

"You accepted? How do you plan on chairing something like that from South Gloucestershire? You didn't want to talk to me first?"

"I have to do this, Gid. You don't get second chances in my world, and the most important woman in fashion just offered me one. I can't say no. This is my shot to come back from the royal wedding and G. Malone and finally stand on my own two feet."

Gideon shook his head and sat down on the couch. "I thought you were done with all of that."

"Designing isn't just a whim or hobby for me. It's what I do. It's who I am."

He looked up at me and sighed. "God, you must think I'm a chauvinistic jerk."

I rushed over to his side. "No, no, of course not. I don't think that at all."

He took hold of my hands and looked deeply into my eyes. "I love how your brain works. I've never been prouder of anyone than I was of you the night of Victoria and Alexander's wedding. Don't misunderstand me, I want you to keep designing and creating."

I searched his face. "You just want me to do it from Badgley Hall?"

"Everything you touch, everything you put your spin on becomes something extraordinary. The teahouse was an old stable before you came in and made it something beautiful and special. Badgley Hall needs you." Gideon stroked the side of my face. "*I* need you."

What was I doing? Self-sabotaging my relationship with Gideon? Running away again? Deep down, I knew his apprehensions weren't *really* about location or logistics. In this modern age, it was possible to be almost anywhere doing almost anything. I could easily set up a studio and design my line from Badgley Hall. With a better Internet connection, I could probably even chair the Met Ball from there. No, what Gideon wanted was for his wife to be the Countess of Harronsby, dedicating her life and purpose to everything that comes with the title. We were engaged. I committed to spending the rest of my life with him, and when I made that promise, I understood that his life was at Badgley Hall. Being with him should mean honoring that promise no matter what the cost.

I buried my face in Gideon's chest before he could see the tears brimming in my eyes. He tilted my chin up and kissed me softly on the lips. "We're on the same page, aren't we?"

"Of course we are," I whispered.

"Good."

Gideon slowly rose from the couch. He glanced at his watch and said, "I should go shower and freshen up. I'm meeting Asher at his office in about an hour. Can we come back to this conversation later?"

"Meet me at 79th and Central Park West at 5:00."

He leaned down and kissed me again. "We'll figure all this out, Gigi. I promise."

"Hey, sorry I'm running so late. Did I ruin anything?" Gideon asked, rushing over to me.

I looked down at my watch. "No, no, it's okay. We can still make it. Everything okay? I thought you'd be done with your meetings hours ago?"

"I walked around Central Park for a while."

"You've been walking around Central Park all this time? Why didn't you call me? I could've met up with you."

"I wanted some time on my own."

He was only in town a couple of days and he wanted some time on his own? That didn't make any sense at all unless maybe the meetings hadn't gone well?

"Are you sure everything's okay?" I asked again.

"Yeah. Fine. So where are we headed?"

"Follow me."

He motioned for me to take the lead, and we crossed the street toward the American Museum of Natural History.

"Are we checking out the dinosaurs?" he asked.

I shook my head no.

"The whale?"

Gideon was referring to the famous and huge fiberglass model of a blue whale suspended from the museum's ceiling. "Patience, young grasshopper. We aren't going to the museum."

He scrunched up his nose. "We aren't?"

"Nope," I said excitedly. I could hardly wait for him to see what I had planned.

We turned the corner and walked through a courtyard, until we came to a large glass building with a huge circular dome in its center.

"A planetarium?"

I took a half bow. "The stars at your disposal, sir. I know the light pollution of the city makes it harder to see the stars here than at Badgley Hall, but where there's a will... "

"There's a way," he finished. "This is great, thank you."

I thought he'd love the surprise, but his reaction was lukewarm at best. "We can do something else if you'd rather? I just know how much you love astronomy. I thought this was right up your alley?"

He held the door open for me. "It's cold. Let's go inside."

We hurried into the large auditorium, where the 6:00 show was about to begin. An usher directed us to two reclining seats off the aisle. We settled into our chairs and leaned back, so we'd have the best view of the show. A few minutes later the room went dark, and a booming voice came over the speaker, welcoming us to the Hayden Planetarium at the Rose Center for Earth and Space as the ceiling gave way to the stars. I reached my fingers over the armrest to hold Gideon's hand. He pulled back and away, resting his hands on his lap.

I looked up. The narrator was explaining the phenomenon of the Supernova.

When there is a crack in the core, or center, of a star, eventually the core becomes so heavy, so weighted down, it cannot withstand its own gravitational force. The core collapses, and a blindingly bright star bursts into view in a corner of the night sky—it wasn't there a few hours ago, and now it burns like a beacon. That bright star isn't actually a star, at least not anymore. The brilliant point of light is an explosion of a star that has reached the end of its life before finally and gracefully fading from the sky.

I glanced over at Gideon. He was shifting uncomfortably in his seat, barely paying attention to the show. When the presentation ended, I followed him out to the courtyard.

I pulled out the museum map. "Do you want to go back inside and check out any of the exhibits? The one on Mars looks pretty interesting."

"No, that's okay, we can head downtown to dinner," he mumbled.

"Rush hour's over, so we'd probably fly down the FDR if we grab a taxi to Chinatown."

"Whatever you want," he muttered, and walked ahead of me toward the corner to hail a cab.

I reached for the crook of his arm. "Hey, are you going to let me in on what's wrong?"

He whipped around to face me. "When were you going to tell me?"

I racked my brain to figure out what he was talking about. "Tell you what?"

"When were you going to tell me about G. Malone and the money?"

I closed my eyes. "Asher told you didn't he? I went to Alicia for some financial advice. I should've told her not to say anything yet."

"Asher was pretty surprised that I was still going after investors, considering the money you're about to come into."

"Jamie accepted another job and wants to dissolve G. Malone. If we do it now, we both stand to walk away with a good deal more than our initial investment."

"How much more?"

"Just shy of two million dollars each."

"This morning I was going on and on about needing to raise capital for Badgley Hall, and you didn't think to mention any of this?"

"Nothing's final. I haven't even signed the dissolution papers yet."

He looked up at me. "Asher said Alica told him you're considering using the money to finally start your own label."

"It was just something I threw out there. Jamie mentioned the idea, and I don't know, I started to think maybe I could. But, it was *just* an idea, and that was before I knew anything about your plans for Badgley Hall."

"Do you know how stupid I felt when Asher mentioned the dissolution like it was common knowledge?"

"I'm sorry. It wasn't on purpose. I was processing everything, trying to figure out my next move. I was waiting until you got here so we could talk about all of this in person. But the answer's simple. You need the money for the improvements, so take it. Take all of it."

"Asher's pretty confident one of the investors from this morning will come through. I don't need your money."

"That's wonderful. If we add that money to the money from G. Malone, then we can absolutely transform the property. It can be everything you've dreamed of."

"You aren't hearing me. I think you should *keep* the money, Gigi."

I continued talking over him. "We can do what you suggested and turn the apartment above the carriage house into a small studio for me. Maybe I'll even keep the shag carpets and popcorn ceiling. A little seventies inspiration can't hurt. With my other responsibilities on the estate, it could never get to the scale of G. Malone, but I can certainly create some pieces for the shop. Eventually, we could even blow out one of the walls of the gift shop, and I could use the extra space as a small boutique."

"Georgica, stop. *Please* just stop."

I nodded and moistened my lips. We were standing beside one another, but he already felt a million miles away. I reached out to touch his arm and he recoiled.

"I pushed you. I was jealous of Perry and afraid of losing you. That night in the Whispering Gallery, you thought the whole world had turned against you. I wanted you to know I was on your side. But we rushed into all this. *I* rushed into all this. I hardly knew you. The press was at your heels and I didn't want you taking off. I thought with enough time we could find our middle ground. If I'm honest, I thought you might welcome the change of pace and we'd be partners in Badgley Hall." He took a step closer to me. "I do love you, but we both know that's not enough. At first, yes, I suppose it could be, but over time we'll come to resent each other, and I don't want that. This morning, I asked if we were on the same page. You said yes, but we're not, are we?" He brushed the tears off my face and cupped my chin. "Are we?"

I shook my head. "I don't know."

"I do know. And, I'd never forgive myself if I let you stifle your dreams for me. We shouldn't get married. Hard as we've tried, we both want different things, different lives. It would be a mistake."

"I can make it work, Gid. I can be everything you want me to be."

He pulled me into his arms. "I don't want you to be anything other than who you are. It's my fault. You've been trying to tell me who you are. You tried over and over again but I didn't want to listen. Now we're trying to force something that doesn't feel right. It should feel right for us both and not be riddled with all these obstacles and compromises."

I stared into his gray-green eyes. In the very depths of my soul and hollows of my heart, I knew he was right. We were a Supernova, cracks in our core, weighing us down until we couldn't fight the gravitational force any longer. Gideon being pulled to Badgley Hall and me back to my first love, design. I thought of the quote Perry gave to the *New York Times* last year, the one that had hurt me to my core. Nothing summed Gideon and me up better.

"Some of the best relationships challenge you to be a better, different person. They're usually the ones where you don't start off on equal or sure footing, but, eventually, you find your way there. Those relationships are never the lasting ones, though. They require too much compromise, too many concessions. Some romances are intense and wonderful, but are simply doomed from the start."

"Are you sure this is what you really want?" I asked.

"No, but I am sure this is what's best for us both," he said.

I slipped the engagement ring off my finger and held it firmly in the palm of my left hand. "Here," I said, handing it back to him. "This ring's been in your family for generations. It belongs on the finger of the future Countess of Harronsby."

He closed his fist around it. He brought his hand up to his mouth, closed his eyes, inhaled deeply, and slipped the ring into his breast pocket. "I'll go back to the apartment, get my things, and be on the first flight back to London."

I wiped my nose and cheeks with the back of my hand, while Gideon tucked a stray hair behind my ear. "We can't send you back to South Gloucestershire without at least one meal at Wo-Hop. What do you say Viscount Satterley?"

He pulled me back into his arms again and we stood together in an embrace for what felt like forever, each of us silently saying goodbye to the other. When we pulled apart he smiled, put his arms around my shoulders, and stepped out into the street to hail us a cab downtown.

CHAPTER FIFTEEN

Jamie opened the door of his apartment. "Christ Gigi, you look like shit."

Considering I'd been crying on and off for the last forty-eight hours and hadn't slept for more than fifteen or twenty minutes at a clip, saying I looked like shit was probably a wild understatement. I passed Jamie a bouquet of flowers and the carefully wrapped housewarming and baby gifts from Barney's, his favorite store. "Thanks. It's nice to see you too," I said, folding my coat over my arm.

He leaned in to get a better look at me. "What happened?"

"Nothing happened. Maybe this is just my face now."

"No, you didn't look like this the other night. Thom, come check out Gigi's face," Jamie yelled into the hallway.

"I can't. I'm feeding Oliver. Bring her face into the nursery," Thom called back.

"May I come in now?" I asked sweetly, still perched in the doorway.

He bowed to the door. "Entre, mon amie."

I stepped into a beautiful marble foyer that gave way to an impressive living room. Even only having taken a few steps into the apartment, it was obvious Jamie had a heavy hand in decorating. The couches were a gorgeous electric blue velvet, which brought out the vibrant colors of the hand-painted de Gournay wallpaper. The herringbone floors were stained a rich brown to tie in the large oak beams overhead. It was sophisticated and eclectic all at the same time—the perfect mix of Thom and Jamie.

"The place is incredible." I rushed over to the large windows. "And these views of Central Park are *amazing*."

"You know what they say, the best things in life are free, and the second best are pretty fucking expensive. Thom found the place. He dragged me here kicking and screaming. I was determined not to move above Fourteenth Street. But, this apartment's spectacular and the Upper West Side is definitely more kid-friendly."

"Speaking of kids, can I pleeeaasse finally meet them? I brought gifts from Barney's and everything."

"This way," he said, motioning toward the far hallway.

I followed Jamie into a pastel sunlit nursery. Thom was feeding Oliver, while Clara was playing on a colorful mat on the ground.

I covered my mouth with my hand. "They've gotten so big since those first pictures Thom sent after they were born. And more beautiful, if that's even possible."

Jamie bent down and lifted Clara off the floor. "Clara, meet your Auntie Gigi," he said, handing her over to me. "Auntie Gigi's going to be countess, but don't worry, you'll outrank her one day when you become a princess."

"Are you sure that's what you want for her? After having a front-row seat to her life, I'm not so sure I'd trade places with Victoria."

"Yeah, I was thinking more of the jewels and castles, but she'll be able to spend her summers with you at Badgley Hall, which is pretty much the same difference."

I smiled uncomfortably and handed Clara back to Jamie. He placed her into the crib, while I walked over to Oliver. "And what about you, little man? What's your story?"

"He's a fighter, this one. The doctors discovered a small hole in his heart after he was born that required surgery, but he's doing great now," Thom answered.

I turned to Jamie. "I can't believe I didn't know anything about it. I would've been on the first flight over. Helped with Clara. Whatever you needed."

"I know you would've," Jamie said. "We didn't tell anyone what was going on. It was too hard to talk about."

"He's okay now, though?"

Jamie picked Oliver up from Thom's lap and placed him over his shoulder to burp him. He rubbed his back in a circular motion before patting it gently. "He's amazing."

Oliver let out a few small burps, and Jamie placed him down in his crib, while Thom switched off the light.

"Naptime," Jamie whispered.

I followed him out of the room, closing the door softly behind me.

"You and Gigi go relax on the balcony. I'll dig up some snacks," Thom said.

"I can come help," I offered.

"I got it. You two have some catching up to do," Thom insisted, waving us off.

We stepped out onto a beautiful balcony overlooking Central Park. It spanned almost the whole length of the apartment.

"I can *certainly* see why you were kicking and screaming all the way here," I ribbed.

"Well, it's no Badgley Hall—please tell me you decided to hold the wedding there. The wedding dress I designed for you isn't going to work in any other venue."

I spun around to face him. "You designed a wedding dress for me? What? When?"

"As soon as Jordana told me you and Gideon had gotten engaged. Hold on, let me go get my sketchpad."

I was in shock. All these months, I thought I was the only one desperately missing our friendship, but he was too.

A few seconds later Jamie came back onto the balcony, hugging the pad tightly to his chest. He passed the book to me. I looked down at the sketch. The gown was gorgeous, with a boat neck bodice giving way to long sleeves in a French Chantilly lace. It had three-dimensional floral lace appliqués and beading along the hemline for a touch of modernity and sparkle.

"The floral appliques—" he started.

"Are a homage to the dress I wore to the royal wedding," I said, completing Jamie's thought.

He nodded. "Exactly. If Gideon wasn't already in love with you at that point, that Valentino dress sealed the deal."

I studied the sketch again. The dress was simple and classic. Nothing about it was over-the-top or showy. It was the complete opposite of Jamie's usual and more theatrical aesthetic.

"It took all the restraint I had not to cover the skirt with feathers, but with this particular dress, I thought less was more," he said.

"It's perfect. Really."

"Then why do you look like that?"

"Like what?"

"Like you're about to collapse into a puddle on the ground."

"I'm just so touched. I never expected you'd do this."

"Jordana said the wedding's July 4th weekend? We don't have a lot of time, but if I get your measurements today, I can get it finished. Maybe I'll outsource the beadwork. It's never been my strong suit anyway. For the material, I was thinking satin. It's just richer-looking. It doesn't breathe all that well, though. How warm does it get in England in July?

"Jamie, there isn't going to be a wedding."

His eyes opened wide as he did a double take. "Wait, what do you mean there's not going to be a wedding? Don't tell me you two are going to elope - that is so déclassée."

"We're not eloping, we broke up."

I held my left hand up, and Jamie pulled my bare ring finger closer to examine it. "What happened?"

"Our lives were pulling us in different directions. We decided to let go rather than get torn apart."

"Oh Gi, I'm so sorry."

Jamie put his arms around me as Thom walked in holding a tray of cheese and crackers. "Did I miss something?"

Jamie let go and took the tray out of Thom's arms. "Our Gigi's single again."

Thom shook his head. "Men are such bastards."

"No, Gideon is one of the good ones. It just wasn't meant to be. I'll be okay."

"Of course, you'll be okay. But in the meantime, let me scrounge up a bottle of something we can all drown our sorrows in," Jamie said.

Thom put a hand on my knee. "How are you really holding up?"

"I've been better, but it was the right decision for both of us. I know it was."

"Can I ask, does this have anything to do with Perry Gillman?"

"Perry? No. No. I haven't even thought about Perry."

"Really? I think of him daily. Of course, I do pass that billboard for *Elizabeth* on my way into the office every morning. You must know it, the one where he's dressed as Dudley, wearing those tight camel colored riding pants and silky white V-neck shirt. God, I love those period costumes."

I laughed and wiped my nose. Thom put his arm around me. Jamie returned with the bottle of wine and some stemware and poured us each a glass.

"A toast," Jamie said.

I set my glass down on the mosaic table. "Hold on one second. Let me go get something from my bag."

I hurried back into the living room, retrieved the manila folder from my tote, and carried it out to the balcony.

I handed the documents over to Jamie. "The signed dissolution papers."

He picked up my wine glass and passed it over to me.

"To new beginnings," he said.

"To new beginnings."

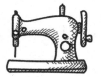

"We have Elizabeth II's Norman Hartnell wedding gown. The Dior dress Rita Hayworth wore when she married Prince Aly Khan, and the Balenciaga drop-waist dress Queen Fabiola wore for her wedding to King Baudouin of Belgium. Where are we with Elizabeth I's Rainbow Portrait Gown?" I asked.

Planning the Met Ball had proved to be a much larger undertaking than I ever imagined. I'd spent the last several months working with the curators and art historians in the museum's Costume Institute to finalize the exhibits and compile a list of artifacts we hoped to acquire for the show. The theme, *Fashion Queens, The Royal Influence on Style* was so broad, the committee felt we needed to bring in as many examples of royal dress as possible, spanning the entire globe. The logistics alone were keeping me up at night.

"That one's a little tricky," Jordana answered. "The British government considers the Rainbow Portrait Gown a national treasure. That dress has only been exhibited twice in the last four hundred years. Long story short, there are a lot of hoops to still jump through to secure it, but we're closer than further. I'm waiting on a final quote from the museum's insurance company, but if they sign on the dotted line, we should have it over here in time for the Met Ball."

"We absolutely *have* to have it."

Jordana typed furiously on her laptop. "I know, and we will. You've been obsessed with that dress since we got this gig. In better news, the Elie Saab is being flown over from Luxembourg, Princess Madeline of Sweden's Valentino wedding gown came in last night, and Victoria Ellicott's dress will be here before the ball."

"Thank you for offering to be the one to reach out to Gemma for it."

Jordana stopped typing and looked up. "Of course. Besides, what would an exhibit about the best royal fashions in history be without Victoria Ellicott's one-of-a-kind G. Malone wedding gown? We even got Cartier to loan us back the real jewels for the show."

I put my hand over hers. "You have no idea how grateful I am that you agreed to help me take this on."

"It was this or barista at Starbucks," she teased. "I have to admit, I prefer having an office at the Met, even if it's only a temporary one."

Jordana took the news of G. Malone's dissolution far better than I expected. In some ways, I think she may have even been relieved. There was no question Jordana had been the glue holding the business together these last few months. Her dark circles and extra-thin frame didn't hide the fact she was in need of a serious break from G. Malone. When I proposed the idea of assisting me with the Met Ball, she jumped on it. I don't think either one of us were ready to part ways just yet.

I looked over my inventory list. "Where do we stand with all of the museums?"

Jordana flipped to a new page of her notebook. "The Victoria and Albert Museum is loaning us several pieces, as are the

Ermitage, The Louvre, The Royal Museum of Scotland, and the Muse de Traje in Madrid. You know, I never say things like this, but I actually think we're in excellent shape." Jordana looked at her phone. "I'm running late for a meeting with the *Vogue* marketing team. Do you have everything handled here?"

"I think so. Jan's going to present the final renderings of the galleries, and I'm announcing the list of exhibits. Do you think I should include the Rainbow Portrait dress in the presentation?" I asked.

"Did you forget who you're working with?" Jordana asked with a smile. "Of course include the gown—it'll be here in time."

"What would I do without you?"

"You'd be just fine. I don't think you've left this room for as much as a coffee in months."

"To be honest, given everything with Gideon, I've been glad for the distraction."

Jordana put her arm around my shoulder and squeezed. "I'll swing by to check on things after the meeting."

I turned on my laptop and pulled up the excel sheet itemizing all the gowns and other pieces promised for the exhibition. My idea was to pair the royal ensembles with the more modest garments they influenced to show how the royals inspired the fashions and trends of the day. For example, the curator from the Louvre explained that Marie Antoinette's lavishly decorated heels, complete with sensuous fabrics, ribbons, lace, bows, and jewels became so popular it was common to see both men and woman wearing them in the streets. The Louvre generously loaned us a pair, along with the much less ornate version worn by the masses, which I planned on displaying alongside them.

I gathered up the dossiers for the meeting. It was the first time I was presenting to the complete Met Ball committee, including the honorary celebrity chairs. Every year since Anna Wintour's first year as Met Gala chair in 1995, the event featured honorary hosts from the worlds of entertainment and fashion.

Their job was to rally donations, finesse the theme, and generally bring even greater awareness to the event. Anna Wintour was announcing her chair selection to the press in a couple of days but giving the committee a chance to become acquainted with her picks at today's meeting. Taylor Swift and Bradley Cooper were among the names I'd heard thrown around most, but as Trini reminded me, Anna also liked to go with the unexpected.

I took the staff elevator up from the basement into the Greek and Roman gallery of the Met. The meeting was taking place in the Leon Levy and Shelby White Court, a peristyle court with a soaring two-story atrium that had been sectioned off for the gathering. The entire space evoked the feel of a Roman garden, with statues and sculptures lining the walls, and a large black onyx fountain in the center of the room. I walked to the back of the gallery to greet the statue of the Roman God Janus, my favorite, in his usual spot by the fountain, his two faces welcoming visitors from every direction.

I leaned in close to the statue. "Hello, old friend," I whispered.

"Hello," a familiar voice whispered back. I closed my eyes and spun around. Every single hair on the back of my neck stood up.

"Hello, Georgica," Perry said again, his smooth British accent punctuating every syllable of my name.

Before I could respond, Jan approached us. "Perry, I see you've already met our chairwoman, Georgica Goldstein. Georgica, this is Perry Gillman, writer, creator, and star of *Elizabeth*. He's also graciously agreed to be one of the celebrity hosts for this year's ball."

Perry and I eyed Jan suspiciously, unsure if Jan was making a joke or was genuinely unaware of our past connection to one another.

He continued. "Perry, Georgica was the designer of Victoria Ellicott's wedding gown and has been an absolute lifesaver in helping orchestrate this event."

"We've actually met before," Perry said.

Jan smoothed down his mustache. "Oh, really? Where? How?"

"It was in another life," Perry answered, his eyes never leaving my face. "We haven't seen each other in quite a while."

Trini Bower walked to the center of the gallery and clapped her hands together to get the attention of the rest of the attendees milling about the room. "I know the art in here is a pretty great distraction, but if everyone could take their seats we'll get started," she said.

"After you," Perry said, smoothly extending his arm toward the table.

I found my name and took a seat at the far end of the table. Perry sat down directly across from me. He looked great in a dark blazer over a distressed *Elizabeth* T-shirt and fitted dark jeans. His wavy hair was loose, falling just past his chin. He was wearing round-rimmed tortoise glasses, and his beard was neatly trimmed. I caught at least three of the *Vogue* staffers gawking at him.

Trini stood up on her tiptoes and waited for the room to quiet down before she began speaking. "Thank you all for joining us this afternoon. With just six weeks left until the ball, we wanted to share the final renderings of the space, as well as the list of exhibits we've been able to secure. Without further ado, let me turn this presentation over to Jan Klaus and Georgica Goldstein."

The room clapped politely as Jan turned his attention to the large screen set up behind us. He nodded to the AV team to start the presentation.

"As everyone knows, this year's theme is *Fashion Queens, the Royal Influence on Style*. To capture the essence of the subject matter, we are going to display the bulk of the artifacts in the Costume Institute, the Medieval Galleries, and the Renaissance Galleries. We'll utilize the gate from the Valladolid Cathedral in the Medieval Sculpture Hall as the backdrop for the special exhibit on the royal clothes of the Tudor dynasty."

Jan flashed through renderings of those galleries, which had been reconfigured to look like royal courts, and continued, "The architecture of these galleries, along with the imported textiles, provide the perfect context for these remarkable fashions. Taking a page from Perry Gillman and *Elizabeth*," he said, nodding in Perry's direction, "we designed these galleries to be a full immersive experience. We want our audience to become familiar with not only the clothing and designers, but the incredible monarchs that wore them."

Jan held his hand up to his forehead and squinted into the spotlight. "If there are no questions, I'll turn the presentation over to the honorary co-chair of this event, Georgica Goldstein."

I stood up and felt every eye in the place on me. Jan may not have known my past connection to Perry Gillman, but the rest of the room sure did.

"Thank you, Jan," I said, my voice and hands trembling. I took a sip of water and pulled a stack of index cards from my pocket. "Royals needed an impressive collection of garments to display their majesty and send a powerful message to their subjects. For example, Queen Victoria might have become known for her darker mourning garments in later life, but she was quite the trendsetter in her youth. She was one of the first women to opt for a white wedding dress—an unusual choice for any bride at the time, and especially so for a queen, who was expected to wear official royal robes when she tied the knot. Characteristically, Victoria rebelled against expectation and wanted her wedding day to be about her as a woman, not a public figure. As such, she inspired a fashion that has survived for women and royals to the modern day."

I took a sip of water and continued, "I am pleased to announce we've secured Queen Victoria's white wedding gown for the exhibition."

The room clapped politely as I advanced the presentation a few slides. "Looking at more modern monarchs, Princess Margaret, the only sister of Queen Elizabeth II, was glamorous, beautiful, and vivacious, and those qualities showed up in her appreciation of fashion. The wasp-waist designs of Christian Dior's New Look suited her perfectly, as did the elaborate evening wear of Norman Hartnell. Both designers will be prominently featured in our show."

I set the cards down on the table. "Today, as in the past, royal fashion is as much about politics as it is about elegant attire. In this exhibit, we will peel back the layers of monarchs' outfits, past and present, to reveal how fashion has been used by kings and queens to reflect their power and their reign. I now ask everyone to turn to their dossiers to view the complete catalog of secured pieces for the exhibit."

I gave the room a few minutes to peruse through the books. I took another sip of water and set the glass back down on the table. "I'm now happy to take any questions?"

Perry shot his hand up.

I raised my eyebrows. "Mr. Gillman?"

"How the hell did you manage to get a hold of the gown from the Rainbow Portrait?" he asked, a satisfied smile sweeping across his face.

Perhaps the most heavily symbolic portrait of Queen Elizabeth, the Rainbow Portrait was painted just three years before Elizabeth's death. In the painting, a young, vibrant Elizabeth appears dressed in a linen bodice embroidered with spring flowers, her hair loose beneath a fantastical headdress. Her cloak was intentionally decorated with painted-on eyes and ears, so foreign leaders would understand that, as ruler, she sees and hears all. Her headdress was an incredible design decorated lavishly with pearls and rubies supporting her royal crown. The pearls symbolizing her virginity; the crown, of course, her royalty.

Perry knew the Rainbow Portrait well, having even written a

song for the second act of *Elizabeth* based on the painting. Perry had explained his vision for the scene to me back when he was creating the show, the younger Elizabeth from the painting coming alive to taunt the older Elizabeth on her life choices and missed opportunities. The two women would then go on to sing a gorgeous duet about ambition, love, and regret.

The dress was housed in the most secure archive vaults of the Victoria and Albert Museum, and for years, Perry tried desperately to arrange for us to go and see it up close. But back then, Perry was a no-name composer without a hit musical, trying to view one of the most important pieces in fashion history. He was denied access again and again. Eventually, we made do with photocopied pictures from the New York Public Library, and whatever images the Internet could provide. He leaned on my experience as a designer to understand the dress's construction and symbolism. I even sewed a replica of the dress so he'd have something tangible to serve as inspiration. We worked on those lyrics for weeks, maybe even months, until Perry was satisfied we'd captured the essence of the scene and what the Rainbow Portrait would've meant to the aging queen trying desperately to hold onto her power.

I looked out into the audience, my eyes locking with Perry's, and flashed back to our encounter at The Goring Hotel just about a year ago, when he pleaded with me to give him a second chance. On his knees, he told me I was in every melody of *Elizabeth,* every moment and every measure. I'd just about forgotten our collaboration on the Rainbow Portrait song and how back then, I let my work, my goals, and ambitions take a backseat to his. Jamie used to say G. Malone would've gotten off the ground a full year earlier if there was no Perry Gillman and no *Elizabeth.* Maybe he was right.

Jan stood up to field Perry's question. "I've been curator of the Costume Institute since 1977 and have tried unsuccessfully for years to bring the Rainbow Portrait gown to the Met. When

Gigi said it *had* to be in this show, I practically laughed in her face and told her it couldn't be done. The British government simply does not lend out that artifact. In fact, it hasn't been in a public exhibition since 1865. But, she insisted we had to have it and has been relentless in her pursuit to bring the dress to this year's ball. Thanks to you, Mr. Gillman, Elizabethmania has taken hold of our fair city, and it seems only right that the Rainbow Portrait Gown be the star of our show."

Trini rose from her seat. "Thank you, Jan. Thank you, Gigi," she said, nodding in our direction. "I would now like to introduce this year's honorary celebrity chairs, neither of whom even require an introduction. First, she's an American songwriter, singer, actress, philanthropist, dancer, and fashion designer. She's graced the cover of US, French, and Italian *Vogue*, and her current hit, "Get With It" has been number one on the Billboard Top 100 for twenty-two consecutive weeks. Please join me in welcoming Emmy J."

A girl in at least ten-inch sky-high black patent leather platform boots and a hot pink latex dress stood up from the table. Even after living in South Gloucestershire these last few months, I instantly recognized her. Emmy J. was one of the hottest, if not *the* hottest, acts in music right now. Her message of "female empowerment" was resonating, as was her hit song "Get With It," an anthem for women, demanding their men to "get with it" or get out. Emmy J. stood up and nodded politely to the room before sitting back down.

"Next, he's the British composer, lyricist, playwright, and actor best known for creating and starring in the West End hit, now a Broadway phenomenon, *Elizabeth,* a musical about the life of Queen Elizabeth I. *Elizabeth* won a record number of Olivier Awards and is rumored to break the record for most Tony Award nominations. It is the winner of five Outer Critics Circle Awards, fifteen Drama Desk Awards, including Outstanding Musical, and the New York Drama Critics' Circle Award. Perry Gillman was named as one of *Time* magazine's Most Influential People in the World and graced the cover of our highest-selling issue of *Vogue*. We are thrilled he is not only one of our celebrity chairs this year but is also performing a number from the show at the ball. Let's be honest, it's the only way most of us are going to get to see any part of *Elizabeth* in this century. Perry?" Trini motioned to Perry, who stood up and gave the crowd a small wave.

It was hard to believe there was a time Perry was more mine than anyone else's. Now, it seemed with all his mounting accomplishments, he belonged to the whole world.

After he sat back down, she lifted her water glass and said, "Thank you all for your time and involvement. Here's to what I know is going to be the best Met Ball we've ever put on. Please feel free to enjoy the Greek and Roman galleries. We have them closed off to the public for another half hour."

As the audience dispersed in different directions, I went to talk to Trini, who was organizing papers into her portfolio.

After a few seconds she noticed me standing there.

"Wonderful presentation, Georgica. Just wonderful."

"Trini, do you have a minute to talk?"

She looked down at her watch and then up at me. "I have about ten until I'm supposed to meet Anna for lunch. What's up?"

"In private?"

"Uhh, sure," she said, looking around. "Let's slip into the hallway."

I followed her out into the hall, which was crowded with museum tourists.

"I assume when you said in private, you meant away from the prying eyes and ears of the committee," she said.

"This is fine."

She crossed her arms over her chest. "What's going on?"

"Perry? Really, Trini? Of all the possible celebrities you could have asked to chair the ball, you asked Perry Gillman?"

"Shh!" She pulled me to the corner of the hallway. "The Perry Gillman thing hasn't been announced yet."

I lowered my voice. "You know how hard it's been for me to separate my name from his in the press! I can't even imagine the feeding frenzy that'll be waiting for me when this nugget comes out."

"The powers that be might kill me for telling you this, but Perry approached us about chairing the ball, not the other way around. He was on the short list, of course, but nobody thought he'd ever say yes with *his* schedule."

I shook my head. "Why would he volunteer?"

"Maybe publicity for *Elizabeth*?"

I tilted my head to the side. "You and I both know *Elizabeth* doesn't need any more publicity."

"What do you want me to say, Georgica? Do I think he volunteered so he could get closer to you? It's possible. He approached me a few days after we announced you were coming on as co-chair. Truthfully, I'm not sure what his motives are, but he's the hottest celebrity in the world right now, and we'd have been crazy to turn him down."

I understood where she was coming from. To have Perry Gillman headlining the Met Gala in a year where the exhibit was focused on royal fashions was an opportunity nobody in their right mind would pass up.

Trini took hold of my hands. "If you make it a big deal, they'll make it a big deal. Go on doing the same fabulous job you've been doing, and the headlines will be about this incredible exhibition you orchestrated, nothing else."

"I hope you're right."

She slipped on her signature oversized tortoise frames. "I'm Katrina Bower, I'm always right."

CHAPTER SEVENTEEN

I walked back into the Greek and Roman gallery to collect my things. It was virtually empty, except for a few stragglers from the meeting checking out the marble sculpture of Hercules on the far side of the room. I walked around the table and collected the secret dossiers, piling them on my chair to bring back down to my office along with my laptop.

"Do you need any help?" Perry asked.

I turned around from the table and caught Perry looking at my left hand. I slipped it into my suit pocket. "What are you still doing here?"

"These days, I rarely get any time on my own. I thought I might wander the museum a bit," he answered.

I nodded and tried balancing the rest of the binders with my right hand. Perry looked me square in the eye and raised an eyebrow. "Are you sure I can't give you a hand first?"

I relaxed my stance. "Okay, sure, if you could grab my laptop, that would be a big help."

He picked up my laptop and tucked it under his arm. "Lead the way."

Perry followed me to the staff elevator and down to the lower level that housed most of the museum's corporate offices, including the one I was borrowing until the Met Ball. I set the binders on the ground and dug around my pocket for my set of keys to open the door.

"Where should I leave the laptop?" Perry asked once we got inside.

I cleared some space on the desk, which was overflowing with Art History books and museum catalogs. Perry set the computer down beside a pile of notebooks. He stood back to survey the large amount of research piled everywhere.

"Reminds me of what our apartment looked like back when I was in the throes of writing *Elizabeth*."

My mind drifted back to our apartment living room, the floor littered with takeout containers and stacks of books from the New York Public Library. On those days when Perry hit a wall or stumbling block, I'd spend hours combing through volumes of research to help him find the perfect quote to use in a lyric or moment to build into a song. When I struggled with a design for G. Malone, he'd make one small suggestion or tweak that would instantly put me right back on course. When it worked, our partnership was pure magic. Maybe that's why it'd hurt so much when he walked away from us.

"Putting together this show's been way more work than I ever expected, but I'm really loving it," I said.

"That doesn't surprise me. Remember the wedding dress you designed for *Fiddler on the Roof*? You were so committed to making sure every single detail was authentic."

Even though we were standing inches apart, hearing Perry talk about the summer we met at Camp Chinooka made me miss him in a way I hadn't allowed myself to in a long time. Certainly not when I was with Gideon, and now, even all these months later, it still felt like some sort of betrayal of the heart. I turned from him and noticed the time on the desk clock.

"Shouldn't you be getting back to the theater for the matinee performance?" I asked.

"I'm not going on today."

I turned back to face him. "I know about fifteen hundred people who are about to be sorely disappointed."

Perry hopped up on my desk, letting his legs swing into the file cabinet. "Nah, my understudy's pretty great. I doubt anybody will even notice. They may even like the show better with him in the part. Hey, do you have some time? I thought if you weren't too busy, maybe we could grab lunch?"

"Do you think that's such a good idea? Victoria and Alexander's televised interview is airing Sunday night. If you hadn't noticed, we're back in the headlines again."

"How about lunch in the park? Like old times? Two hot dogs and a park bench? What do you say?"

Back when Perry was writing *Elizabeth* and Jamie and I were struggling to get G. Malone off the ground, money was tight, and all we could afford for a date night were a few hot dogs and the best scenery New York City had to offer. We'd take our picnic up to Belvedere Castle, a Gothic-style fortress, smack in the middle of Central Park, with panoramic views of the Manhattan skyline. We'd fantasize about how perfect our lives would be if *Elizabeth* made it to Broadway or G. Malone could get even *one* collection shown in the tents.

"Jan and I have a meeting with the architects in the Medieval Galleries around two," I answered.

"More than enough time to get to Belvedere Castle and back. Look, we're going to keep running into each other. We can go on avoiding one another, but that didn't exactly work out well for us last go 'round. What do you say? I'll even spring for some ice cream from one of those carts."

"A Chipwhich?"

A tiny smile crept across his face. "Whatever you want, Princess."

We stopped at a food cart, and Perry ordered two hot dogs and two bottles of water.

"Mustard and sauerkraut, just the way you like it," Perry said, passing me a hot dog wrapped in tinfoil.

I slipped my sunglasses on and glanced behind me.

"There's nobody trailing us, I promise. As far as anyone's concerned, we're two people taking a stroll in the park on a beautiful day."

"Except that one of us just happens to be wearing an *Elizabeth* T-shirt and looks remarkably like Perry Gillman," I joked.

Perry looked down and pulled his shirt away from his body. "This shirt's our best seller. It's all over the city." He pointed up to the tower. "Those people are getting up. Let's grab their bench. Best views of the Great Lawn from up there."

I followed him up a few steps to the observation deck of Belvedere Castle and took a seat on the empty bench.

"Your parents came to see *Elizabeth* a couple of weeks ago," he said.

"Yeah, I know, they told me."

"It was good to see them. Your mum mentioned you and Gideon are getting married this July."

There was no point in concealing the truth. He'd hear about me and Gideon soon enough. I slid my left hand out of my pocket. "We're not, actually. We called off the engagement. We were in two different places, literally and figuratively. You'd think I'd have learned my lesson after what happened with us. Who knows, maybe I'm a glutton for punishment."

Perry pushed a piece of hair out of my eyes. "Or someone who loves unreservedly."

Our eyes met for a moment before I broke contact.

"Was it really all so bad with us?" he asked.

A lump formed in my throat. "No, not so bad."

"Do you ever think about what would've happened if I didn't write *Elizabeth* and you hadn't started G. Malone?"

I swallowed hard. "Umm, I don't know. You'd probably still be playing piano in that jazz bar in the West Village. Maybe I'd be designing for small boutiques. Who knows, we may even have gone back to work at Camp Chinooka over the summers to make ends meet."

"Think we'd have been happy?"

"Maybe? A different kind of happy, I suppose."

He tucked his hair behind his ears, and a faraway look swept over his eyes, like he was almost imagining the other version of us —tucked away in my small Hell's Kitchen apartment, enjoying each other and the life we were building together.

"I think we could've been happy," he said softly.

I elbowed Perry's side. "What about the Gillman Girls? Just think about all those tweens who'd never have had the chance to adore you."

"Don't you forget who was named hottest counselor at Camp Chinooka four years running." Perry leaned in closer to me. "Tweens have *always* adored me."

Just like that, we were back in our easy rhythm, and every one of my senses was reminded of how at home Perry could make me feel.

I balled up the tinfoil from the hot dog in my hand. "It's late. I should probably be getting back for my meeting."

"Before you go, I have a proposition for you. It's the reason I wanted to have lunch. It won't be announced to the trade papers until tomorrow, but I've sold the film rights to *Elizabeth*."

"Wow, that's amazing. Congratulations."

"I want you to join the project as a creative consultant. You understood my vision right from the beginning. You were the only one."

"I'm not sure I'm the right—"

He pulled a ticket from his back pocket. "Before you say no, come to *Elizabeth* Saturday. You've never seen the revised second act."

"We're mounting the Tudor gallery on Saturday."

He handed me the ticket. "Then come for *just* the second act. Curtain goes up at four thirty."

I waved the ticket around and teased, "Do you know how much I could scalp this for? At least two first-class tickets to Bora Bora."

"Bora Bora, huh?"

"I don't know, it was the first place that popped into my mind."

"Crystal-blue waters, white sandy beaches, huts over the ocean. I wouldn't blame you one bit. But, if you decide to stay stateside, I hope you'll consider my offer."

"I'll consider it."

"Good."

CHAPTER EIGHTEEN

I raised my coffee cup and tried to get the waitress's attention. There were probably hundreds, if not thousands, of brunch spots in New York City, but, of course, Jamie would have to pick the most popular one. Finally, the waitress spotted me and swung by with the pot for a refill. Mid-pour, Jamie finally arrived and dropped a huge pile of newspapers on the table. "Just when you thought Perry Gillman couldn't get any more famous, he's starring in and producing the movie version of *Elizabeth*."

I sipped on my coffee. "I know."

He pulled his chair out from under the table. "You know?"

"Guess who's also been named celebrity chair of the Met Ball?"

Jamie sat down and unfolded his napkin on his lap. "Perry? What's next? Is *E!* going to offer him his own reality show? Keeping up with Perry Gillman?"

I laughed and passed Jamie a menu. "The Tony Award nominations come out next week. They say *Elizabeth* is going to break the record for most nominations."

"Christ, he's going to be an EGOT before the age of forty, and I still don't know how to parallel park."

I tried to decipher the acronym. "EGOT?"

"Someone who wins an Emmy, Grammy, Oscar, and Tony. I don't begrudge him his success, but even *he* must be over himself by now."

I thought back to the conversation we had at the park, where Perry asked if I'd ever thought about what our life would be like if there was no *Elizabeth*. I couldn't say for certain he was *over* himself, but I could tell he wasn't fully settled into his success.

Jamie ran his finger down the specials. "I think I'll have the challah French toast."

"Complex carbs? What's the big occasion?" I teased.

"This is," he said, sliding an envelope across the table. "The money from G. Malone."

I picked the envelope up off the table. "This is it? The end of an era?"

"Or the start of a new one. Did you get the garment bags we messengered over from the office?"

"They're hanging on a rack in my living room. I haven't had the heart to open them yet. Those are all that remains of G. Malone."

"All that remains of G. Malone is in a storage unit in Williamsburg. What I messengered
over were the pieces from *your* unfinished collection. The appraiser wants them kept separately for insurance reasons. You know, I'd never looked at any of the garments until this week. You really could have something there. Have you given any more thought to using the money to start your own label?"

"I've been so busy with the Met Ball, thankfully, I haven't had time to give *anything* much thought."

"No word from Gideon?"

"It's been months. I won't hear from him. Besides, the way we left things was pretty final."

"You know what you need?"

"Complex carbs?"

"A crazy night out. When was the last time we really let loose?"

I strummed my fingers against the table. "Maxwell Fleichman's Bar Mitzvah?"

"That's how sad we've become? Our last night out was G. Malone's CFO's son's Bar Mitzvah? That is completely unacceptable."

"You know what, you're right. Hey, Jamie, want to be my date to the Met Ball? I don't know if it'll be a crazy night out, but Emmy J.'s performing, and so's the cast of *Elizabeth*."

"That depends. Who's dressing us?" he smirked.

Every year, major designers handpicked the celebrities they want to dress for the ball, the ensembles typically reflecting the gala's overall subject matter and theme. Given my involvement with the event, a few houses had already reached out, but I hadn't made any decisions yet.

"Don't worry, a couple of your favorites are in the running," I answered.

"Puh-lease just don't pick a designer who wants to do a more literal interpretation of the theme. We can leave the breeches and puffy sleeves to Perry Gillman."

"Deal."

The waitress came over to take our order.

I motioned to Jamie. "You know what you want, so go ahead and order. I need another minute."

He put down his menu and looked up at her. "I'll have an egg white omelet, dry, with spinach, tomatoes, and mushrooms. No potatoes and no toast. You know what, throw in a wheatgrass shot."

I did a double-take. "What happened to challah French toast, complex carbohydrates be damned?"

"*That* was before I was invited to the Met Ball."

When I got home, I placed the envelope with the check from Jamie on my drafting table and hit the blinking red button on the answering machine. I plunked down on the couch while the messages played. The first was from the New York Philharmonic, asking if Mr. and Mrs. Gillman were interested in re-upping their season subscription. I snickered, almost two years later and the Philharmonic remained wildly optimistic about our future together. I'd call them tomorrow and correct our names... again.

The second message was from my mother. "Geor—" I turned down the volume before she could even get the last syllable of my name out. "It's Mom. Oh, good, you're out of the house. I was worried you'd be home watching the Victoria and Alexander interview, drowning yourself in a pint of ice cream."

I slapped my forehead. The interview! I *had* forgotten. With everything that'd happened with Gideon and all the craziness of the Met Ball, it very fortunately slipped my mind. I hit the off button and flew back to the couch in search of the remote, which I finally found in the back of a drawer of the entertainment unit. I searched through the channels until I landed on BBC America.

The camera was aimed at Victoria and Alexander seated together on a cream-colored couch. I instantly recognized Victoria's dress as a Stella McCartney, the much-beloved British designer. The message was clear, at least to me. Victoria broke with tradition when she selected an American designer for her wedding gown, and that decision came back to bite her. Stella McCartney was a longtime friend of Victoria's, so she could trust there would be no skeletons jumping out of the closet to ruin her first public appearance since the wedding.

She looked positively radiant. Her skin was dewy and glowing. Her amber hair fell into thick waves across her slim shoulders. There was no question, marriage agreed with her, and so did pregnancy.

A reporter I didn't recognize thanked the duke and duchess for the opportunity to speak to them in their first televised interview since their engagement and wasted no time shooting off her first question about how the first six months of marriage were treating them. Alexander took the lead, telling the reporter that being married to Victoria exceeded every one of his expectations.

The reporter smiled and turned to Victoria and asked how she shared the news of the pregnancy with Prince Alexander.

"It was New Year's Eve day, and we were getting ready for an evening out. Alex brought me a glass of champagne, so we could have a private toast to the New Year. I passed the glass back to him and told him I'd be toasting with sparkling cider these next nine months. It took him a few minutes to catch on to what I meant, but once he did, well, I wish I had a video of the smile that erupted across his face."

"It's true," Alexander added. "I was stunned. Absolutely thrilled but stunned."

"And what about both of your parents? They must be over the moon?" the reporter asked.

"Oh, both of our families are absolutely ecstatic. As I'm sure you know, it's the first grandchild on both sides," Alexander answered.

"Speaking of both your families, might I ask about your sister, Annabelle?"

Victoria folded her hands into her lap. "Annabelle's wonderful. She's so excited to be an auntie."

The reporter leaned forward. "It's no secret that the night of the wedding, your one-time friend and designer of your wedding gown, Georgica Goldstein, was caught in what appeared to be a compromising moment with your sister's then boyfriend, Perry Gillman. What, if anything, do you have to say about the matter?"

Victoria took a sip of her water and brushed some hair away from her face. "Gigi was a consummate professional the entire time we worked together. The gowns she created for our wedding were *everything* I'd dreamed of. I know she's taken a pause from designing, but hopefully not too long a pause."

"And what about your sister and Perry Gillman? Is there anything else you'd wish to say on that front?"

"I'll let Annabelle discuss that matter when she's ready. All I'll say is, the press made quite a bit more out of that relationship than there really ever was. Let's be honest, there's only really been one woman in Perry Gillman's life this past year, and that's Elizabeth I."

The reporter nodded knowingly. "You've become increasingly involved in charities focused on refugee relief, can you talk to me a bit more about some of those causes?"

I switched off the TV. So that was that. For almost six months I'd been waiting for Victoria to pass sentence, and in the end, she absolved me. And while I knew many of her words had been carefully massaged and crafted by the royal family's PR machine, I also knew Victoria. She was her own person, fiercely independent, and not afraid to speak her own mind, even if it occasionally went against what was expected of her. The press would soon back off the story, Victoria had made sure of that.

I leaned over my coffee table and grabbed the binder of sketches of the looks the designers submitted as ideas for my Met Ball gown. Flipping through the pages, I carefully studied each one. Though the dresses were beautiful, none captured the overall theme and history the way I imagined.

I picked up the binder and took it over to my drafting table. I dumped over the pencil holder on top of my desk and sorted through the pencils, paperclips, and erasers, until I found the little gold key I was looking for. Kneeling down, I unlocked the small file cabinet under the table and wrenched out the sketchbook buried under stacks of papers and fabric samples. Leaning back against the wall, I drew my knees up close to my chest and wiped the accumulated dust off the top page.

It'd been close to six years since I last looked at these sketches, the solo collection I'd started working on while I was seeing Joshua but abandoned soon after our relationship ended. Inspired by the great movement of writers and artists to Paris after World War I, my designs celebrated the vitality of the artistic and intellectual scene of the 1920s. From the rich and unusual fabrics, I'd sourced from dealers in Paris, Lyon, and Marseilles, to the trims and unique embellishments I found in flea markets and consignment shops all over New York, each piece told its own story.

I flipped through the pages and landed on a sketch of one of my favorite gowns, a silver beaded semi-sheer tulle dress with an exposed décolletage. The gown had full-length sleeves and a slim silhouette that faded into glittering fringe cascading from mid-thigh to the floor. My modern take on a 1920s flapper.

That dress was here! I'd almost forgotten Jamie had my collection messengered over this morning. I hurried to the rack, unzipped the garment bag, and delicately removed the garment from inside. I held the hanger up to my body and stood in front of my floor-length mirror. It'd taken me almost five weeks to construct this gown, the sequined fringe alone taking close to one hundred thirty hours. No question, the dress was a showstopper. The silk I threaded with metal to produce a sheen was different from any other textile in the marketplace. The art deco-inspired gemstones carefully placed on the bodice to create a subtle pattern. But the bare neck, which was beautiful, still called for something. Then, it hit me.

I hurried to my bag and pulled out my massive research binder for the Met Ball, skimming through the pages until I found the section on Queen Mary of Teck, famous for her massive jewelry collection. Queen Mary was known for pairing her already beaded and patterned dresses with tiaras, brooches, rings, bracelets, and then throwing on as many necklaces as it took to create an almost bejeweled turtleneck.

I draped the silver gown onto a dress form and went into my kitchen pantry, long ago turned into a makeshift sewing cabinet. I dug around until I found the box of vintage jewelry I'd been collecting over the years and spilled the contents onto my drafting table. After separating out the necklaces, I arranged them on the form so they created a glittering bib over the dress's neckline. Standing back to appreciate the whole look, there was no question, this interpretation was the perfect homage to Queen Mary, and the perfect dress for me to wear to the Met Ball.

I slid the dress off the form and onto the table, along with the necklaces. While some designers loathed hand-sewing, I had always loved it. Couture seamstresses relied heavily on hand-stitches for accuracy and to maintain absolute control of the fabric. Although I wasn't formally trained, I'd spent years studying and learning these classic techniques, so I could execute a similar quality in my own creations.

Hunched over my kitchen table, I spent the next few hours affixing the jewels to the gown, building a sparkling neckline much like the ones Queen Mary wore during her reign. There was a buzz in my fingers and toes I hadn't felt since I was at Camp Chinooka completing the look book for Victoria's wedding. When I finally finished in the early hours of the morning, I shot a text off to Jamie.

I've chosen the designer we're wearing to the Met Ball... Georgica Goldstein.

CHAPTER NINETEEN

"Can I open my eyes now?" I asked.

"Not yet. We're almost there," Jordana answered.

I was beginning to panic a bit in the darkness. "Now?"

"Just a couple more steps. Okay," she said. "Open them."

I blinked my eyes open and let them adjust to the dim light of the climate-controlled warehouse. A larger gentleman wearing a navy suit and silver mirrored aviator shades was guarding a large wooden crate.

I took a few steps closer to the box. "Is this what I think it is?"

Jordana nodded excitedly. "May I present to you, the Rainbow Portrait Gown."

I shook my head in disbelief. "How did this happen?"

"I hate to say it, but Jan's right, the whole world's been swept up by Elizabethmania. Though the government was still reluctant to lend out the dress, Perry's show has apparently done wonders for British tourism. Visitors to the UK are up almost forty percent. They conceded there was likely no more appropriate

157

time or place to exhibit the Rainbow Portrait Gown than this year's Met Ball. There *are* some conditions, though."

I jerked my head toward the larger gentleman. "I assume he's a condition?"

"The name's Archie, ma'am."

I turned to him. "Nice to meet you. I assume Archie's one of the conditions? What is he? Part of the Tower Guard?"

"Or MI6? I haven't been able to get it out of him," Jordana answered.

I caught Archie cracking the smallest of smiles before going right back to deadpan.

"So? Do I get to see the dress or what?" I said, practically jumping up and down.

"Jan's already on his way down to meet us."

A few minutes later, Jan burst through the warehouse door, panting. He must've run down the four flights of stairs to the subbasement.

"Is the gown really here?" he gasped.

Jordana stepped to the side so Jan could get a good look at the crate. He slapped his hand to his head and started laughing. "Christ, I never really thought you'd make it happen. You know this gown was the one that made me want to be a fashion historian?"

Jan passed me a pair of white gloves and laid acid-free tissue paper across the table.

"Ready?" he asked.

I nodded, and Jan gently removed the dress from inside the cotton sheeting. Inch by careful inch, he slipped the sleeves off the padded hanger and set it down flat on the paper to avoid creasing the garment. Once he was finished, we stood back to take in the gown's grandeur.

Jan whispered in my ear, "Well, Georgica, what do you think?"

My eyes swept over the delicate needlework, rich brocades,

and bobbin lace. This wasn't just a dress, *this* was the statement of a powerful woman who wanted the whole world to understand the reach of her influence and strength of her resolve.

I turned to Jan. "I think she'll be the belle of the ball."

He winked at me. "I do too."

Jordana stepped forward. "If you'll both excuse me, I want to let the PR team know the dress is here, so they can send out the press release they've been sitting on."

"What about Archie?" I asked.

"What about him?"

"Does he just stay down here with the gown?"

"I'll be fine, ma'am. Don't worry about me."

"You heard him, he'll be fine," she repeated.

I shook my head. "And I thought *you* were devoted to your job."

CHAPTER TWENTY

Obtaining the Rainbow Portrait Gown for the exhibition completely changed our plans for the Tudor galleries. There was no question that piece would be the focal point of that particular showcase, but also the entire ball. Jan and I spent several hours with the museum engineers reconfiguring the space and pacing of the show to accommodate the addition of the dress. The morning flew by, and before I realized, it was almost time for me to leave if I was going to catch the second act of *Elizabeth*.

"Jan, about how much longer do you think we'll be?"

"Go. You've been here since six a.m. You must be exhausted."

"No, I'm okay. I want to stay until we're done."

"The visual arts team is on their way up to finish stenciling the walls. We shouldn't be in here when they're working anyway."

"Are you sure?"

"I'm positive. All this will be waiting for us in the morning." Jan sat down on the marble bench in the center of the gallery and leaned forward to stretch out his back. "I'm looking forward to going home, opening a nice bottle of wine, and putting my feet up. What are your plans for the rest of the day?"

"I have tickets to see *Elizabeth*."

"Why didn't you tell me you had tickets? All this could've waited."

"No, it couldn't. The gala's in two weeks."

Jan shook his head. "But tickets to *Elizabeth*—go. What are you waiting for?"

Jan practically hurled me out of the gallery. I hurried out of the museum and hopped on the first bus I could find heading downtown. I got off in Times Square and pushed my way through the massive crowds and over to the St. James Theater, where, surprisingly, nobody was standing outside. I checked my watch. Perry said the second act started at four thirty. It was four twenty. Where were all the smokers and people checking their cell phones during intermission?

I walked into the lobby, where a single ticket taker was waiting to greet me. I dug my ticket out of my bag and handed it to him.

"Is intermission over?" I asked.

"No, Miss," he answered curtly.

I peered around the entrance. "Did they give the five-minute warning already?"

He pointed to a set of doors. "Your seat is right through there. Enjoy the show."

I walked through the doorway and was met by an usher. She handed me a Playbill and said, "This way, Ms. Goldstein."

I did a double-take. "How do you know my name?"

She remained silent and motioned for me to follow her down the aisle to my seat. I looked around and stopped dead in my tracks. The theater was completely empty.

"I don't understand. Where's the rest of the audience?"

The usher stopped and pointed to a row and chair. "Lucky girl, best seat in the house. Enjoy the show."

My eyes darted around the room as I slowly lowered into my seat. There wasn't a single other person in the theater. Fifteen hundred seats empty, save mine. Moments later, the familiar first notes of the overture started to play and Perry, as Robert Dudley, came out from behind the stage's crimson curtain to give the audience (in this case, just me) a brief history lesson and recap.

The First Act ended in the winter of 1559 with Mary I's death and Elizabeth's accession to the throne. The second act began with a country in turmoil and a queen hopelessly in love with Dudley, already married to another woman, Amy Robsart.

I thumbed through the Playbill until I came to the show's song list and ran my finger down to the second act and the first song, "Court of Public Opinion." I vaguely remembered the number from when Perry was workshopping *Elizabeth*. When Dudley's wife dies under mysterious circumstances, the finger of suspicion points at Dudley and Elizabeth. Perry wrestled with including Amy Robsart's death as a subplot in the show. Ultimately, he decided to scrap the idea *and* the song when he couldn't work out how to weave the narrative into the central story.

I was surprised to see the narrative had found its way back into the Second Act… until I listened more closely to the lyrics all about scandal and speculation, rumors, and gossip. Sung by minstrels playing harpsichords scattered across the stage and throughout the audience, each musician told a different and inaccurate accounting of Amy Robsart's untimely demise.

Finally, a frustrated Dudley rips a harpsichord away from one of the minstrels to tell his version of what really happened to Amy, but unfortunately it's too late. The scandal had already reverberated not just around the kingdom, but across the courts of Europe. Elizabeth is obliged to distance herself from Dudley in order to avoid being implicated any further. As the song suggests, after the court of public opinion passed its sentence, Dudley and Elizabeth's relationship is never quite the same.

Perry must've seen the parallels between their plight and our own experience with the unrelenting paparazzi and decided the number belonged back in the show. I leaned back into my seat and watched the forlorn Dudley plead his case to the people, and then to Elizabeth, who loves him, but will not jeopardize her position.

Unable to accept the reality of the situation, Dudley breaks into a ballad, a brand-new number Perry must've added between the West End and Broadway run. While the lyrics spoke of Dudley's devotion to Elizabeth, Perry's gaze let me know he felt every word he was singing. As he delivered his confessional, I realized why I was the only person in the St. James Theater. Perry didn't want me to *assume* his words were meant for me, he wanted me to know that they were. I closed my eyes as verses about regret and redemption soared into the back balconies.

When *Elizabeth* premiered in London, the reviews hailed Perry's acting and musicality, but weren't as fond of his singing abilities. The New York critics didn't share this sentiment, though, and I could see why. This new song showcased the best qualities of his voice, particularly the way he could break your heart with one small turn of phrase. It was hard to know anymore where Dudley stopped and Perry began, or if, after all he'd poured into the show, there wasn't much of a distinction to be made anymore.

The rest of the act flew by, touching on many pivotal events in Elizabeth's reign, including the execution of Mary Queen of Scotts and the defeat of the Spanish Armada. Then, the entire company came out for "Dudley's Petition," the same number Perry presented at Alexander and Victoria's wedding reception, though it was an entirely different experience seeing the song performed in the theater the way Perry had conceived it.

By 1575, Dudley decided to make one last plea of marriage to Elizabeth and staged a masquerade at Kenilworth Castle, in which an actor playing the "messenger of the gods" would ask for Elizabeth's hand. In the number, Dudley and a band of traveling troubadours come bounding down the aisles, while the rest of the cast, dressed in exquisite masquerade masks, watches from the stage. Historians say, the spectacle at Kenilworth influenced Shakespeare's *A Midsummer Night's Dream,* and in a stroke of pure theatrical brilliance, Perry wove lines from the Shakespeare play into the already complex lyrics of the song.

In the next big number, "Semper Eadem, Ever the Same," a phrase Elizabeth affectionately used to end her letters to Dudley, the audience learns of Dudley's death, and then, in one of the final scenes, old Elizabeth and the young Elizabeth from the painting perform "The Rainbow Portrait Song." Examining all the moments and choices of Elizabeth's life, we finally understand her inconsolability at the loss of the one person she ever truly loved.

From what I recalled, the show ended shortly after the "Rainbow Portrait Song," with Elizabeth clutching Dudley's last letter to her. But Perry must've made some significant changes when *Elizabeth* opened in the West End, because this ending was very different than the one I remembered from when he originally wrote the show.

In this new ending, Elizabeth, on her deathbed, is visited by the ghost of Anne Boleyn, who recounts all of Elizabeth's triumphs and victories. She praises Elizabeth for holding to her own convictions and being the heroine of her own life. Elizabeth, having never really known her mother, dies at peace, finally trusting she made the right decisions for her life and her people. It's a powerful moment, and the right ending for the show that, while many thought of as the story of Dudley and Elizabeth's star-crossed romance, really was about a woman reclaiming her power and exerting her influence.

The company came out for their curtain call, and I sprang to my feet. Clapping my hands together with sheer abandon, I practically forgot I was the only person in the theater. Perry was the last of the cast to take a bow. Although the actress playing Elizabeth had equal or even more stage time, as the show's composer, lyricist, playwright, and star, Perry deservedly got top billing. He walked to the center of the stage for the final time. Our eyes locked, and he didn't take his off me until the orchestra squeaked out their last note and the red velvet curtain fell.

Wiping the tears away from my cheeks, I waited to see if the usher had any other instructions for me. After about ten minutes, I reached over to collect my things from the seat next to me and head out of the auditorium.

"Hey, Gigi," a voice called from behind the curtain.

I turned around. Perry, dressed back in distressed jeans and an *Elizabeth* T-shirt, hopped down from the stage and came up the aisle to greet me.

"I'm so glad you could make it," he said.

I held my hands open. "Me too, but what happened to the other fourteen hundred ninety-nine ticketholders?"

"They were offered tickets to a very special performance of *Elizabeth* in exchange for me canceling this one."

"God, I can't even imagine what it cost you to do this. It's quite the gesture."

"I wanted you to experience *Elizabeth* the same way you did back when we were working on it in our apartment. No outside influences. No expectations. Just you, me, and our wild imaginations."

"Well, you deserve every accolade and every award. The show... it's... well, the most beautiful, moving thing I've ever seen."

"Come, let me give you a tour of the theater."

I followed him down the aisle and through a side door leading to a small set of stairs running up to the stage.

"This is obviously the revolving floor," he said, pointing down to the rotating turntable taking up three-quarters of the stage. It allows us to get the set pieces on and off pretty quickly."

"And serves as a pretty good metaphor."

"Exactly. The axis of power keeps shifting on *Elizabeth*," he said with a knowing smile. "Up in the rafters are some of the larger backdrops, like the Tower of London and Whitehall. Come, I know you're going to enjoy this next room."

Perry took my hand and led me down two metal flights of stairs to the costume shop that housed the close to three hundred different looks used in the show. When we walked in, the dressers were working with the costume supervisors to get Elizabeth's gowns cleaned, steamed, and inventoried for the next performance later that evening.

I stepped closer to examine Elizabeth's coronation gown, which was placed over a large dress form in the corner of the room. One of the seamstresses was kneeling on the ground, repairing a small rip in the hem.

I lifted up the sleeve to examine the workmanship more closely. "The detail in the dress is just amazing."

Perry came up behind me. "The movie's costume budget will be about ten times what we had to work with for the stage production."

I turned around to face Perry. "Is anyone from the cast still here? I should really thank them for giving their all to an audience of just one."

"Sure. Let's head up to the dressing rooms. It's a two-show day, and most of the actors stick around between performances."

As we hiked back up the steep stairwells built into the belly of the St. James Theater to the suite of dressing rooms, Perry explained that most of the principal actors came over from the West End production, while the bulk of the ensemble were local hires. Making our way down the winding hallways, Perry stopped to introduce me to every single cast member of the production. When we finally got to his dressing room, he pushed his way inside.

"You'll have to excuse the mess," he said, picking books up off the couch and chairs so I could take a seat.

"Research for your next show?"

"Maybe. I have the smallest nugget of an idea I've started working on. I'm not sure if it'll amount to anything."

All around the room were pictures of Perry with different celebrities who'd come to see the show. Perry with Madonna, Barak Obama, Jay-Z, Helen Mirren, and even Elton John.

I pointed to a picture frame on his dressing table. "Who are they?"

Perry picked up the frame. "Those are Annie's parents. I invited them to opening night. I never thought they'd come, but I'm glad they did." He set the frame back down on the table. "Hey, would you care for a cup of tea? I usually have some this time of day."

I nodded, and he reached over his dressing table and plugged in a hotpot. "There are a few extra cups on that shelf over there," he said, pointing to an old bookcase.

I pulled two mugs off the top of the mantle, passed them to him, and then ran my finger down a row of colorful vinyl record sleeves. "You've downsized a bit."

"Nah, these are just the ones I had shipped over. Most of my collection's still in my London flat. One of these days I'm gonna take a ride up to Camp Chinooka, though. I donated a bunch of records to Gordy my last summer there. I didn't realize I'd have such a tough time replacing a few of my favorites."

"You know, they're all still in your old cabin. I saw them when I was there last year."

He poured me a cup of steaming tea and passed the mug over. "There's milk in the mini fridge and sugar in that canister shaped like the Phantom of the Opera."

I picked up the tin. "The Phantom of the Opera?"

Perry raised his shoulders. "It was a gift from Sir Andrew Lloyd Webber when he stopped by backstage. Why were you at Camp Chinooka?"

I poured a little milk into my cup and stirred it around. "I went up last year, when I was experiencing severe designer's block. I needed to get away for a few days. Camp Chinooka seemed like the perfect refuge."

He tucked a couple of stray curls behind his ears and rubbed his neatly trimmed beard. God, he looked handsome. His hair was pulled back off his face, showing off his chiseled cheekbones and long eyelashes.

He flashed his dimples and set his teacup down. "And a couple of gooey s'mores helped you find your way again?"

My lips broke into a small smile. "Always."

Perry reached past my head to get a better look at the records. Inches away from me, I breathed in his familiar scent, the 2-in-1 shampoo and conditioner brand he'd been using since he was a counselor at Camp Chinooka mixed with the piney smell of the rosin he rubbed on his violin bow.

"That's the one I was looking for," he said, pulling out one of the records and setting it down on the turntable.

Seconds later, the hauntingly memorable first notes of *Rhapsody in Blue* drifted out of the speakers and into the room. Even though I knew the tune better than I knew my own name, I couldn't help but ask anyway. I wanted to hear him say the words.

"Copeland? Bernstein?" I asked.

"Gershwin, Gigi, always Gershwin," he said softly.

I looked up and into his eyes. "I know."

He let the words hang in the air for a moment before clearing his throat. "Have you given any more thought to my proposition? Pre-production on the movie is set to start in a couple of weeks. I'm going to finish out my contract with the show, and then I'll join the rest of the team in London."

It was a tempting offer. Getting to work on a feature film with a healthy budget to execute every idea Perry had for the telling of Elizabeth's story was beyond anything either one of us could have imagined. I stood up to get a better look at a dress form that'd caught my eye in the far corner of his dressing room.

"That isn't—"

"It's the replica of the Rainbow Portrait Gown you made for me when we were first working on the show together."

I walked over and ran my hands up and down the fabric. "I have to be honest, now that I've seen the real thing, we didn't do half bad."

"*You* didn't do half bad."

"I really can't believe you kept this."

"She's been everywhere with me. From the flat I rented in London when I was finishing writing the show to my West End dressing room and now Broadway. Here," he said handing me a binder. "This is the film treatment and proposed filming schedule."

I tucked the book under my arm. "Can I have a little more time to think about the movie? Right now, I have nothing but Met Ball on the brain."

"Of course, darling. Take whatever time you need."

The way he pronounced darling so it sounded more like *dahling* could still make my heart ache.

A stagehand wearing a walkie-talkie and attached earpiece poked his head into Perry's dressing room.

"Perry, man, we need you on stage in fifteen for the fight call."

"Fight call?"

"We have to have a run-through of all the choreography of the fight sequences before each show. You Americans and your union rules. In England, we take it on the chin," he teased.

I laughed. "I'm *sure*." I gathered up my things. "I should get going."

"Hey, Gigi, I'm glad you didn't scalp the ticket and take off to Bora Bora."

"I am too."

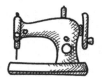

CHAPTER TWENTY-ONE

"**A**re you going to put down your phone and actually *enjoy* your pedicure?"

"I *am* enjoying it."

Jamie had arranged for a day of pampering at his favorite spa inside the Peninsula Hotel.

Jamie rolled his eyes. "Coulda fooled me."

I set the phone down beside me. "I'm sorry. Jordana's been sending emails nonstop since six a.m."

Jamie took a sip of his champagne. "I thought Jan told you to take the day to get ready? Everything was done?"

"It's all the last-minute stuff. I'll run back to the museum for a bit after we finish up here."

He reached over and lifted a piece of hair off my shoulders. "Are you sure you don't want to take advantage of the extra primping time?"

I smoothed the hair back into place. "Do I really look that bad?"

"After a breakup, don't women usually shake it up a bit? You've been sporting that look since the day we met."

"I have not. Have I?"

Jamie took out his phone and typed in *Top Designer Season One*. He pulled up a picture of me and flipped the screen around.

I leaned in to study the photo. "My hair's a drop darker in this picture. And I have a few layers now."

"You look exactly the same."

"And that's a bad thing?"

"It's not bad, but it might be time for a change, don't you think?"

I eyed him suspiciously. "You haven't been talking to my mother, have you? She's been trying to get me to cut my hair for a decade now."

"No, although your mother has impeccable taste. Second only to you... minus your hair."

"That might just be one of the nicest things you've ever said to me."

"I mean it, Gi. My tuxedo for the Met Ball, perfection."

I grabbed his hands. "You like it? Really?"

"No, I don't like it. I *love* it. You nailed it."

I'd spent every spare second of the last few weeks completing both of our looks for the ball. Jamie's tuxedo came out far better than I ever imagined. I sourced the most incredible brocade fabric from London that had silver threads running throughout the pattern to complement the metallic finishes of my own gown. Henry VIII was said to have had his most formal capes lined with brocade, one the finest fabrics one could find in Tudor England. This design was the perfect nod to the ball's theme without being too literal in my interpretation. The suit was sleek, modern, and just a little bit over the top—not unlike Jamie himself.

Though I'd completed much of my own gown the night I had the idea to design it as a homage to Queen Mary of Teck, I continued to improve on it by adding even more sparkle to the already bejeweled neckline and attaching a twelve-foot train completely covered in Swarovsky crystals. The additional embellishments took the dress to another level, and for the first time in my entire career, I didn't give a damn what the critics, bloggers, fashion insiders, or the world at large had to say about one of my designs. I loved it. I loved its theatricality and sophistication. The fit and structure of this gown was different than anything I'd done before, and I couldn't wait to get the dress out onto the red carpet.

"What's on tap for the rest of the day?" Jamie asked.

"Jordana got us one of the suites at The Mark Hotel to get ready. I'm going to pop over to the museum to extinguish any last-minute fires and plan to be at the room around three to start getting dressed. I hope it's okay, I invited Alicia to come by?"

"Of course. Thom's gonna try to drop by too."

"He's still coming to the after party, right?"

"Yup, his mom's staying over to watch the kids tonight. I hope he got his beauty sleep, because we are hitting the town, hard."

I giggled and looked down at my feet. "I think I'm almost dry, so will probably head out in a few minutes. What about you?"

Jamie held his glass out for a refill. "Are you kidding? I'm here for the duration. I'm not leaving until I'm scrubbed, rubbed, and slathered in mud."

"Have I told you how much I missed having you in my life?"

Jamie smiled broadly. "Not today."

Jan was pacing up and down the hallways of the Renaissance Galleries shouting instructions at anyone who got in his way. Even though we locked down the exhibit two nights before, ever the perfectionist, Jan was still finding things to tweak and change. Of course, each change created a ripple effect of work. If a gown got moved, then so did all the accompanying artifacts and placards. The museum's logistics team was scattered around the room, implementing Jan's modifications.

Jordana spotted me and came running over.

"We have a *major* problem."

"Oh no, what?"

She shook her head and motioned at the doorframe. "Just follow me."

I trailed Jordana down the large corridor of the Renaissance Galleries, into the Medieval Sculpture Hall, where the gate from the Valladolid Cathedral was currently being used to stage the Tudor Dynasty exhibit. This wing was also where we decided to display the Rainbow Portrait Gown in all its glory.

I inventoried the room. "Jordana, I don't see anything amiss. What's the big issue?"

"He is," she said, pointing at Archie.

Archie was wearing the same, or at least a very similar, navy suit from the day the Rainbow Portrait Gown was delivered, and the same signature silver mirrored aviator glasses. When we walked into the gallery, he was standing at full attention, guarding the priceless dress.

I leaned in close to Jordana so Archie wouldn't hear me. "What's the problem? Everything looks fine to me."

"He's refusing to change for the ball, and let's face it, he sticks out in this room like a sore thumb."

"He's here to guard the dress. He doesn't have to blend in."

"Jan thinks he kills the entire aesthetic of the room, like some big modern eyesore."

"I wouldn't go that far, Jord."

Jordana walked over to Archie and tapped his big, broad shoulder. "Excuse me, but do you think maybe during the event you can stand over in that dark corner?"

"No, ma'am. My orders are to stay within three feet of the gown at all times."

She leaned into him and whispered, "Who's gonna know?"

"I will, ma'am," he said curtly.

Jordana turned to me. "See, Gigi? He's being impossible."

"I think he's just doing his job. It's really going to be fine. As soon as the guests see the Rainbow Portrait Gown, that's *all* they're going to focus on, and they won't give Archie a second glance or thought. No offense, Archie."

"None taken, ma'am," he replied.

Jordana turned to him and threw her hand on her hip. "Can you even string more than three words together at a time?"

"You'd be surprised, ma'am."

"Archie, thank you so much for doing your duty and keeping this priceless gem safe and sound. We're indebted to you and appreciate your steadfast dedication."

"Thank you, ma'am."

"Have you ever met anyone more infuriating?" Jordana asked once we were out of earshot.

"Funny, that's the exact same thing I used to say about Perry Gillman."

CHAPTER TWENTY-TWO

Jamie was already at The Mark Hotel suite getting ready when I arrived. Frankie, my mother's most trusted hair and makeup person, and one of, if not, *the* best stylists in the city, was giving him a quick trim. Tons of celebrities tried to book Frankie for the gala, but he was fiercely loyal to my mother, who had been fiercely loyal to him since they met several decades ago, when she was a young model starting out.

"Perfect timing. Frankie and I were *just* talking about you."

I took two tentative steps into the room. "Never a good thing."

"He was saying how he's been dying to get his hands on your hair for years."

"You know, I've always thought you had the most beautiful hair, Gigi, but you're hiding your even more beautiful face with it," Frankie said.

I threw up my hands. "Ugh, all right. You win."

Jamie whipped around in his chair. "Really?"

"Really?" Frankie repeated.

"Really. But nothing too drastic, and nothing that requires *too* much maintenance."

Frankie practically tossed Jamie out of the seat.

"What are you wearing tonight? That might help provide some inspiration," Frankie asked.

I went to the closet and retrieved the two garment bags with our outfits. I laid Jamie's across the bed and unzipped mine. I shimmied the hanger out of the bag and held the gown up over my head so the bottom just skimmed the floor.

"Boys, here she is."

Jamie gasped, and Frankie covered his mouth with his hand.

Jamie stood up to examine the gown more closely. "Christ, Gi. When did you have time to do this?"

"Once the idea came, I worked on it every spare second I had. The dress, believe it or not, was in that unfinished collection from a few years ago. I've just been improving on it."

Frankie did a full circle around the dress. "Okay, I know what I need to do. Gigi, sit."

Frankie went to work mixing color. He turned me away from the mirror and started on the highlights. He began by painting individual strands of hair using his patented Balayage technique. Even though it felt as though he made contact with every hair on my head, Frankie assured me the result would be beautiful and very subtle. After he rinsed me out, he got to work on the cut.

He completely dried my hair to get a better sense of texture and length. Then, like a precision surgeon, he carefully snipped small sections, standing back to admire his work every few minutes. As locks of hair fell to the white cotton sheet, I started to second-guess my decision to make a change. Frankie rubbed some styling product on his hands and sculpted the rest of my hair into place.

"I am just about finished," he said.

Jamie got up from the bed to look as Frankie turned my chair back to face the mirror.

I blinked hard. I was completely transformed. Frankie took my hair up several inches, so the ends sat just past my shoulders, with honey-colored highlights throughout. Frankie was right, the highlights were subtle, adding just the slightest pop of color to brighten up my features. The cut was edgy and sophisticated and completely complemented the look of my gown.

"You, my friend, are an artist. Gigi hasn't looked this good in years. Maybe ever," Jamie said.

I shot Jamie a dirty look.

"You know what I mean."

"Now for your makeup. Let's do some contouring. If the Kardashians have provided any value to the world, it was bringing contouring to the masses. After that, I'm thinking a less intense eye, so we can go for a really bold red lip? With all those jewels across your décolletage, we'll need something to draw their attention upwards and to that gorgeous mug of yours. What do you think?"

"After this haircut, I am completely in your hands. Whatever you want."

He flashed a naughty grin. "That's what I was hoping you'd say."

For the next forty-five minutes, Frankie applied different brands and shades of makeup to get his desired effect. Finally, he handed me a tube of M.A.C Retro Matte Lipstick in Ruby Woo.

"Here, this is so you can reapply later. Ready to see the whole look?" he said, passing over a hand mirror.

I held it up to my face. "I look like a movie star. Thank you."

Frankie leaned in and whispered, "No, you look like a real queen."

Jamie walked Frankie out of the suite, while I answered a few more emails that'd come in from Jan. A minute later he walked back in with Alicia.

"Look who I found in the hallway," Jamie said.

Alicia dropped her bag on the floor. "Your hair!"

I fluffed up the bottom. "You like?"

"Love. Plus, your mother's going to be thrilled. Seriously, though, you look stunning. Perry Gillman's gonna lose his mind."

Perry. With everything else going on, he was practically the last person on my mind. *Practically.*

Alicia popped a bottle of champagne and passed me a glass.

I waved my hand. "This is a work event. I need all my faculties."

Jamie swiped the glass from my hand. "Well, I'm off duty, hand it over."

Alicia laughed and filled up Jamie's flute as Jordana came tearing through the door.

I looked down at my watch. "Jord, you know we have to be on the red carpet in a half hour? Where have you been?"

"There was a crisis at the museum."

"Why didn't you call me?"

"It doesn't directly involve the exhibit."

I searched her face. "I don't understand."

"There was a last-minute addition to the guest list. We were trying to figure out where to seat her."

"A last-minute addition? Who?"

Jordana took deep breath and said, "Annabelle Ellicott."

CHAPTER TWENTY-THREE

My heart began racing as my stomach sank. "Annabelle Ellicott?"

"You know they were hoping to get some real-life royals at the event to bolster the theme. She was on the original invite list, but she declined, so I never thought to mention it," Jordana said.

"What do you think changed her mind?" Alicia asked.

She shrugged. "I don't know. But she's coming, and Tom Ford's team is dressing her. Trini was going to come by to tell you, but I told her it'd be better if I broke the news."

I could feel Jamie, Alicia, and Jordana's eyes on me, anticipating my reaction. "Her name being attached to the event will bring even more international attention, so that's a good thing, right?"

Jordana drew in a sharp breath. "Agreed."

Jamie took a few steps toward me. "I won't leave your side all night."

"You're sweet, but it's fine. Really. It's a huge event, and I'll be running around most of it. I doubt my path will even cross with hers."

"And if they do?" Alicia said.

"If they do... they do."

"Okay, good. Now that that's settled, why doesn't everyone get dressed so we aren't late," Jamie said.

I nodded and took my dress into the bedroom. Alicia followed me and sat down on the bed.

"It's just us in here, so you can tell me what you're really thinking," she said.

"I'm a little thrown, but no more thrown than when I heard Perry was the gala's celebrity chair. I've spent most of the last six months in hiding. I don't want to hide anymore. Can you help me zip up the back of this?"

Alicia jumped up from the bed and came around behind me. She slowly slid the zipper up the track, and then fastened the hook and eye. I turned around to face her as she put her hand up to her forehead like she was blocking out the sun.

"You are literally blinding me with all that bling. There's certainly no hiding in that gown," she teased.

"It's good, right?"

She nodded her head up and down, smiling. "Oh, it's better than good."

"I'm sorry I couldn't wrangle tickets to the gala for you and Asher."

"Between the *Elizabeth* performance, Emmy J., and the especially fabulous fashions this year, the buzz around this thing is out of control. Word on the street is that you guys have had to turn down *actual* celebrities. You got us on the after party guest list, and for that, we will be eternally grateful. I haven't had an excuse to get a new set of eyelashes in months."

We walked out into the living room, where Jamie was waiting in his brocade tuxedo and Jordana in a gorgeous hunter green silk organza Carolina Herrera gown with a high Elizabethan collar and lace cuffs. Her red hair was pulled back in a chic chignon, and she was wearing the most incredible emerald and diamond statement necklace. She looked like a young Elizabeth I.

"Cartier?" I asked.

"They offered to lend it to me when they brought over the jewels for Victoria's gown."

"Well, it's perfect. You look positively stunning."

Jordana placed her hand on the necklace and smiled.

Alicia pulled her phone out to snap some pictures. "May I just say, you three clean up nice."

"Don't post anything yet," Jordana warned. "The first time people see Gigi's dress should be on the red carpet."

You had to hand it to Jordana, even without the office or title, she was still running the show.

"Don't worry, these are just for me," Alicia said, holding up her phone. "This shot will go right next to the one I have of Gigi at our senior prom."

Jordana looked down at her phone. "The car's downstairs. We should go."

We started walking out of the hotel suite when Jamie suddenly said he left something and ran back inside to retrieve it.

"I can't believe I almost forgot. When you told me the dress you were wearing was a nod to Queen Mary of Teck, I got this for you."

Jamie passed me a large blue velvet box. Inside was an antique diamond bandeau tiara interlaced with oval and pave diamonds and a large center diamond brooch.

"This isn't—"

"Real. No. I didn't get *that* rich off the sale of G. Malone. But, it's an exact replica of the one Queen Mary commissioned in 1932."

"How did you do this?"

He winked at me. "I called in a couple of favors."

Jamie slid the tiara into my hair. "There, now you look every bit the part. Let's go before we turn into a pair of pumpkins."

Even though we were among the first to arrive, the steps up to the Met were already packed with photographers, fashion commentators, and media outlets all clamoring to get the best shots of the celebrities entering the gala. The Met Ball's red carpet has always been the known epicenter of the fashion world. With every new and unexpected gala theme, came new and unexpected fashion.

When I was a teenager I used to cut school and camp out across the street from the museum just to get a firsthand glimpse of the avant-garde looks. I'd sit on the hard sidewalk with my white notebook and black pencils, making rough sketches of any gown that moved me. The next day I'd walk to the corner bodega and buy all the newspapers that covered the event, ripping out the pictures and adding them to my scrapbooks. I was having a tough time wrapping my head around the fact that this year, I was not only attending the ball, but walking it's red carpet in one of my very own creations.

Within seconds of our feet touching the famous staircase, the paparazzi were screaming our names. On the way over, Jordana had fed me and Jamie a few soundbites we could use when fielding questions from reporters. I was trying to recall some of them when a correspondent from the *New York Times* pulled me over.

"Can we get a couple of quotes for the style section of the *Times*?" the reporter asked.

I smiled politely. "Of course."

"Tell us a little bit about this year's theme, *Fashion Queens, the Royal Influence on Style* and what you hoped to achieve with the exhibition."

"Royals were really the celebrities of their day. They had the money and power to influence trends and fashion in a way that was completely unique to their position. This exhibit celebrates some of the most important and significant looks of their reigns, and the ripple effect they had on popular culture and trends."

"Getting the Rainbow Portrait Gown is quite the feather in your cap. Why was it so important to you that this particular gown be part of the show?"

"It's no secret there's a renewed interest in Queen Elizabeth, thanks in part to Perry Gillman. That particular gown captures everything this year's exhibit is about, a great monarch using fashion to make a statement more powerful than words could ever convey. The minute I was asked to be a part of this year's gala, I knew we had to have the Rainbow Portrait Gown and am so pleased we were able to make it happen."

"Speaking of powerful fashion statements, talk to me about who you're wearing and how it ties into this year's theme."

"I'm actually wearing one of my own designs. It pays homage to Queen Mary of Teck, who was famous for wearing several pieces of dazzling jewelry all at one time."

"G. Malone's designing again?"

The corners of my mouth rose upward. "*This* is a Georgica Goldstein."

As the reporter furiously scribbled away in his notebook, his accompanying photographer took pictures of the dress from every possible angle. I don't know if it was the stiffness of the jewelry collar or the tiara, but I felt regal and commanding, owning every square inch of the look.

Jamie leaned into me and whispered, "Drop the mic, Perry Gillman in da house."

An army of photographers refocused their lenses to catch a shot of him coming up the stairs.

Likely tired of his period costumes, Perry decided to forgo his Dudley puffy shirt and breeches for a classic tuxedo, complete with bow tie, tails, and a top hat. Channeling a European prince from the 1920s or '30s, he looked dapper and devastatingly handsome.

"You didn't talk to Perry about what your gown looked like, did you?" Jamie asked.

"No. Why?"

"Your looks just perfectly complement each other, that's all."

Jamie and I continued making our way up the staircase, stopping every couple of steps to chat with a reporter or get our picture taken. As the official host of the ball, Trini was standing at the very top landing, greeting all the guests as they entered the Great Hall.

"So, you decided to wear a Georgica Goldstein?" Trini said, her face beaming.

I hadn't told her who I was wearing. "How did you know?"

She tapped on my nose. "That dress is utterly fabulous, and quintessentially you."

CHAPTER TWENTY-FOUR

Even though I'd seen the facilities team working on the Met's Great Hall and Grand Staircase all week, walking into the finished product was a completely different experience. The Great Hall was recreated into a formal English rose garden, like you'd find in the great palaces of Europe, complete with perfectly manicured evergreen hedges, raised flower beds, and gorgeous stone trellises.

The reimagined space reminded me of the maze at Badgley Hall, green moss covering the walls, and long lines of ivy and climbing roses ascending the Grand Staircase. Servers dressed as Regency footmen, wearing long blue coats and powdered wigs, were walking around carrying champagne and hors d'oeuvres on silver buffet trays.

Jamie and I took a few steps into the space, and a butler standing in the frame of the doorway announced us into the room just like at the royal wedding.

"This is just incredible," Jamie said.

"Wait 'til you see the European Sculpture Court."

The Carrol and Milton Petrie European Sculpture Court was designed to resemble a classical French garden, presenting large outdoor Italian and French sculptures dating from the seventeenth to the nineteenth centuries. After considering the Temple of Dendur in the Sackler Wing and The Charles Engelhard Court in The American Wing, there was no question the European Sculpture Court was the perfect place to host the gala dinner.

Inspired by the extravagance and grandeur of the eighteenth-century French nobility, the court had been decorated with pastel flowers, ornate candelabras, silk table coverings, decadent desserts, and gold accents. Jan brought some of the best examples of fashion from Marie Antoinette's court to display in the space alongside the sculptures. The space was like nothing I'd ever seen before. The guests were going to lose their minds when they were seated in the room for the banquet.

"Where should we begin?" Jamie asked.

"The Medieval Sculpture Hall. I want you to see the Rainbow Portrait Gown before the gallery gets too crowded."

Jamie took my arm, and I led him down the center corridor off the Great Hall to the Medieval galleries, which were virtually empty. Most of the invitees were still walking the red carpet or mingling in the Great Hall. As we turned the corner to the room housing the Rainbow Portrait Gown, Jamie grabbed my arm and jerked me into a dark corner.

"What are you doing?" I whispered.

"Jordana's in there," he said.

I raised his eyebrows. "And?"

"Jordana's *in there* making out with a security guard."

"What?"

"Big guy. Navy suit."

"Archie?" I squealed.

I peeked around his shoulder and into the room. Jordana was in a full-fledged make-out session with Archie, the Rainbow Portrait Gown guard.

"Do you think we should interrupt them? I don't even know the last time I saw her let loose like that," Jamie said.

"I do. It was the Camp Chinooka Color War karaoke contest."

"Well, that's just sad," Jamie replied shaking his head.

"If we don't break it up, someone else will, and the poor girl will be mortified. Let's just clack our shoes against the floor loud enough for them to hear that someone's coming."

Jamie and I stamped our feet on the ground a few times and raised our voices as we came down the marble hallway. By the time we entered the room, Jordana and Archie were standing on opposite sides of it.

"Jamie, Gigi, hi! How are you guys?" she said, smoothing her hair back.

"We're good," Jamie answered. "How are *you* guys?"

"I'm just making the rounds. Everything looks good in here. Archie, thank you for being so on top of me—er, so on top of *things*, rather."

I'd never seen Jordana so frazzled or red-faced. Her cheeks glowed almost the exact same color as her hair.

"Not a problem, ma'am."

"I'm gonna go check on the Tudor exhibit. Jan said he's expecting the most traffic in there," she said.

"Great," I answered.

"Okay, catch you both later," she said, and scurried out of the room.

Jamie turned to me. "So *this* is the famous Rainbow Portrait Gown? I can certainly see why."

I moved up next to him. "Notice the snake embroidered up the arm sleeve? It symbolizes fertility, while the heart at the top right—"

"Symbolizes love," a voice said from the back of the gallery. Perry took two steps toward us. "Hello, Jamie. It's been a while, mate. Congratulations on becoming a father."

Jamie reached out to shake Perry's hand. "Congratulations on *your* baby. *Elizabeth* is a triumph. How many Tony Awards is it up for?"

"Thirteen."

"Guess it'll be *another* few years 'til I can get my husband a ticket. He still hasn't forgiven me for seeing it in London without him."

Perry pulled a card out of his wallet. "Call my publicist. She'll get you hooked up with some seats."

"Are you sure?"

"Believe it or not, there aren't too many people in New York I consider real friends. You're one of them."

"Well, thank you. Thom is going to be thrilled." Jamie turned and gave me a little wink. "I'm going to go check out the Tudor exhibition. Gigi, I'll meet you back at our table for dinner."

Jamie walked out of the gallery, leaving me and Perry alone with the Rainbow Portrait Gown.

"Pretty great getting to see the dress in real life, huh? Things don't always live up to their hype, but this does," he said.

"It sure does."

"You look beautiful." He reached out and stroked my hair. "You cut it?"

"It was time for a change."

"Well, it suits you."

I reached up to smooth out his satin lapels. "In these get-ups, I feel like we should be headed to a speakeasy to dance to some of your favorite jazz standards."

He flashed his dimples. "Darling, we don't need a speakeasy."

Perry pulled me into his arms to dance, and started humming Gershwin's "They Can't Take That Away From Me." I laid my head on his broad chest as he twirled me around the room singing the lyrics into my ear. I closed my eyes and was transported to a club from the 1920s. I could see the dark wood paneled walls, velvet banquets, and crystal chandeliers. The Duke

Ellington Orchestra playing on the center stage, while we slow danced in the center of the room.

I was so absorbed in the reverie, I barely heard the voices and footsteps coming down the hallway. Seconds later, as the voices grew closer, we backed away from one another as if the moment never happened.

"I should get going. We're performing a song from *Elizabeth* after dinner. I'm already late for the sound check."

"Which number?"

"'The Rainbow Portrait Song.'"

"Right, of course."

Perry leaned in close and stroked the side of my face. "Thanks for the dance, doll face."

After he was out of earshot, I turned to Archie. "You didn't see any of this."

"Any of what, ma'am?"

CHAPTER TWENTY-FIVE

As I made my rounds through the exhibitions, several members of the museum's board of trustees came up to personally congratulate me on one of the best galas they'd ever attended. In the end, the event spanned over twenty different galleries, covering close to sixty thousand square feet of the museum. Most of the board, true art aficionados, couldn't stop gushing about getting to see the Rainbow Portrait Gown in person.

I wandered over to one of my favorite exhibits featuring the fashions of British designer Norman Hartnell. Hartnell designed clothing for members of the royal family, starting in 1935, and continued all the way through the late sixties. In 1947, he designed Princess Elizabeth II's wedding dress and, six years later, her coronation robes.

I absolutely loved his aesthetic. Hartnell relished the symbolism and pageantry of British ceremonies and found embroidery the perfect medium for conveying the gravity and glamour of the monarchy. I couldn't agree more. His archives generously lent us several of his best pieces, and the crowds were going crazy over the fashions.

I looked up and reread his famous quote, which Jan had stenciled across the wall of the gallery.

I despise simplicity, it is the negotiation of all that is beautiful.

As a designer, I wasn't sure I completely agreed with that notion, although, some of the ideas I'd been mulling around for a new collection were far more intricate, ornate, and as a result, more beautiful than anything I'd designed before. I didn't know if I had the necessary technical skills to even construct a few of the looks but was finally game to try.

I stood back to admire Elizabeth II's wedding gown, when I heard a laugh I would have recognized anywhere. I spun around. Annabelle Ellicott was standing with a small group of people, wearing a stunning but simple crisp white gown with an elegant cape feature. Being so closely associated with the royals, I assumed she didn't want to take the theme too literally and instead opted for a more subdued kind of elegance.

Our eyes met, and suddenly, it felt as if we were the only two people in the very crowded room. She excused herself and made her way toward me. I scanned the space. There was no way to escape without making a scene. I smoothed my dress and adjusted my replica tiara, which suddenly seemed ridiculous in the presence of a woman who'd very likely seen the real one.

"Georgica, darling, how are you?" she said, giving me a double kiss on the cheek.

"I'm good. I've been good. You?"

"Wonderful. I'm in town for a few weeks, and I'm so glad I was able to make it to the ball. It's a smashing event, many congratulations. I'm actually on my way to go see Vic's dress."

"We really appreciate that Victoria was willing to lend the gown to the museum."

"Of course, her wedding gown should be on display. That dress is far too beautiful to be locked up in the Buckingham Palace archives."

"Thank you, Annabelle."

She started to turn to leave. "Well, it's been nice catching up."

I knew this was my moment, otherwise I might never have the opportunity to apologize to her face-to-face. I took a step closer to her and lowered my voice. "I want you to know, for whatever it's worth, nothing happened between me and Perry that night at the Goring Hotel."

She moistened her lips and looked down.

I continued, "We were very wrong to conceal our past relationship, and I'm truly sorry for any hurt or embarrassment we caused you or your family."

She looked up and into my eyes. "He's not an easy person to get over, is he?" She gave me a soft, but sad smile. "If you'll excuse me, I'd also like to sneak a peek at the Rainbow Portrait Gown before dinner."

She slid past me and out the door, trailed by a small entourage and some of the event photographers, who'd been snapping away during our conversation.

Trini sidled up to me. "That didn't look too painful."

"It wasn't. She was very complimentary and gracious."

"She was being *very* British is what she was being. And I can say that because I'm Scottish."

"No, she's a good person. She didn't deserve any of that fall out."

Trini took me by the crook of the arm. "No doubt about that. Come, let's find our seats for dinner."

Emmy J. was already on stage performing a number in the sculpture garden when we walked in. Trini and I checked the seating chart. As hosts of the event, our table was in the center of the room, up close to the stage so we'd have a great view for the show. We took our seats, and Jordana found us a few minutes later.

"Here," she said, handing me a few sheets of paper.

"What's this?"

"Your welcome speech just in case there are any issues with the teleprompter."

Trini took Jordana by the hands. "Jordana, darling, you're wearing Carolina Herrera and Cartier, you look gorgeous, and you're at the Met Ball, for god's sake, please try to have a good time."

Jordana nodded and left to go chat with some of the *Vogue* staffers.

Trini unfolded her napkin into her lap. "She's a real treasure, that one. I hope you'll give her a big promotion."

"Promotion?"

"When you start your own line, of course."

"You never give up, do you?"

She scrunched up her nose. "Would you really want me to?"

Jamie sat down beside me. "So, what'd I miss?"

"Not much, just a run-in with Annabelle Ellicott, *that's* all," Trini said.

"It was fine. She was perfectly lovely to me," I said.

"And now it would appear she's being *lovely* to Perry Gillman."

Jamie pointed over to the corner of the room, where Perry and Annabelle were knee-deep in conversation.

"I should go look over my speech one more time before Jan introduces me. Excuse me for a moment."

I picked up my clutch and walked out into the hallway. My bag was vibrating. I dug out my phone and did a quick scroll through my texts. I tapped open the one from my father. Not usually one to put his feelings in writing, I was surprised by his message.

Georgie, you look like a million bucks. Couldn't be prouder. Love you, Dad.

I smiled and slipped the phone back into the bag as Jordana came out to find me.

"I've been looking all over for you. Jan's finishing his intro. You're up next."

"I'll be there in one minute."

She nodded and headed back into the party.

I pulled out a compact and reapplied the deep red lipstick. I straightened the layers and layers of jewels across my neck, and then my tiara. Exhaling, I walked back into the garden and waited for Jan to introduce me.

CHAPTER TWENTY-SIX

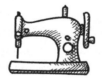

Stepping up to the podium, I looked out into the audience. George and Amal Clooney, Rhianna, Madonna, the Kardashian sisters, movie stars, theater stars, political figures, the who's who of the fashion world, and the most elite members of New York Society were all gathered together in one room, and I had their full and undivided attention. My voice steady and strong, I started with one of my favorite Francis Bacon quotes, "Fashion is the only attempt to realize art in living forms and social intercourse."

I highlighted some of the most remarkable and notable pieces from the exhibit, and then, launched into the story of how I created Victoria Ellicott's wedding gown. For the first time, reveling in all the carefully chosen historical details and complicated construction of the dress. For months, I'd done all I could to separate myself from every detail of the royal wedding, afraid that to acknowledge my role in any way would somehow be an admission of guilt. But, seeing Victoria's wedding gown on display alongside some of the greatest examples of fashion of our time, I finally owned my achievement, and it felt wonderful.

I thanked Jan and Jordana and the dozens of fashion houses,

museums, and archives that lent us so many incredible pieces for the show. Finally, I recognized Trini, who joined me onstage. She stepped forward to the podium to acknowledge several other teams at *Vogue* instrumental in mounting the event, and then turned the microphone over to the President of the Board of Trustees.

We sat back down at the table as waiters dressed as traditional French footmen in long red coats with gold embroidery served the entrees. Lobster and king crab stuffed with caviar, baby lettuce and heirloom tomatoes, or baby lamb chops with fresh mint and almond pesto, and branzino with lemon caper brown butter.

Jamie pulled out his phone and stealthily slid it to me underneath the table. I glanced down.

"Is that a selfie of you and Kim Kardashian?"

He nodded. "Thom is literally losing his mind."

"Jamie! I told you, that's Anna Wintour's only rule, no selfies at the Met Gala."

"Oh, puh-lease, what do you think everyone's doing in the bathroom?" He took his phone back and slipped it into his pocket.

I looked around the garden. "Where's Jordana? Her dinner's getting cold."

Jamie cracked his lobster tail. "I have one guess."

"Archie? You think?"

"Oh, yeah."

I nodded and smiled. "Good for her."

"Did you notice the outline of his pecs under his suit? Great for her."

Emmy J. came back to the stage and performed a few more hits off her new album before asking Perry Gillman to join her. Perry, back in his Dudley costume, came up to the podium. Emmy J. handed him a violin and stepped back and away from the microphone as an accompanist sat down at the grand piano.

"In this sculpture garden meant to evoke the beauty and splendor of France, I wanted to play a song that always brings me right back to the city of lights, Gershwin's 'An American in Paris.' I compose more than I play these days, so please excuse me if I'm a bit rusty."

Perry tucked the violin under his chin and began playing the jazz-inspired orchestral piece by his favorite composer.

"Rusty my ass," Jamie whispered.

The room was enraptured, even the servers were stopped in their places, listening to him play. Perry might be a huge star now, with tons of honors and awards, but the man standing on the stage, eyes closed, feeling every note soaring out from his violin, was the person I fell in love with in the middle of the Pennsylvania woods, and it was disarming to see *him* again.

When he finished, Emmy J. returned to the stage in a costume replica of the Rainbow Portrait Gown, taking her place inside a painting frame for the number. The crowd went absolutely crazy. It was a brilliant move to replace the actress who normally played the "portrait version" of Elizabeth with the superstar.

Perry turned to the audience and gave a brief synopsis of the events leading up to the number. Then, two Elizabeths, the aging queen and the younger one from the portrait, launched into an incredible duet followed by a short sequence, where different scenes from the show were rewound via staging and choreography to highlight the most significant choices and decisions of Elizabeth's life. The scenes between Dudley and Elizabeth, the most heartbreaking to relive.

I couldn't help but think of me and Perry, all the moments I'd gladly do over, especially those last few months of our engagement. When Perry was in London working on *Elizabeth*, he all but disappeared into his work. I was so positive he wanted out of our relationship that I never stopped to consider all the other reasons for his behavior. I mailed back the ring and did my best to move on.

I glanced back up at the stage. Elizabeth in a masquerade mask, and Dudley on his knees proposing for a final time. Of course, the audience knows what her answer will be, but even still, the small glimmer of hope that in this alternate version she might give a different one had everyone holding their breath. After she gives her decision, the younger Elizabeth from the Rainbow Portrait and the older Elizabeth, come together, one force, both in the gown symbolizing the queen's strength and power.

When the song ended, the entire room was on its feet. The performance perfectly captured every sentiment of our exhibit. Even Trini, not usually one to display her emotions, had tears running down both cheeks.

She turned to me. "Remind me, Georgica, what was the thing that came between you and Perry Gillman?"

"To tell you the truth, I don't even know anymore."

CHAPTER TWENTY-SEVEN

Unlike fairy tales, the Met Ball didn't end at the stroke of midnight. The celebrations continued until the wee hours of the morning at the different after parties hosted by celebrities and designers all around the city. After the gala, Jamie and I hurried back to The Mark Hotel to change for the rest of the night's events.

I switched into another dress from my unfinished collection, a two-piece liquid silver ensemble with a full skirt and cropped bejeweled top meant to evoke the more formal Queen Mary inspired gown. Jamie traded his tuxedo for a slim-cut gunmetal gray three-piece suit and Swarovski crystal-encrusted smoking slippers.

Frankie generously offered to come back to refresh my hair and makeup, this time opting to give me a sexier, sleeker look. He flat-ironed my hair until the strands were bone straight and added tons of dark rich eye shadows and individual lashes to give my eyes a smoldering quality.

Jordana was supposed to meet us back at the hotel so she could change and get touched up, but was nowhere to be found. Even more unlike her, she hadn't answered a single text or call in the last couple of hours. After waiting for her for close to a half hour, we headed downtown to the first after party at the Standard Hotel.

I slid into the car first. "Is Thom on his way?"

Jamie looked down at his phone as he climbed in behind me. "He's in an Uber. What about Alicia?"

"She and Asher just got past the red velvet rope."

"Still no word from Jordana?"

I shook my head. "Nope."

"I'm sure she'll turn up at the party. Do you happen to know who else is going to be in attendance?"

I eyed him with a sideways glance. "Is that your way of asking if I know whether or not Perry's going to be there? I didn't see him again after the *Elizabeth* performance. Come to think of it, I didn't see Annabelle either."

"I was actually asking if you knew whether or not my best friend, Kim Kardashian, was going to be there," he teased.

"Oh, right. I'm not sure."

Jamie tilted his head to the side. "Gi, what do you think? That Perry and Annabelle sneaked off together?"

"That would be crazy, right? And even if they did, why should I care?"

"You shouldn't. You're *clearly* very over him."

"I am."

Jamie held up his hands. "Clearly."

The car stopped in front of the hotel, and we got out. A huge line of people trying to get into the party stretched from the entranceway all the way around the block. We walked up to the front.

"I always feel like such a jerk cutting the line," I whispered to Jamie.

"I don't. I spent most of my early twenties in line trying to get into Bungalow 8. But, back then I was a fresh-faced boy from Griffin, Georgia, who didn't know a soul in New York. Now, I'm on the arm of the chairwoman of the Met Gala." He proudly turned to the bouncer. "Georgica Goldstein and Jamie Malone."

"Right this way," he said, holding the door open for us. "Take the elevator up to the Top of the Standard, eighteenth floor."

The Top of the Standard was a penthouse-style bar and lounge perched atop The Standard High Line Hotel in the Meatpacking District. The vast space had floor-to-ceiling windows, cozy fireplaces, and leather couches, all of which surrounded a grandiose bar in the center of the room.

We stepped out onto the crowded floor. Most of the gala attendees had changed into completely different looks and found their way to the after party. Alicia, Asher, and Thom were sitting by the bar sipping on martinis. We walked over to join them.

Alicia kissed me on both cheeks.

I stood back to admire her. "Ali, you look incredible."

She stood up and did a full turn. "Vintage G. Malone."

"From our spring line two years ago," Jamie said, appreciating his work.

Alicia clapped her hands together. "How was the ball? Tell me everything."

"The ball was a smashing success. They'll be talking about this one for years to come," Jamie chimed in before I had the chance to answer.

"I saw some of the photos from the red carpet. Annabelle Ellicott looked pretty," Alicia said, her voice going up so her statement sounded more like a question.

"She did," I answered.

Alicia's green eyes widened. "You saw her, then? You two talked?"

"We spoke for a few minutes. She was actually very nice."

Thom glanced around the space. "Think she's here?"

"We lost track of her when she left the gala with Perry Gillman," Jamie said.

Alicia covered her mouth. "She left the gala with Perry?

I shot Jamie a look. "We don't know that for sure."

Alicia peeked around and over my shoulder. "Is that Jordana walking in? Who's she with?"

I turned toward the entrance. Jordana was coming off the elevator, walking arm and arm with a tall gentleman wearing aviator sunglasses.

"No way. Is that Archie?" Jamie asked.

Alicia tapped my arm. "Who's Archie?"

"I'll fill you in later," I muttered.

Jordana spotted us from the doorway and came over.

"Sorry I didn't make it back to the hotel. Archie was waiting on his replacement."

"You're off duty, then?" I asked Archie.

"Yes, ma'am," he replied curtly.

"You don't have to call me ma'am. Gigi's just fine. When do you head back to the UK?"

"Not for a few more weeks. I'll stay with the dress while it's on exhibition with the Met. My replacement's coming in tomorrow, so he'll be on for a few days, and after that, we'll alternate the post."

"You have a whole week off in New York, then? Jordana, you'll have to show young Archie around our fair city," Jamie said.

She shook her head. "I don't know. We have a lot to do to make sure all the artifacts get back to their proper homes."

"Don't worry, I'll take care of all that with the staff from the Costume Institute," I said.

"And I have some follow-up meetings with the *Vogue* PR team."

"Just leave me whatever you need taken care of." I nudged her arm and lowered my voice. "Have some fun. You've more than earned it."

"Emmy J.'s new song's playing. Let's go." Jordana took Archie's hand and pulled him out onto the dance floor. I hadn't seen her look so carefree since we lip-synched to "Summer Lovin'" at the Camp Chinooka dance.

"Want to join them?" Asher said, taking Alicia's arm.

"When in Rome, right?" she said and leapt off her bar stool to meet them on the dance floor.

The bartender leaned over the counter. "What can I get you?"

Jamie raised his eyebrows. "You're officially off duty, and you've more than earned a cocktail."

I held up my fingers. "Three champagnes, please."

The bartender passed the glasses over to us. Jamie and Thom leaned back into the bar to people watch, treating it almost like an Olympic sport.

Thom pointed out a fresh-faced supermodel in a very revealing dress. "Well, she certainly feels good about herself."

"If I looked like her, I wouldn't even bother with clothes," Jamie joked.

I turned around to see who they were talking about and locked eyes with Perry, who was walking into the party with Annabelle.

"Is that—" Thom asked.

"Annabelle Ellicott," I answered.

Jamie passed me his glass of champagne. I waved it away with my hand. "That's the absolute last thing I need."

He nodded in agreement and set the flute down.

We watched Perry and Annabelle make their way around the room, stopping to say hello to different celebrity cliques.

Thom leaned into me. "I didn't realize Perry knew George Clooney?"

"Annabelle knows Amal. Longtime family friend." I placed my flute down on the bar. "You know what, I think I'm going to go make my rounds. There were a lot of people I didn't get a chance to talk to at the gala."

I left Jamie and Thom at the bar and made my way through the room, stopping every couple of feet to chat with another group of people. Most gushed about how wonderful the gala had been and how exciting it was to get to see the Rainbow Portrait Gown and a performance from *Elizabeth*. And although I never made it all the way over to where she was standing, when Anna Wintour lifted her sunglasses and gave me the slightest hint of a smile from across the room, I knew the gala had truly been a success.

After another hour of making small talk, I popped up on my tiptoes to scan the room for Jamie and Thom, who were deep in conversation with Kim Kardashian. Alicia and Asher were still on the dance floor, and Jordana and Archie were snuggling on a blue velvet banquette in the far corner of the room. Then I saw them. Perry and Annabelle were getting on the elevator, leaving the party, together.

CHAPTER TWENTY-EIGHT

I rolled over and hit ignore on my phone, which had been buzzing and ringing the better part of the last hour. I was experiencing complete déjà vu. The night of the royal wedding I went to bed on top of the world and woke up to my phone practically blowing up with messages and texts about me and Perry. Burying my head deeply under the pillow, I wondered how long I could really hold out before looking at my phone this go-around. I already knew what was waiting for me, photos and stories about Perry leaving the after party with Annabelle Ellicott. I could even imagine the colorful headlines. *The Princess's Sister Rekindles with her Prince at the Ball,* or something equally cringe-worthy. My phone rang again. This time, I picked it up and chucked the phone across the hotel room.

I swung my legs over the bed and stretched my arms up over my head. My whole body felt sore. Too many hours on too high of a heel had taken its toll. I heard a knock at the door and got up to answer it.

"Ms. Goldstein, we have complimentary room service for you," a voice said.

I let the bellhop inside, where he carefully laid out coffee, fruit, and a Greek omelet. Then, he set a stack of newspapers on the table beside the plate.

"I thought you might like to see some of the news from last night's gala. Can I get you anything else?"

"That was thoughtful, thank you. I think this will be all."

"Wonderful."

He left the room, and I sat down at the table to pour myself a cup of coffee. I slowly pulled the first paper from the pile and closed my eyes. *Now or never*, I thought to myself, and turned *The Post* over to the front page.

Royal Triumph, the Stars and Exhibitions Shine at this Year's Met Ball.

Where was the picture of Perry and Annabelle leaving together? Where were the screaming headlines about their inevitable reconciliation? I thumbed through the rest of the papers. The articles were all positive reviews of the exhibit and fashions, especially my own. My gown got rave reviews across the board, the *New York Times* Style Section calling it, "the single most innovative and elegant dress to walk a red carpet in years."

I didn't understand. If all the coverage was so positive, why was my phone blowing up? I picked it up off the ground and scrolled through the messages. There were several from Alicia, Jamie, and Jordana, each asking me to call them, plus at least ten missed calls from my mother. I started to dial her back when the hotel phone rang.

"Gigi, finally," Jamie said when I answered.

I looked down at the receiver. "Sorry. I must've had the hotel phone on *do not disturb*."

"I know, I've been trying it *and* your cell all morning. Have you spoken to your mom?"

"She tried me a couple of times, but I'm just waking up." I could hear him exhale into the phone. "What's wrong? What happened?"

The other end of the phone went silent for a moment before he said, "Your father had a heart attack last night."

"What! I don't understand. He just texted me last night during the Met Ball. When?"

"I'm not sure. Your mom's been trying to get a hold of you. She didn't realize you were spending the night at The Mark."

"All my stuff was here, so I decided to just stay. Oh my God, is he okay? Jamie, you have to tell me, is he okay?"

"I don't know much. She's at Lenox Hill Hospital with him. That's all I know. Do you want me to meet you there?"

"I appreciate it, but maybe I should just get to her and see what's happened."

"I'm just a cab ride away if you need me, kiddo."

"Thanks, Jamie, that means the world to me."

I hung up, threw on my clothes, and debated whether to get into a cab or just run there, unsure of which would be faster this time of day. When I got downstairs, the hotel doorman hailed me a taxi, and I jumped inside, giving the address for Lenox Hill Hospital. We pulled up to the hospital, and the driver asked me if I wanted him to circle around to the Emergency Room entrance. I wasn't sure but nodded yes.

I ran inside and immediately spotted my mother curled up in a chair beside the admittance desk. Her normally perfectly coiffed hair was lying in knots and kinks on her delicate shoulders, and there was the slightest remnant of her signature Chanel cherry red lipstick across her mouth. She looked up at the clock and saw me walking in. I rushed over to her.

"I'm so sorry, Mom. I had no idea you were trying to get a hold of me."

"Oh, Georgica," she said, practically crumbling into my arms.

"Mom, is he... ?"

She wiped the tears from under her eyes and smoothed out her shirt. "No, thank God. He's in surgery. He needs a quadruple bypass."

"When did he go in?"

"Umm, about an hour ago. They said the procedure could take as long as four hours."

We sat down. "I don't understand. He was texting with me last night."

"He mentioned that he was exhausted, beyond exhausted, actually. But, you know him, always burning the candle at both ends. I begged him to go to bed, but he wanted to watch you walk the red carpet. A little while later, he said he was hot and a bit nauseous and got up to lower the thermostat. He collapsed right there in the living room."

I put my hand over my mouth.

"I dialed 9-1-1 and started performing CPR," she said.

"I didn't even know you knew CPR."

My mother picked up a piece of my hair. "Did you get it cut?"

"Mrs. Goldstein?" a voice called into the waiting room.

My mother raised her hand and jumped up. "I'm here."

A woman in scrubs approached us. "I wanted to come out to give you an update."

"This is my daughter, Georgica," my mother said.

The nurse smiled politely. "We've finished the graft to the aorta and cleared two of the four blockages. He's still on the heart-lung bypass machine, but stable. We hope to close in another hour and a half, give or take."

"So, he's out of the woods?" my mother asked.

"So far, everything's gone as planned, and the team's happy with the progress. We're at the halfway point."

"I understand," my mother replied.

"You're welcome to move over to the cardiac waiting area. It's more comfortable and less noisy. Plus, the coffee's fresher. I'll come by there with my next update."

"Thank you," I answered.

"Yes, thank you," my mother muttered.

My mother sank back down into the chair.

"Mom, we should probably go to the cardiac waiting area, like she said. That's where they'll look for us if they have any news."

She picked up her jacket. "Of course."

We wound through the long, twisty halls of the hospital, following the signs to the cardiac unit. The waiting room was a vast improvement over the Emergency Room, with brown pleather couches, Keurig machine, and a television mounted to the wall. We found some space on the far side of the room and settled in.

"Can I get you some coffee, Mom?"

"No, nothing. Thank you."

"Is there anyone I can call for you?"

"I already let his office know what happened. What's funny is that they didn't sound at all surprised. They want to send some food over to the house. I'm supposed to call them when he's out of surgery." She took her phone out of her pocket and glanced down. "It's Aunt Bea. I promised to give her an update. I'll be right back."

Bea was my father's sister. She was a painter and lived in Ojai, California. She and my father were night-and-day different, but extremely close. He used to say I got my artistic and independent streak from Aunt Bea, which I always took as high praise.

I pulled out my phone and shot texts off to Jordana and Alicia, letting them know I'd connected with my mom and giving them a quick update on my father's condition. I scrolled through the rest of the messages and saw texts and missed calls from Perry. There was also a text from Trini, asking me to give her a call as soon as possible. I turned the screen off and tucked the phone back into my bag. Closing my eyes, I leaned my head back against the wall. The adrenaline that'd been coursing through my veins was slowly waning, and suddenly, I felt very tired and very empty.

"Aunt Bea is taking the red-eye tonight. She'll be here in the morning," my mother said, walking back toward our couch. "I told her not to, but she couldn't be dissuaded."

"Dad'll be happy to see her when he comes to," I said.

"Yeah," she agreed, the word catching in her throat. "I'm sure he will be."

We sat in silence as different doctors and nurses came out to talk to other families and provide them with updates. We both jumped at least two feet in the air every time we heard the click of the surgical wing deadbolt open.

I stood up and stretched. "I'm gonna make a cup of coffee. Sure you don't want one?"

She shook her head no as I walked over to the machine. I picked out a K-Cup and leaned closer to choose a portion size.

"Don't bother with that. I come bearing overpriced lattes," a voice said from behind me.

I smiled and turned around. "Jamie, I told you, you didn't have to come here."

He passed me the coffee cup. "When have you ever known me to listen?"

"Never, and I'm so glad," I said, giving him a hug.

"How's your mother holding up?"

"It's hard to tell. She seems more shell-shocked than anything."

We walked over to where she was sitting. She'd put on her reading glasses and seemed to be trying to send an email from her phone.

"Gigi, remind me, how do you send an email so the list of recipients is hidden?"

"You blind copy everyone. Add the email addresses next to where it says BCC," I answered.

"Hello, Mrs. Goldstein," Jamie said.

She pulled off her glasses. "Jamie, what are you doing here?"

He passed her the latte. "I thought you might need a decent cup of coffee. How's Mr. Goldstein?"

"He's still in surgery."

Jamie sat down and took both our hands into his own. "He's a rock. He'll be fine. Just fine."

I leaned my head into his shoulder, and for the first time all morning, let myself cry.

CHAPTER TWENTY-NINE

The nurse adjusted the IV and made some quick notes on my father's chart before leaving the room. My mother was fast asleep in a chair by the window. She'd been up all night, but the relief of knowing my father made it through his surgery had finally allowed her to get a few minutes of rest. The doctor informed us that the next few hours could be a bit touch and go, but overall, he felt the surgery had gone well, and my father had every hope of a meaningful recovery.

I sat down in a chair beside the bed and took hold of his hand. His fingers were warm to the touch, and I was relieved to know his heart was doing its job again.

"How long have I been asleep?" my mother asked.

"Not too long. The nurse was just in here, said Dad's vitals look good."

"Did Jamie leave?"

"He had to get home to the twins. He said he'll try to swing by again later."

"He's a wonderful person. I'm so glad you two are back on good terms." She stood up and stretched. "What do you think? Should we go get something to eat?"

"The nurse said Dad will be asleep for hours."

She nodded, and we carefully tiptoed out of the room.

We took trays and moved to the back of the hospital cafeteria line. I reached for a chef salad and passed my mother the same. We paid at the register, found an empty table, and sat down. I opened my salad and pushed the lettuce around in the container.

"I guess I'm not very hungry," I said.

My mother pushed her tray away from her. "No, I guess I'm not, either."

She looked exhausted. There was the kind of tired that could be fixed by a good night's sleep, and the kind of tired that comes from feeling the weight of the world on your shoulders. I'd never seen her so drained.

"Mom, if you want to go home for a few hours and freshen up, I can stay with Dad."

"No, I want to be here when he wakes up." She leaned back in her chair to take me in. "You know, you look stunning. Really stunning," she said.

"I didn't have a chance to wash off my makeup from last night. You know Frankie, he applied it with shellac."

She laughed. "How was the gala?"

"Truthfully, I don't think it could've gone any better."

She sipped on some hot tea. "Your dress was fabulous. Who designed it?"

"I did."

She set down her mug. "I didn't know you were designing again?"

"Jamie thinks I should take the money from G. Malone and finally start my own line. What do you think?"

"Is that what you want?" she asked.

"I'm not sure I ever thought it was a possibility before."

"You should. It's time for you to step out on your own."

"What if I fall on my face? I've had my share of stumbles already."

"You won't. You're your father's daughter."

Suddenly, all the tears she'd been holding back came flooding out like a dam giving way. I jumped up and ran to her side.

"Oh, Gigi, things have been so good for us these last few years. He's the man I fell in love with at eighteen. I can't lose him."

"He's okay. He's going to be okay," I said, even though I still wasn't sure myself.

She nodded and blotted her face with a tissue. Her phone buzzed, and she reached into her purse for it.

"Aunt Bea was able to squeeze onto the afternoon flight. She lands at six," she said, reading off the text message.

"Want me to go to your apartment and get you some things?"

"Maybe I'll run home, change, and get the guest room ready. The nurse said your father would be asleep for a few more hours, right? I'll go now, so that I can also get a few of his things to bring back for when he's feeling better. I'm sure he'd prefer his own robe and toiletries." She bent down, kissed my forehead, and forced a brave smile. "I'll be back soon."

I threw away the rest of our lunch and stepped outside for some air before going back up to the cardiac ICU. I had several more missed calls from Trini on my phone. I dialed her back.

"Trini, I'm so sorry, I wasn't avoiding you—"

"I know, I know. I spoke to Jordana. How's your father?"

"He's out of surgery. The doctors are very optimistic about his recovery."

"That's wonderful. I'm so glad to hear it. Look, I won't keep you long, but I wanted to share some good news. A private equity firm's reached out to Anna's office to get your information. They're interested in investing in your label. Georgica, between that and the money from G. Malone, you'd be well on your way."

"Trini, I—"

"You don't have to make any decisions today. Right now, just be with your family. When things calm down, we'll go over the details." Her voice softened. "You did it. You rose from the ashes to become a phoenix. Try to enjoy the moment."

"I will, I promise."

"Good," she said and hung up.

I cradled the phone against my ear for a moment, then hurried back inside.

While my father slept, nurses and aides rotated in and out of his hospital room every thirty minutes like clockwork. They checked his vitals, the monitors, and scribbled notes into his chart before passing the baton to the next person. My father was a tall man, almost 6'2", but he looked small and frail lying in the bed hooked up to half a dozen machines.

When I was a little girl, maybe eight or nine, my mother convinced him to let me tag along to the courthouse, so I could see him give the closing arguments in a huge case he was involved with. I remembered how he held my hand as we navigated the confusing subway tunnels leading to the courthouses Centre Street. When we got out from underground, we stopped at a small bodega, where everyone behind the counter seemed to know his name and how he liked his coffee—light and sweet. He bought me some orange juice and promised if I behaved in the courtroom we'd have lunch together at Wo-Hop.

I sat in the row directly behind the plaintiff's table and watched how the other attorneys looked to my father every time they addressed the judge or made a motion. He was clearly the one in charge, and my heart was practically bursting with pride. When he stood up to give his closing argument, the jurors hung on his every word and movement. He charmed them with his charisma and authority. Without understanding much about the case at all, I knew for certain he'd won them all over.

During the lunch recess, we walked the few blocks from

Centre Street over to Mott Street and down the long staircase to our favorite table at Wo-Hop, where he ordered us Hot and Sour soup, egg rolls, and lo mein to share. While we ate, he reviewed the case, explaining the plaintiff's position and the legal precedents he was using to prove their argument. He let me ask dozens of questions, taking the time to answer each and every one. When we finished, he told me he was sure I'd make an excellent lawyer one day. I'll never forget the look of disappointment that registered firmly on his face years later when I finally got up the courage to tell him I let my law school acceptances lapse and was going to FIT to follow my dream of becoming a designer instead.

A nurse tapped me on my shoulder. I'd closed my eyes for a few minutes and apparently had fallen asleep.

"We've removed the ventilator, and he's breathing well on his own." She motioned toward the bed. "He's starting to stir. You may want to move closer, so he sees a familiar face when he opens his eyes."

He was fluttering his eyelids and licking his dry, cracked lips. I stood up from the corner chair and took a seat in the one beside the bed.

"I feel like I've been hit with a Mack truck," he said. His voice was hoarse and gravelly from the intubation tube.

"You basically were," I said.

"Did they give me the full roto-rooter?"

"Oh, you got the works. But the doctor says you'll be good as new."

"Funny, I feel anything but." His eyes darted around the room. "Where's Mom?"

"She ran home to get you a few things and get the guest room ready for Aunt Bea."

"Bea's coming? Things must've *really* looked bleak for me. I can't remember the last time your Aunt Bea was in New York."

"Can't blame her for preferring the California sunshine."

"No, I suppose you can't." He coughed to clear his throat. "Was it terribly awful for your mother?"

"Mom's tougher than she looks, but it sounds like you gave her a bit of a scare."

"Georgie, when the pain shot up my left arm, I wasn't sure I was getting out of this one. My life didn't quite flash before my eyes, but everything that mattered to me came into clear, exquisite focus."

I took him by the hand. "You don't usually wax poetic?"

"I was so thankful for your mother, our last few years, and how wonderful they've been. And I was so grateful I'd had a chance to see you doing the thing you love most in the world. You designed the gown you were wearing at the Met Ball, didn't you?"

My eyes brimming with tears, I nodded.

"I knew it. Georgie, if I ever made you doubt yourself, or your choices, I'm truly sorry."

"Dad, are you getting all sentimental on me? You know, they just repaired your heart, you didn't get an entirely new one," I teased.

"I love you, sweetheart. I just want to see you happy. You know that, right?"

I leaned in, smoothed some hair out of his face, and kissed him on the cheek. "Get some rest. Mom will be back soon, and if she thinks I've done anything to derail your recovery, there'll be hell to pay."

He smiled, closed his eyes, and drifted back to sleep.

"Hey, Dad... love you too," I whispered.

CHAPTER THIRTY

Five days later my father was released from the hospital with strict orders to take it easy over the next six to eight weeks. Almost immediately, my mother whisked him away to their South Hampton house, where she thought the fresh air and quiet would help him heal more quickly. Though they hired a private nurse, I planned to pack up my apartment to go with them for a few weeks as an extra helping hand. I knew it would take all hands-on deck to keep my father sedentary. Plus, I thought a change of scenery might even do me some good.

I was exhausted from the Met Ball. Besides the weeks of preparation leading up to the event, I'd spent the last few days dismantling parts of the exhibition and moving pieces to their temporary home in the Met's Costume Institute. Except for a few pieces, which were returned to their owners at the end of the week, the majority of the exhibit would be open to the public through the summer. The show was so well received, hundreds of people were lining up daily to view the exhibition, especially the Rainbow Portrait Gown. Jan told me he hadn't seen crowds like this since their Alexander McQueen showcase in 2011.

Before heading out East, I met Trini for lunch and to go over the details of the offer from the private equity firm. As soon as I walked into the restaurant, she pulled me in for an uncharacteristic bear hug.

"How's your dad?" she asked after finally letting go.

I took a seat and set my sunglasses on the table. "He's doing well. Recouping in the Hamptons."

"There are worse places," she teased.

"My mother's put the kibosh on most of his favorite things—cigars, scotch, red meat, and work, so we'll see how long he lasts under her thumb."

She laughed and said, "Speaking of work, should we cut right to the chase?"

I bent down, pulled a portfolio out of my bag, and slid the folder across the table. "They had this messengered over to my apartment. I picked the package up this morning but haven't had a chance to review any of the information." I ran my hand over the embossed leather cover and the words, BLD Capital. "Bold Capital?"

"Baume, Levine, Dawson Capital," she answered.

I nodded and turned to the first page of their prospectus.

BLD Capital is an independent private equity firm that focuses on businesses in the lifestyle segment. Our primary objective is to secure profitable equity investments and manage third-party investment in fashion.

Our hands-on approach combines a keen understanding of branding and the lifestyle segment, a powerful global network, and a dedicated and experienced team of industry specialists to ensure complete alignment and a transparent working relationship.

I looked up at Trini. "I'm impressed so far."

"They're a newer firm, but they've launched several up-and-coming designers. Their reputation's stellar."

I turned to the page listing the three main partners in the firm, and that's when I saw his face. Sandy-blond hair, light blue eyes, and a thousand-watt smile I'd know anywhere. Joshua Baume. I took in a sharp breath and pushed the folder a few inches away from me.

Trini pulled the folder closer to her side of the table. "What's wrong?"

"One of the founders of the firm is Joshua Baume."

She slipped on her signature oversized tortoise reading glasses and began perusing the page. "Who's that?"

"Joshua-Joshua. Alicia's Joshua. The guy I was in love with during the first Season of *Top Designer.*"

"You didn't know this is where he worked?"

"We've lost touch over the years."

"Well, there's no possible way he didn't know he was reaching out to you. But, six years is a long time, and this *is* what his firm does. They invest in new designers. I'm sure his intentions are pure." The waiter set our entrees down on the table, and Trini laid her napkin down in her lap. "They're offering a significant amount of capital and backing. The money would allow you to take the brand beyond ready-to-wear but expand into luxury goods as well."

I took a few sips of water. "Crazy enough, this isn't the only offer I have on the table."

Trini set her glasses back down on the table and shifted in her seat.

"Perry Gillman's asked me to consult on the *Elizabeth* movie."

"That's quite the feather in your cap. How'd you answer him?"

"I told him I needed to think about it, and that I'd let him know after I finished up with the Met Ball."

"No doubt about it, working on *Elizabeth* is a very appealing offer from a very appealing person, but, if you want any advice, don't wait too long to make your decision. The positive press you received from the ball has a shorter shelf life than you might think. *If* you're serious about starting your own label, you have to strike while the iron's hot."

After lunch I met up with Jamie for a walk in Central Park with the kids. He was enjoying his brief sabbatical and spending time with Clara and Oliver so much, I wasn't completely sure whether he ever wanted to go back to work.

"Let's park ourselves here in the shade," he said, steering the stroller over to a bench under a large tree.

I opened two bottles of water out of my bag and passed him one.

"When are you heading out to the Hamptons?" he asked.

"In a few days. I have a couple more meetings to wrap up the Met Ball."

"I'd offer to drive you, but we aren't headed out East until next week."

"You broke down and let Thom trade in the Audi A6 for a minivan?"

"Of course not. You'd have to squeeze between the car seats in the back of the Audi." Jamie turned the double stroller around so the bassinets were facing us. "They really are amazing, aren't they?"

I tucked the blanket more tightly around Oliver's feet. "Are you really going to want to go back to work after being home with them all this time?"

"It won't be easy, but I am excited about this role and taking on some new challenges. Designing's in my blood. I don't think I could ever really give it up. Well, unless, of course, I'd been the one engaged to a viscount."

"I'll be honest, even *that* life isn't all it's cracked up to be."

"Well, Caroline Barker will just have to learn for herself, won't she?"

My head shot up. "Caroline Barker?"

He closed his eyes. "Oh, shit."

"Gideon's seeing Caroline Barker?"

"Jesus, of course, you've been off the grid this last week with your dad being in the hospital. I wasn't thinking or I never would've blurted the news out like that."

Jamie pulled out his phone and opened up a tabloid site. He scrolled through a few pictures, found the one of Gideon and Caroline, and reluctantly passed his cell over to me.

Viscount Satterley and new girlfriend, Caroline Barker, step out at the Victoria and Albert Museum Summer Garden Party along with Spencer Howle and Linney Cooper.

Gideon was wearing a light gray herringbone summer suit, open collar, his arm tightly wrapped around Caroline's tiny waist. Linney, standing right beside Caroline, was beaming from ear to ear. They looked *so* right together—all four of them.

I handed the phone back to Jamie. "I guess I shouldn't be surprised, right?"

"Isn't Caroline Barker that ice princess who gave you hell? *Of course,* you should be surprised! But, if you're asking me, this whole situation screams rebound." Jamie put his hand on my shoulder and squeezed.

"I'm fine, really, I promise. Caroline's the perfect candidate to be the future Countess of Harronsby. Truth is, Gideon and I were never right for each other."

Jamie raised his eyebrows.

"Don't give me that look. Perry and I weren't right for each other, either."

"Have you heard from him?"

"He's left a few messages. I'll reach back out when things settle down with my dad."

"Look, I saw the two of you dancing in the Rainbow Portrait Gown gallery. If you ask me, he's still madly in love with you."

"*So* in love with me that he left the ball with Annabelle Ellicott?"

"We don't know the whole story. You above all people should know that things are not always what they seem, and to not make assumptions based on a single moment from afar."

"I'm pretty sure I can fill in most of the gaps. Either way, I think it's high time I swear off British men entirely, don't you?"

A group of shirtless runners sprinted past us.

Jamie lowered his sunglasses. "When there are so many excellent possibilities right here in the good old US of A, why not?"

CHAPTER THIRTY-ONE

The last time I saw Joshua Baume was four and a half years ago, right around the time Perry told me he was staying in London to finish *Elizabeth* and Alicia announced her engagement to Asher. We decided to meet up for drinks, two old friends looking for some consolation. Joshua suggested we meet up at one of our old haunts, a small, family-owned Italian restaurant off Mulberry Street, where wannabe opera singers would treat the diners to performances of arias from *La Boheme* and *Tosca*.

Over several bottles of their house red wine and at least two renditions of "Quando men vo," we talked, we reminisced, and we fell right back into old patterns. When dinner ended, he hinted at the idea of us going back to his apartment, and I'll admit I was tempted. Perry'd broken my heart, and I was looking for comfort wherever I could find it. But, in the end, I decided that was a door better left closed. We didn't speak again, until last night, when he called to schedule a lunch to discuss BLD Capital's possible investment in my new label.

Staring into my closet for what felt like hours, I finally settled on a black sundress and wedge sandals for the meeting. I applied simple makeup and let my hair dry in soft waves. Down in the lobby of my building, I gave myself a last once-over in the vestibule mirror.

"Big date?" Albert teased.

I spun around. "Huh? What? No. Just a lunch meeting. A potential investor. I might be starting my own label."

Albert looked confused by my ramblings. "Can I hail you a taxi, Ms. Goldstein?"

"No, thanks. It's a beautiful day. I think I'm just gonna walk," I answered.

He nodded and held the door open for me. I stepped out onto the sidewalk and turned east. I was meeting Joshua at a small Greek restaurant a few blocks from his office on 50th and Park. I figured I'd use the walk to get my thoughts together. At one time in my life, Joshua occupied every one of my feelings and decisions. In my pursuit of him, I piled on so many mistakes that, even six years later, in some ways it felt like I'd *just* gotten out from under the wreckage.

I stepped inside the restaurant, and Joshua was already seated at a corner table. The hostess guided me through the crowd and over to him. He stood up to greet me, kissing me on both cheeks before sitting back down. The hostess's eyes were locked on Joshua as she handed me a menu and told him not to hesitate to let her know if there was anything else she could do to make his dining experience more enjoyable. *Unbelievable.* He still made the ladies weak in the knees.

"I was beginning to think you were going to stand me up," he said.

I raised my eyebrows. "Joshua Baume getting stood up? That'd be a first."

He laughed, which instantly put me at ease. "It took a little longer to walk here than I planned. I'll admit I might've been dragging my feet a bit. I'm not entirely convinced this meeting's a good idea."

Joshua held up his hand. "My motives are entirely professional. Scout's honor."

"You were *never* a Boy Scout."

He ignored my comment and motioned for the waiter. "Want anything to drink?"

I shook my head no, and he ordered an iced tea for himself. He leaned forward and clasped his hands together. "I have a confession to make. I've been following your career for a while now. When it was announced in the press you were designing Victoria Ellicott's wedding gown, BLD reached out to Jordana Singer. We were prepared to invest a significant amount into G. Malone."

"And then the scandal happened," I said, folding my napkin into my lap.

"And then the scandal happened," he repeated. "But, look, the press on the Met Ball's been amazing. You have the whole world talking about you for all the right reasons, and I want you."

I set my water glass down on the table. "You want me?"

"For our portfolio. BLD Capital believes, with the right management, your brand could go far."

"You didn't do your homework, Mr. Baume. I don't have a brand, just some half-finished sketches."

Joshua leaned back and crossed one leg over the other. "Gigi, I know you. Better than most. If you decide to move forward with this, there'll be no stopping you."

His words hung in the air as the waiter came by to take our orders.

"I'll have the cobb salad," I said.

"Sounds good, I'll have the same." Joshua snapped his menu closed, took mine from my extended hand, and handed them back to the server.

The waiter scribbled into his pad. "I'll be right back with some bread."

Joshua slipped off his suit jacket, hung it over his seat, and leaned into the table. "Would it be crossing a line if I were to tell you how great you looked?"

"Probably, but when has that stopped you before?"

Years ago, a throwaway comment like that would've sent me into a complete tizzy. I'd have spent the next several days dissecting his every inflection and intention. Now, I knew he was just a perpetual flirt.

"I'll keep it to myself, then," he said with a coy smile. "I saw Perry Gillman was celebrity chair for the Met Ball. That must've been awkward."

"Surprisingly, it wasn't."

"I'm glad to hear it."

I narrowed my eyes. "You are?"

"Means you might not hold our past *against* me."

"Joshua... "

"Gigi, I was an idiot. We were in an impossible situation. I know that now."

I tilted my head to the side. "Joshua, we knew *that* then."

"So, why'd we do it?"

"I can only speak for myself. I thought I was in love with you."

His eyes hovered over my face. "You weren't?"

My mind drifted to Perry. "No. Love is something very different. I know that now."

The waiter set our salads in front of us. Joshua asked for some pepper and the drink menu. He ordered himself a Macallan 18 neat.

His eyes crinkled in the corners. "I hope you don't mind. I needed something to take the sting out of hearing you say that you were never really in love with me."

There was no denying he was still sexy. Perfectly chiseled features, an impossibly good tan for this early into the summer, and eyes that were both familiar and a little bit dangerous. Looking into them could always bring me right back to that moment on the camp bus when he sat down next to Alicia and I felt the first real pangs of heartache.

Joshua bent down, pulled the prospectus out from his briefcase, and set the papers down on the table.

"Gigi, this is BLD Capital's strategy to grow your label and take you public. We see you as a major player in the fashion world and would want to have you in the tents by the spring and in all the major department stores by fall next year."

"I've been down this road with G. Malone, and it's a long, hard road."

"With all due respect, when you started G. Malone, you and Jamie were two no-name designers with no real experience or financial backing. Now, you have both."

I slid the folder closer. "Can I keep this to look over?"

He sipped on his scotch. "Please."

I pushed the papers into my tote. "It may be a few days before I get back to you. I'm heading to the Hamptons for a bit. I don't know if Trini told you about my dad?"

He reached over and squeezed the top of my hand. "She did. I'm so glad to hear Mitchell's doing better."

I pulled my arms back down and into my lap.

"Am I skirting the line again?" he said with the same boyish grin that used to charm the hell out me.

"No, I just realized what time it is. I told my parents I'd be on the four-o'clock Jitney."

Joshua tapped on his glass. "Go. I'll finish this, pay the check, and head back to the office. Give this some real thought, Gigi. You need us. We can take this thing places you'll never be able to on your own."

I stood up and reached for my tote under the table. "It was good to see you, Joshua."

I hurried back to my apartment for my bags and rushed to catch the Jitney. The summer was in full swing and the Jitney was packed with people. I squeezed into a seat in the very back of the bus and pulled the BLD prospectus out of my tote. The first few pages outlined their aggressive growth plan for the brand and a two-year turn around to recoup their initial investment. Much of the strategy involved the brand's expansion into accessories and luxury home goods. While that was something I could imagine doing one day, I wasn't sure if it was the direction I wanted to go in from the outset. Even in these first few pages, I could see if I signed with BLD, I would be making a lot of creative concessions.

I tucked the binder back into my bag and dug out my headphones. I slipped them on and skipped to "Semper Eadem" a song from *Elizabeth's* second act. I closed my eyes and let the words and music wash over me, Perry's haunting and remorseful voice in my ear. Jamie used to say that nothing hurts more than having someone in your heart that you cannot have in your arms. That pain was the reason I'd closed my heart off to Perry all those years ago. I hadn't meant to let him back in, but there were so many moments these last few weeks where I could swear there was something developing between us again. But clearly, I'd misread all the signs. He was back with Annabelle. Whatever interest he may have had was strictly professional and for better or worse, if I wanted him in my life, that would have to be enough.

CHAPTER THIRTY-TWO

I carried the tea tray out to the patio and set the platter down on the table, along with some light snacks and fruit.

"I should stop expecting an afternoon meat and cheese plate, shouldn't I?" my father asked.

I passed him a cucumber sandwich. "I think your days of brie and prosciutto are far behind you, I'm sorry to say."

He took a bite of the sandwich and spit most of cucumber out into a napkin. "Yeah, I'm sorry too." He eyed me up and down. "You didn't happen to smuggle any Wo-Hop onto the Jitney, did you?"

I squeezed his right shoulder. "Maybe next time." I sat down and poured us each a cup of tea. "So, this is new. Afternoon tea? I know tea doesn't quite replace your mid-day martini, but it is one of the things I miss most from my time at Badgley Hall."

"Your mother thought our company might enjoy some tea also," he said.

"You're having someone over to the house?"

"You'd be surprised at how quickly almost dropping dead can rekindle old relationships. People have been in and out of here all week."

I laughed and swiveled around in my chair. "Should I go back in and see if Mom needs more help? She didn't mention that anyone was coming by."

"No, I think your only job was to be my babysitter."

I tilted my head to the side. "I'm here to keep you company. That's all. Hey, Dad, have you ever heard of BLD Capital?"

He shook his head. "I don't think so. Why?"

"It's Joshua Baume's private equity firm. He's a partner there."

"Joshua Baume. That's a name I haven't heard in a while."

"BLD invests in new fashion labels, and they're interested in helping me launch mine." I pulled the prospectus out of my bag and passed the binder to my father. "I had lunch with Joshua today. He shared this with me."

He pulled a pair of glasses out of his robe pocket.

I raised my eyebrows. "Are those *reading* glasses?"

"What can I say, your mother had me at a weak moment." He slipped on the glasses and skimmed through the document. "Do you think it's a good idea to get into business with someone whom you had a relationship?"

"That was six years ago."

"I'm not sure it would matter if the relationship was sixty years ago. Besides all that, they have some pretty aggressive plans for you. Are you sure you want to give up so much control of your company so early into the game?"

A few moments later my mother called out to me from the back-patio door.

"That must be the company. Do you mind bringing him out to me? I don't feel like going inside just yet," Dad asked.

I left my father and hurried back to the house. I opened the screen door and could hear my mother chatting away with someone in the kitchen.

"Hey, Georgica, is that you?" she called out.

"Dad wants to stay outside a little longer," I hollered back.

"Can you see our guest out to the back patio then, please?"

I stepped into the kitchen and stopped dead in my tracks. "Perry, what are you doing here?"

"If the mountain won't come to Muhammad..." He took a few steps in my direction. "Hello, Gigi."

"Isn't it lovely Perry took a night off from *Elizabeth* just to pay a visit to your father? Can you take these flutes outside with you? I think Perry's visit calls for some champagne, don't you?" She turned to him. "I didn't think we'd ever get a chance to personally toast you on your record-breaking number of Tony nominations."

"I can help you with those," he said, taking a few glasses out of my hands.

"Let me grab a bottle from the cellar. I'll meet you all out back," my mother said, practically floating out of the kitchen. I could only imagine all the things she was presuming from his seemingly impromptu visit.

"What are you doing here?" I asked again.

"When you didn't return any of my calls, I reached out to Jordana. She told me about your father, and I don't know, I needed to see you."

"Did you tell my parents not to tell me that you were coming?"

"I didn't want to scare you off. I know you're upset with me, and you have every right to be. I know how things must've looked at the Met Ball."

"You reconciled with Annabelle, and I'm happy for you. For both of you."

Perry took the flutes from me and placed them on the counter. He took hold of my hands. "I didn't get back together with Annabelle. She asked me if we could be seen at some of the parties together to show the press we're on good terms. Look, her name was dragged through the mud along with ours, maybe even worse than ours. She wanted to take the narrative back and prove none of what went down was as big a deal as it was made out to be."

"I don't understand? It was all an act then?"

"Look, after everything that happened, it was the least I could do for her. All these months, the press has portrayed her as the poor unsuspecting fool, cheated on by her boyfriend and good friend right under her nose. Walking out with me arm and arm was her way to show them once and for all that the story was more smoke than it was fire."

"So, you're saying that nothing happened between the two of you?"

"She's dating one of the band members from One Direction, less than nothing happened. I tried to get a hold of you that night to explain, but you were so busy I couldn't catch you. And then, by the next day when I tried to reach out, you were dealing with all the stuff with your dad."

My mother came back up from the cellar holding two bottles of Dom Perignon.

"What are you two still doing in here? Let's take these down to the pond," she said.

We followed her out the back doors and down to the shore of Georgica Pond, where my father had started a small bonfire.

"Mitchell, why didn't you wait for our help?" my mother asked.

"Kate, I am perfectly capable of bundling up some twigs and tossing in a match. Besides, I knew I'd have Perry for the heavy lifting."

"Hello, Mr. Goldstein," Perry said, shaking his hand. "You look well."

"There was one time I was going to be your father-in-law, you can certainly call me Mitchell."

I elbowed my dad gently in the side. "Dad, don't."

"There's no need to be coy, Gigi. We all know what you two meant to each other at one time. And I'm grateful that after all that's happened, we can still spend time together as friends."

My mom looked down at her watch. "Mitchell, it's time for your afternoon meds. Why don't you come back inside, and then we'll rejoin them in a few minutes?"

My father followed my mother back to the house, leaving me and Perry alone by the fire. The afternoon sun was starting to go down over Georgica Pond, and the only sound was the low, soothing hum of the cicadas in the White Oak trees across the lawn.

"She certainly timed that well," I said.

"I can't help it if I was the favorite of all your boyfriends and your mother wants to see us back together."

"Oh, I don't know. The viscount was a front-runner for a little while, but you may have slid into the lead *after* you gave them tickets to see *Elizabeth* and a backstage tour. She was the envy of all her friends."

He laughed and sat down in one of the big white Adirondack chairs along the pond.

"Speaking of *Elizabeth*, have you given any more thought to my offer? Please say you have."

In my heart, I knew the very best chance of us getting back together would be for me to sign on. Annabelle wasn't in the picture and distance would no longer be an issue. We'd be a team again. But Trini was right, I might never be given another chance to strike out on my own if I didn't do it now. I had to take my shot.

I turned to him. "You know how proud I am of you, right? In those early days, we couldn't've even dreamed of anything this big. *Elizabeth* surpassed every single hope we had for it, and I am in awe of how far you've come." I stood up and took a few steps away from him. "Perry, I love you. I do. I don't think I ever stopped, and I'm not sure if I ever will. But, I need to love *me* more right now. It's taken me a long time to realize that, let alone say the words aloud. I know this might be jeopardizing the possibility of us, but I can't accept your offer. I finally have the opportunity to go out on my own and start my own label. I have to try."

His eyes focused on an empty space in the air between us while trying to digest my words.

"Gigi, Perry, let's have that toast now," my father called out from the patio, snapping us back to the present. We walked back up the lawn to greet them.

"Here we go," my mother said, doling out the champagne. "Mitchell, you can have a small taste, since it would be bad luck for you not to toast."

My father raised his glass. "A wise man once said, the most wonderful thing in the world is somebody who knows who they are and knows what they were created to do. Perry, you found your calling, and the world is grateful. Congratulations on all your Tony nominations, and cheers to a very bright future ahead."

Perry's big brown eyes brimmed with tears, and I knew he wasn't hearing my father's praise, but finally, his own father's approval. He cleared his throat, thanked my father for his kind words, and lifted his own glass.

"I have a toast as well. Georgica just shared the wonderful news with me that she's starting her own fashion line. She's finally doing the thing *she* was created to do, and I couldn't be more pleased. To Gigi."

"To Gigi," they all exclaimed.

CHAPTER THIRTY-THREE

The next morning, I tiptoed down to the kitchen and turned on the coffeepot. It was just after five a.m., and the sun was slowly starting to inch over Georgica Pond. My mother practically strong-armed Perry into spending the night, convincing him to crash in one of the guest rooms and head back to the city in the morning. Knowing he was just a few doors down had me tossing and turning all night long. Finally, when I couldn't take it anymore, I got up, grabbed my sketchpad out of my bag, and headed downstairs. I poured myself a cup, took the warm mug and a fleece plaid blanket out to the back, and settled down in a spot on the grass. I opened my notebook and flipped to a clean page.

When I started this collection over six years ago, I had been inspired by the great movement of creatives to France after World War I. I called the collection "The Lost Generation," a term Gertrude Stein coined to describe the artists, authors, and poets that would congregate in her Paris salon. A youth culture that glorified fast-living, dancing, and the exciting sounds of syncopated jazz, the Lost Generation completely changed the face of fashion.

I still believed in the collection as a concept, but all these years later, my take on the premise was different, less literal and more abstract. The pieces would still incorporate the general trends of the day, dropped waistlines, shorter hemlines, and low backs. I even held to the idea of incorporating some Egyptian-themed pieces. The discovery of the tomb of Tutankhamen in 1922 set off an instant craze for all things Egyptian. Clothing styles and embellishments reflected designs and patterns of ancient Egypt, and I loved the idea of bringing those looks back in a more modern way.

I turned to the front page of my notebook and crossed out the word *Lost* and replaced it with the word *Found*. The title of my new and first collection would be "The Found Generation," and would combine the decadence of the jazz age with the simplicity of modern wear. Just as I'd done with my dress for the Met Ball, I'd mix heavily beaded pieces and delicate embroideries with more modern textiles and minimalist designs.

As I flipped back and forth between old and new sketches, it became increasingly clear that the enormity of the work involved to bring these pieces to life would crush every deadline in Joshua's prospectus. Maybe, if I hired some ateliers to assist with the beadwork, I'd finish in time to show in the tents next spring, but it was a big maybe. Either way, these weren't the kinds of pieces intended for mass production and department store racks. One day, I'd transition to ready-to-wear, but I wanted this first collection to make a splash. I was aiming for over-the-top avant-garde innovation the likes of which the world had never seen. The *Elizabeth* of fashion shows.

I heard leaves rustling behind me and turned to look. Perry was walking out of the house, a cup of coffee in one hand, and his laptop in the other. He sat down, setting his mug beside me on the grass.

He pushed some bedhead out of his eyes. "I hope your mum doesn't mind. I remembered where she kept the coffee mugs."

"Are you kidding? She's still doing a victory dance that she got you to agree to stay over."

"What can I say, she's very persuasive."

"That's putting it mildly." I motioned toward the laptop. "What are you working on?"

"The *Elizabeth* movie script. Obviously, not everything we do onstage is going to translate to film, so I'm working through a massive revision." He leaned back on his elbows. "You know, I forgot how pretty it is out here. What are we, two hours out of New York City, and it's like another world."

"You know what this reminds me of?"

He sat back up and shook his head.

"Remember the first time I stayed in your cabin at Camp Chinooka? I had to sneak back into my bunk in the morning. You walked me through the hidden path behind the lake so Gordy wouldn't catch us."

"That's right! Wasn't that the very same path I caught the Cedar girls using to bunk hop the very first night of camp?"

"Still gonna hold that one against me?"

"Look, Princess, it wasn't my fault you couldn't control your campers."

"Okay, okay, I'll admit it. You were a better Head Counselor."

He turned to me and raised his eyebrows. "Wow, I never thought I'd hear those words come out of your mouth."

"I'm more than happy to give you your due, as long as you admit I was the better Color War General."

"Your team did win, but I don't think we can absolutely one hundred percent say it was because of your leadership skills. There are so many events that make up Color War. It really can't be boiled down to one single, solitary factor."

"Oh, it can. In the case of the Heroes wiping the floor with the Villains, that single solitary factor was—"

Perry leaned in and kissed me, hard.

"Me," I whispered. My lips tingled with anticipation. I looked away so I could concentrate on breathing normally.

He cupped my chin gently and tilted my face back toward him. "Is it okay I just did that?"

"Very okay."

"Would it be okay if I kissed you again?"

I didn't give him a reply, instead, I leaned over and kissed him back, just as hard. Every square inch of me instantly remembered just how good it felt to be in his arms, my fingers tangled in his black wavy hair.

I pulled back, and Perry stroked the side of my face, tracing my lips with the tips of his fingers.

"Georgica, can I ask you something?"

I looked up into his eyes and nodded.

"Will you be my date to the Tony Awards?"

I thought back to a few years ago, when Perry was asked to be a presenter at the Olivier Awards in London and didn't want me as his date. His publicist thought it would be better for Perry's career and *Elizabeth* if he bolstered his reputation as the hot new *eligible* actor hitting the London theater scene. Back then, Perry was so desperate to get the show off the ground, he followed his publicist's advice and went solo. That decision was the first nail in our relationship's coffin. Now, he wanted me to be his date to the Tonys?

The buildup for the award show was out of control. *Elizabeth's* popularity, Perry's notoriety, and the fact that the show was set to break every record on the books, had the press out in droves. Walking the red carpet on Perry's arm would bring the white-hot spotlight right back into our lives.

"Perry, are you really sure that's what you want?"

"I made a mistake when I asked you not to come to the Oliviers with me. A huge mistake that I've regretted every day since. I know it's why you started to doubt our relationship, and I don't blame you. I was so laser-focused, I let everything else in my life fall apart. It wouldn't be like that now. I respect your decision not to work on *Elizabeth*, and I'm so proud of you for wanting to start your own label. You can even design from London. Just while I'm working on the movie, so we can be together. Then we can come back to New York or move to Bora Bora—we can go any damn place you want. I don't care as long as I have you. Please come to the awards show with me. Not because I need you to, but because I want you to. I want to share this with you."

I could see in his eyes that he meant every word.

"Yes, I'll be your date to the Tonys."

"Darling," he breathed and scooped me back up into his arms.

CHAPTER THIRTY-FOUR

I returned to the city a few days later for Sloan's second birthday. Alicia rented out space in the back of a restaurant on the Upper East Side with the goal of transforming the room into a circus for Sloan's big top-themed party. I arrived early to help her finish setting up.

"Gigi, thank God you're here," she said, rushing over to me. "The centerpieces are all wrong, and the party planner doesn't seem to understand the concept I'm going for at all. Can you help? Her name's Rachel."

I set Sloan's present, an American Girl Doll, down on the table. "I can try."

I walked over to a frazzled-looking girl, who couldn't have been any older than twenty-five, struggling to open a bag of sparkly confetti.

I tapped Rachel on the shoulder. "Alicia asked me to check to see if you needed any help."

"We definitely got our messages crossed. I'd been thinking this party should have more of a Cirque Du Soleil feel, but she wants it to look more Ringling Barnum and Bailey. I had to rush order all new props from Amazon yesterday."

"They're two-year-olds. I think Alicia just wants it look more *fun* in here."

"Fun, how?"

"You know, bright colors... streamers." I pointed to the table. "The confetti's a good start. Can I see what else you have?"

She walked over to a huge cardboard box and sliced it open. I peeked inside. "These little stuffed animals are perfect. Each table can be staged to be a part of the circus train. This table can be the elephant table, and this one the lion table."

"Circus train... " Rachel muttered and went back to digging through the box.

I rejoined Alicia, who was separating a large bunch of brightly-colored balloons.

"How'd it go?" she asked.

"I don't think she quite understood the type of circus theme you were going for."

"Yeah, I realized that when the room was starting to resemble the Tao night club in Vegas more than a children's birthday party."

"Everyone seems to be on the same page now. Where's the birthday girl?"

"At the apartment with my mom, finishing up a nap. Asher went to go pick up the cake. Wait 'til you see Sloan's outfit. A tuxedo tutu with a little gold glittery top hat like she's the ringmaster. The getup's completely over the top, but I couldn't help myself."

"She's only two once. If not now... "

"Exactly. Hey," Alicia said, passing me a bunch of balloons to help untangle. "I feel bad to bring this up now, but with your dad and everything, there hasn't been a better time, and I don't want you hearing about it from anyone else today."

"Bring what up?"

"You know how Asher and Gideon have become such good

friends? Well, they've stayed good friends, even though the two of you aren't together anymore."

"Gideon's a great guy. I wouldn't expect Asher to give up their friendship just because we aren't engaged anymore. That was a bromance if ever I saw one. I'd actually feel terrible if it ended because of me."

Alicia smiled. "I'm glad to hear you say that. So, I wasn't sure if you'd heard, but Gideon's been dating Caroline Barker. He told Asher a couple of weeks ago. Asher doesn't think it's anything too serious. Knowing her, she probably threw herself at him the minute she saw an opening."

"I know all about their relationship. Jamie let the news slip the other day."

"I told Asher what a nightmare she was and how terribly she treated you. He's waiting for the right moment to burst Gideon's bubble."

"Asher doesn't have to do that. Maybe Caroline's changed?"

Alicia arched her eyebrow. "Not likely."

"I know this might sound crazy, considering how she treated me, but I'm not all that surprised they're together. She has the perfect resumé for the job, and the truth is, I think she can make him really happy. I hope she can anyway. He deserves to be happy."

Alicia gently patted my arm and passed over a few more balloons from the bunch.

"Speaking of exes, I saw one of ours the other day."

"Since there is only one person that fits *that* particular description, how is Mr. Baume?" she asked.

"He's good. Did you know his firm invested in fashion designers and brands?"

"Yeah, of course. BLD's become pretty well known in that space."

"How did I not know that?"

"They've only become a more major player in the last year or so, and you know, you've been a little far removed from the scene. From what I've heard, they're still on the lookout for one big fish they can anchor their name to."

"He reached out to me about investing in my brand."

"Let's tie a balloon to every chair," she said, passing me a few. "You should definitely consider it. They have a great reputation."

"That's what Trini said."

"Well, she's right."

"You don't think it'd be weird for me to be in business with him?"

"That all depends. How's he looking these days?" Alicia smirked.

"Like Joshua Baume."

She laughed. "If your hesitation has anything at all to do with me, that's just silly. All that's long behind us—both of us. I've moved on, clearly," she said, as she gestured around to her daughter's elaborate birthday setup, "and I truly believe you have as well. I think the question you need to ask yourself is if you're ready to give up that much control of a company you're just starting. I'm sure they wouldn't be involved in the day-to-day operations, but you'd be answering to a board right from the get-go. The capital you have from the dissolution of G. Malone is enough to get you started on your own. If you turn down their offer, you could take things a bit more slowly and build out the brand organically. The only person you'd have to answer to is yourself. Scary but also very exciting."

"Is that what you think I should do?"

Just as she opened her mouth to answer, Alicia's mom walked through the door carrying Sloan.

"Oh my God!" Alicia screeched and rushed toward them. "She looks even cuter than I imagined."

Sloan was wearing a leotard that mimicked a tuxedo top paired with a black, sparkly tutu. Her golden ringlets were practically bursting out from under the top hat.

"Quick, Gigi, get a photo. You know that hat isn't staying on her head much longer."

I jumped up and snapped a picture. "Got it."

A few minutes later, Asher walked in with the cake, a three-tiered fondant replica of a red-and-white circus tent.

I walked over to examine the dessert more closely. "That's not a cake—that's a work of art."

"Might as well be for how much it cost," he joked.

Over the next half hour, a dozen or so two-year-olds and their parents started arriving at the party. Rachel looked like she couldn't get out of there fast enough. As soon as Asher paid her, she bolted out the door, practically knocking over Jamie, Thom, and the twins' stroller on her way out.

Jamie gave me a kiss on each cheek. "Who was that?"

"The party planner. Don't ask."

Thom unbuckled the twins from the carriage and passed me Clara.

"Alicia put out this mat and some toys for the non-walkers," I said, setting Clara down beside a set of stackable blocks.

"Perfect," Thom said, placing Oliver down beside her.

Alicia came over to say hello to Jamie and Thom, Sloan firmly attached to her hip.

"She sees most of these kids in classes all week, but for some reason, she's being extra shy today," she said.

Jamie pointed to Sloan's tutu. "That outfit is fabulous and better be coming to me by way of a hand-me-down."

"Yours, as soon as she outgrows it," Alicia said. "I'm gonna go check on the magician. I'll be right back."

Thom let out a breath. "Oh, thank God. I thought for sure with the circus theme there'd be a clown."

"Thom has a thing with clowns. They terrify him," Jamie said.

I placed my hand on his shoulder. "I don't blame you."

"While we have you on your own, we wanted to invite you to our Tony Awards party," Thom said. "It's *Elizabeth*-themed, *obviously*. Now that I've finally seen the show, I want to celebrate it along with the rest of the world. We're going to drink wine out of goblets, eat dinner with our hands, and try to only speak with English accents."

"And dress in period costume, if you can. I know it's a little late in the game, but I'm sure you have something that'll work. What do you think?" Jamie asked.

"Sounds like a great party, but I'm actually *going* to the Tonys."

"You're what?" he screeched. Half the room turned to look at us.

"Perry asked me to be his date."

"Shut the front door. When? How?"

"He showed up in the Hamptons to visit my father."

Jamie laughed and shook his head.

"What? Why are you laughing?"

"I'm not saying he didn't want to pay a call to your father, but we both know, he went to see you."

Alicia flicked the lights on and off in the room and announced that we should all take our seats for the magic show. Thom motioned us over to a spot behind where the twins were playing, and we settled down on the ground.

"Will we be seeing more of Mr. Gillman?" Jamie asked.

"I think maybe you will."

Jamie pulled Oliver into his lap. "Now, for the most important question of all. The Tony Awards, what *are* you going to wear?"

CHAPTER THIRTY-FIVE

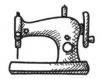

I got on line outside the museum and texted Trini where to meet me. A few minutes later, I heard her calling my name. I waved my arms and directed her to the fountain.

Trini passed me a steaming cup of coffee. "You know we could've just called Jan, and he would've had tickets waiting for us up front."

I'd somehow managed to convince Trini to see the *Fashion Queens* exhibit with me like a regular visitor would. No VIP tickets, no special tour guide. Just us and the artifacts. She seemed to already be regretting her decision.

"I know, but we wouldn't get the complete experience. Part of the fun is waiting on line, hearing everyone talk about the exhibit, and letting the anticipation build. I waited over five hours to get into the Alexander McQueen show in 2011," I answered.

"What anticipation? You know this exhibit like the back of your hand," she said.

"I haven't seen Jan's new design for when the show moved out of the main galleries and into the Costume Institute. Besides, I was so in it when we were planning the gala, I don't think I could fully appreciate all the pieces."

"You really love fashion, don't you?" Trini said.

"I really do."

Trini smiled and sipped on her tea. The museum opened, and they let in the first group of visitors. We shuffled a couple of feet closer to the front entrance.

"How's your dad feeling?"

"Bored more than anything. I think he's ready to get back to the city and his job."

"Your mom's not having it?"

"Honestly, I think she's enjoying having him all to her herself."

"They had a close call. I can understand why she would feel that way."

I reached over and squeezed Trini's hand. She gave me a warm, appreciative smile.

Trini's husband Vince died a few years ago, after being diagnosed with a very aggressive form of brain cancer. We were introduced only a handful of times, but I remembered liking him very much. She told me they met as teenagers in Edinburgh. Trini, by her own admission, worshiped the Edinburgh punk rock music scene as a teenager, and liked to hang around with the roadies, who always had the best access to the bands.

Her husband was a lighting technician who'd sneak her into all the shows. According to Trini, Vince was immediately taken with her shaved head, Vivienne Westwood wardrobe, and her uncanny ability to recite the lyrics to every Sex Pistols song. Gypsies at heart, they never had any children and enjoyed traveling the world and living spontaneously. Trini didn't talk about Vince too often, but whenever she did, it was easy to see she missed him tremendously.

Trini popped up on her tiptoes. "I think we're in this next group."

"This is crazy. The exhibit's been open what, like, almost three weeks, and the line still stretches all the way around the block."

The woman in front of us heard what I said and turned around. "This is my third time trying to see the exhibit. At this point, it might be easier to get tickets to *Elizabeth*," she said, laughing at her own joke. "I finally realized I had to be here by seven a.m. if I had any hope of seeing the Rainbow Portrait Gown before it's shipped back to London. How many times have you guys tried to get in?"

"This is our first time, but we knew to be here early," Trini answered.

"I've had a few girlfriends who were here last week. They can't stop raving about the exhibit. I've always been a fan of Norman Hartnell, so I can't wait to see some of his pieces, and I'm really excited to get a closer look at Victoria Ellicott's wedding gown. My daughter's getting married in a couple of months, and Victoria's dress was all over our inspiration board."

"We can bring in the next group," a docent announced from the door.

"That's us!" the woman practically screamed.

We followed the crowd into the museum, where the docent handed each person a ticket for the *Fashion Queens* exhibit and ushered us into a second line.

I turned to Trini, "You know, when I was a kid my mother took me to the Met Ball exhibit every year. Ironically, we stopped going together when I started making my own clothes and *really* took an interest in fashion."

"Have you asked her to come see this show? You basically orchestrated the whole damn thing."

"Not yet. I was going to, but then everything happened with my dad."

"You need to get her here before it closes. She needs to see what you helped create."

"I'll ask her."

"Good," Trini said. "Okay, I've tried to be patient and let you be the one to bring it up, but I can't wait anymore, how did your lunch go with Joshua Baume?"

"It's hard to say, really."

"Gigi, I've been on pins and needles. Try!"

"He's still Joshua. Charming, flirty, and way way too handsome for his own good. When I'm with him, I remember that twelve-year-old girl holding her breath while she waited to see if he'd want to sit with her on the camp bus."

"Is that the issue? It would feel too strange to be in a working relationship with him?"

"No, aside from a few flirty comments here and there, he kept it pretty professional. Anyway, I don't have those kinds of feelings for him anymore."

The docent directed our group down the stairs and into the Costume Institute. The first gallery highlighted the fashions of the great queens of Egypt. All along the walls were carvings depicting the great pharaohs and their queens in high headdresses, pleated gowns, and ornamental jewelry. Examples of jeweled crowns, beaded collars, and capes lined the gallery.

"These pieces made more of a statement showcased next to the Temple of Dendur at the Met Ball, but I like how Jan was able to show more of an evolution of design with this display," I said.

"I agree," Trini said before turning to me. "So, if you don't have feelings for Joshua, then what's giving you pause? Are you having second thoughts about moving forward with your own line?"

"I'm not, actually. I'm having second thoughts about giving over so much control. I don't know if I need BLD Capital, or Joshua. I think I can do this on my own. I want to at least try. I have the money from the dissolution, which I know isn't enough long term, but it's more than I had when Jamie and I started G. Malone. Hopefully, by the time I need more funding I'll have the collection completed and can find an investor who believes in my vision instead of trying to make my designs fit somebody else's. And if I fall on my face, then I fall on my face. But at least I will have done it on my own terms while creating something I believe in."

"Ladies and gentlemen, we're getting ready to move into the gallery housing the Rainbow Portrait Gown," one of the Costume Institute docents announced. "We remind you, there is no flash photography allowed. In order to accommodate the large number of visitors, we ask that you view the dress and quickly move on to the other artifacts in the Tudor exhibition."

Trini and I followed the crowds into the Tudor galleries. Immediately, swarms of people gathered around the Rainbow Portrait Gown. Since we'd already seen the gown, Trini and I ducked to the side to let them view it.

Trini took off her glasses and wiped the lenses on the bottom of her shirt. "Georgica, I have to say, I never expected to hear you say you wanted to go out on your own."

"You don't think it's a good idea?"

She put her glasses back on. "No, I think it's a bloody fantastic idea."

"You do?"

"I have been waiting over six years to hear you say those exact words."

"What about the financing? Am I a complete fool for not accepting the offer from BLD Capital?"

"When one door closes, another one opens. That's the expression, right? Now that you've told me all this, I have an interesting proposition for you. How would you feel about going back to *Top Designer*?"

"I told you, I don't think I'd have the stamina for *Top Designer All Stars,* Trini."

"Not *Top Designer All Stars, Top Designer Teen.*"

"*Top Designer Teen?* What's that?"

"We're doing a spin-off. Sixteen designers from all over the country competing for the title of *Top Designer Teen,* the catch is that they're all thirteen years old."

"You want me to be a judge? I just don't think I could crush a thirteen-year-old's dreams."

"Not a judge. The mentor. You'd be the Trini Bower of *Top Designer Teen.*"

"Mentor? What business do I have being anybody's mentor?"

"Didn't you tell me you were Head Counselor to thirteen-year-old girls at that summer camp of yours? Didn't you lead them to some sort of victory? The Monty? The Jimmy?"

"The Gordy."

"Yes, the Gordy!"

"Trini, I'm not sure I'm really qualified—"

"Gigi, you were runner-up on the very first season of *Top Designer.* You started G. Malone. You designed Victoria Ellicott's wedding gown. You co-chaired the most successful Met Ball in history, and now you are starting your own label. I'd say you are more than qualified. Just hear me out on this. The show shoots over nine months, but you'd only be required to film about half that time, leaving you the other half to work on your line. The salary's generous. More than enough for you to keep your new business going. It's the best of all worlds. You can keep your name and image in the press, while you're waiting to debut your first collection. Plus, I think you'd really enjoy it. You have so much experience you can pass on, and your eye and knowledge of fashion history is unparalleled. The teens would be lucky to have you."

I shook my head. "Trini, I am so incredibly flattered *and* grateful. You're one of the only people in my life who's always believed in me, always, right from day one. I don't know what I would've done all these years without you."

She cleared her throat and quickly wiped her eyes. "I have a feeling you would have *figured it out*," she said, repeating her famous catchphrase.

"Gigi, hey," a voice called above the noise in the room. I turned to look. Archie was standing guard over the Rainbow Portrait Gown.

I motioned for Trini to follow me as we maneuvered our way through the crowd.

"What are you doing here?" he asked once we got up to the velvet rope.

"Playing tourists," Trini answered.

"It was my idea. I wanted to see the exhibit like a regular visitor would."

I couldn't help but notice how much Archie had loosened up. Last time I saw him, it was all, "Yes, ma'am," or "no, ma'am."

"How are you doing?" I asked.

"I've never been better. Jordana and I have been having a great time together."

"I figured. I haven't seen much of her these last couple of weeks."

"I'm sorry about that. I want to spend as much time with her as possible before I go back to London."

"No apology necessary. I hope you two figure out a way to make it work. Long distance relationships are anything but easy."

"I'm really going to try. I've never met anybody like her." His eyes darted around the room. "The crowds have thinned out a bit, if you want to take a look at the gown," he said, motioning over to the case.

I smiled and sidestepped over. Jan had repositioned the Rainbow Portrait Gown on a mannequin resembling Queen Elizabeth I. The new display really was magnificent, illustrating the true power and influence of not only a dress, but the woman wearing it.

"Hey, Trini, *Top Designer Teen's* going to film in New York, right?"

"At FIT, just like *Top Designer.*"

"And I'd have to be in New York for the production?"

"You know the drill. There's a new challenge every week for the first four months. I don't see how you could do it living anywhere else. Why?"

I took a deep breath and looked up and into Elizabeth's eyes. I could swear she had the slightest smile across her face, and for the first time in my life, without one ounce of reservation, I knew exactly what I was going to do.

CHAPTER THIRTY-SIX

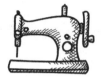

ven though the red carpet on West 50th Street outside Radio City Music Hall had been widened considerably to accommodate more people, the Tony Award's red carpet was even more crowded than the Met Ball. Of all the awards shows, the Tonys was usually the tamest. Most news and media outlets typically sent a leaner crew to snap footage of the New York theater community and the small smattering of Hollywood A-listers usually in attendance. This year was the complete opposite. Photographers and reporters from all over were going absolutely mad trying to capture pictures of anyone in the cast of *Elizabeth*.

Since Perry was performing in a surprise opening number sequence, we arrived on the earlier side. Within seconds of stepping out of the car, a million flashes were going off in our direction. Perry grabbed hold of my hand and waved to the crowd of fans that'd been waiting outside Radio City for hours in the hope of getting a glimpse of him. The Gillman Girls, wearing matching *Elizabeth* T-shirts and holding up signs proclaiming their love for Perry Gillman *and* Robert Dudley had stationed themselves directly across from the theater. I pointed them out to Perry, who ran across the street and posed for a quick selfie with the group. One of the girls practically fainted after he stepped away.

We made our way up the carpet, stopping to speak to reporters, all clamoring to get a few seconds with the man of the hour. The reporter from *Playbill.com* called out Perry's name, and we stopped to talk to him.

"Our readers have been joking that this year's show should be renamed The Perrys instead of the Tonys. How are you feeling about tonight?"

"This show has provided an embarrassment of riches. Whatever happens tonight will be icing on an already pretty great cake."

"*The Producers* won twelve Tonys back in 2001. *Elizabeth's* nominated for thirteen, did you ever imagine you'd be standing here poised to make the record books?"

"When I started *Elizabeth,* it was a true labor of love." Perry glanced over at me. "I sacrificed a lot to get this show off the ground, and I'm just extremely grateful to be standing here surrounded by so many people I care about."

"Word on the street is that you are already hard at work on the *Elizabeth* movie. What can you tell us?"

"I'm in the middle of rewrites on the script. Obviously, the medium gives me some different opportunities than the stage, so I'm working on new songs and other changes to the orchestrations. Damon Chazelle's signed on to direct, and I'll be reprising my role as Dudley."

"Have you found your Elizabeth yet?"

Perry smiled and squeezed my hand. "I think I have."

"Thank you so much, and best of luck tonight."

"Thanks, mate," Perry said, patting him on the arm.

We continued working the red carpet, chatting with the different outlets scattered along the walk. I hung back to let Perry field questions and found I was just as captivated by him as the throngs of reporters. Jamie helped style him for the event, and he looked gorgeous in a deep navy Tom Ford tuxedo with black satin lapels. His hair was pulled back off his face, which was freshly clean-shaven. I hadn't seen him without some scruff in ages, and I'd almost forgotten his perfectly chiseled cheekbones and squared-off chin.

Right after Perry asked me to be his date, I decided I wouldn't wear one of my own designs. I didn't want to put any of the night's attention on my choice of dress or fuel any more speculation about me starting my own label. After careful thought, I settled on a deep almost navy blue bugle beaded vintage Halston dress with a black satin obi sash tied to the waist that I'd seen hanging in my mother's closet for most of my childhood.

It was the dress my mother had worn on her first date with my father to Studio 54 and held a ton of sentimental value for her. The gown was chic, glamorous without trying too hard, and very different from anything I'd ever chosen before. My mother was absolutely thrilled to hear the dress would be making a comeback on the Tonys' red carpet of all places.

Frankie graciously agreed to do my hair and makeup before the event and almost lost his mind when he learned I was wearing my mom's dress. Apparently, he'd met up with her at Studio 54 the night she first wore it, and remembered every square inch of her look, from the matte foundation to the iridescent eye shadows and bone-straight "Cher" hair.

"I want to use your mom for inspiration, but take it to a more modern place," he said, applying highlighter to my cheeks. "For the clubs, we used to do intense makeup, blue eye shadows, and heavy mascara. I want you to look fresher. I'm going to do a light foundation, an eye shadow that has only the slightest hint of a sparkle, and a glossy lip. For your hair, I think I'll blow it out straight with the center part but leave your length as is. No extensions, or the entire look begins to get too costumey."

Two hours later, I was transformed. Perry came to pick me up and, for the first time since we'd met, he was utterly speechless. He took my arm and proudly escorted me to the car. Even with the boatloads of wins already in his pocket, I could tell he was nervous on the ride over to the show. The Tony Awards were still considered the highest honor one could achieve in musical theater, and the hype around *Elizabeth* was becoming almost too much for any person or show to live up to.

On top of all the nominations, Perry had a cameo in the show's opening song, was performing a number from *Elizabeth*, was presenting the award for Best New Play, and, if *Elizabeth* took home best musical, as it was expected to do, the company was closing out the show with one of the show's biggest mainstream hits, "Brave New World," which was currently getting a ton of radio airplay.

When we finally made it through the sea of reporters to the entrance of Radio City Music Hall, Perry handed me a ticket and said, "This is where I leave you."

I looked down and saw his hands trembling. I took them into my own and looked up and into his eyes. "I don't know about you, but I'm having déjà vu?"

He arched his eyebrow. "You are? Here?"

"*Fiddler on the Roof*, Camp Chinooka. Right before the curtain went up, I told you I'd be the one cheering your name from stage left." I stood up on my tiptoes and whispered into his ear, "I'll be the one cheering your name from stage left."

"Do you happen to remember what I said that night?"

I chewed my lip and shook my head no.

"I might be paraphrasing here, but I think I reminded you I was a ringer," he said, winking at me.

"That's right, and I said I'd forgotten just how modest you are."

He pulled me into his chest. "Thank God you're here with me, Gigi."

"There's nowhere else in the world I'd rather be."

"Not even Bora Bora?"

"Not even there."

I took my seat out in the audience beside Perry's empty one on the aisle, which I thought was a very good sign. An aisle seat usually means production expected the person to get out of their chair often. Perry was personally nominated for four awards: Best New Musical, Best Original Score, Best Book, and Best Actor in a Musical.

The Tonys opened with a spoof of the different one-name shows Perry supposedly tried writing before landing on *Elizabeth*. Perry'd helped co-write the opening with Tony host, James Corden, and in the parody, the two of them ran through the one-name contenders. The list of possibilities included Madonna, Oprah, Churchill, and Bono. At one point, toward the end of the song, Sir Andrew Lloyd Webber came out to tell them not to bother with *Evita*, it'd already been done. Then the three of them, Perry, James Corden, and Sir Andrew Lloyd Webber finished off the song with advice to new composers about how the quickest way to winning a Tony was to find the right one-named subject. It got a huge round of laughs from the crowd and was a great way to kick off the evening.

After the song, James Corden jokingly welcomed everyone to the "Perry Awards" and launched into his opening monologue. A few minutes later Perry found his way back to his seat in the audience, a couple of his *Elizabeth* castmates high-fiving him as he came up the aisle. "What'd you think?" he whispered.

"Cheeky, witty, and just self-deprecating enough to get everyone in your corner. It was perfect."

He smiled and put his arm around my shoulder. The first award for the night was for Best Supporting Actress in a Musical and went to Sherri Donovan for her role as Queen Mary Tudor in *Elizabeth*. Her win set the ball in motion, and after that, there was no stopping their train. *Elizabeth* swept every single category it was nominated in. Perry got up to take the stage so many times I practically got whiplash.

An hour plus into the show, he left to join the rest of the cast for the *Elizabeth* number. They were performing the song "Spanish Armada," from the second act. In 1588, Dudley's last great triumph was staging Elizabeth's visit to the army camp at Tilbury. Wearing a steel corselet and helmet with white plumes, Elizabeth famously declared to the troops about to face the Armada, "I know I have the body of a weak and feeble woman, but I have the heart and stomach of a king, and of a King of England, too."

Perry innovatively recorded the quote and had it playing on a loop throughout the song, which told the story of Phillip II's attempt to use the Spanish fleet to take the English throne. The number was brilliantly presented, Elizabeth shouting to the troops from one side of the stage, while the impending ships threatened to overtake the other. Perry, as Dudley, smack in the middle, narrating the action to the audience.

I glanced back up at the stage and immediately felt an emptiness in my heart. Perry was less than twenty feet away from me, but just as easily could've been a million miles away. I hadn't told him about *Top Designer Teen* and staying in New York. I knew deep down he was hoping I'd work on my line from London, while he was filming the movie. Maybe it was selfish of me to want to hold onto the dream of "us" a little bit longer, but I wasn't ready to let go of the fantasy just yet.

When the curtain came down, the entire room was up on its feet. I looked out into the audience, the who's who of the theater world, and all their jaws were on the ground. My eyes welled up with tears. He did it. Perry created something so groundbreaking, so revolutionary that even the so-called experts were reconsidering what musical theater could be. Anyone questioning whether the show was worth all the buzz and attention, immediately had their answer—yes.

CHAPTER THIRTY-SEVEN

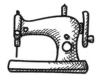

After the *Elizabeth* performance came the *In Memorium* photo montage of all the industry people who passed away over the last year. Perry changed back into his tuxedo and took his seat in the audience.

"You're getting your steps in tonight," I teased.

He winked at me. "You know what, I'm going to cancel on my trainer in the morning. Besides, I'm hoping we have a reason to go out and celebrate 'til dawn."

The rest of the show was a whirlwind. Perry won for Best Book and Best Actor in a Musical. He kept his acceptance speeches short, sweet, and off the cuff, listing off the names of all the people instrumental in *Elizabeth's* success. Then, the category I knew he was most nervous about, Best Original Score. Even though Perry's contributions to *Elizabeth* had been honored in so many ways, deep down, he was a musician. Writing music was always first and foremost his love, and his father's success as a composer, the very high bar by which he measured his own achievements.

When the presenter stepped up to the podium, Perry's entire body stiffened. Perry inhaled sharply, squeezed his eyes closed, and grabbed my hand. She read off the names of each nominee and paused before opening the envelope. When I saw a smile firmly register on her face, I was fairly certain she was about to announce Perry's name.

"I'm sure this comes as no surprise. Best Original Score, Perry Gillman, *Elizabeth!*" the presenter shrieked into the microphone.

He opened his eyes and brought my hand up to his mouth and kissed it. After that, he practically catapulted out of his seat and onto the stage. He accepted the statue from the presenter and wiped his eyes with the back of his hand before reaching into his tuxedo jacket. This was the only category for which he seemed to have prepared an acceptance speech.

He unfolded the paper and cleared his throat. "Most of you don't know this, but in the earliest days of writing *Elizabeth*, I had a co-collaborator. This woman challenged my ideas, conceived some of the best moments, and even acted out every role in the show for my benefit. Much to her horror, those videos do still exist somewhere."

The room laughed at his joke, and I could feel my face heating up. A cameraman knelt down beside me on the aisle in the hopes he might capture my reaction to Perry's words.

"Somewhere along the way, I decided I needed to do this thing on my own. I had something to prove, and I thought the only way to prove it was to cut every tie. I was wrong. I was wrong for so many reasons." His voice started to break. "Dudley and Elizabeth used to end their letters to one another with the letters SE to represent the words, Semper Eadem, Ever the Same. No matter where they were, their two hearts beat as one. Georgica, you are in every note of this score, every measure. It is because of you that I am holding this. It is because of you that I am. Semper Eadem."

When the next presenter came onstage, I ducked out of the auditorium to get some air. Tight pressure began to well in my chest, and I didn't want the cameraman capturing my breakdown. When I got into the lobby, I opened my compact and wiped the smudged mascara out from under my eyes. I took a few deep breaths and tried to recompose myself. I took my phone out from my clutch and looked down at a text from Jamie.

"Are you sure you don't want to change your mind?"

I'd told Jamie about Perry's idea for me to work on my line in London and my decision to accept Trini's offer on *Top Designer Teen* and stay in New York. While he supported my choices, the true romantic in him was still hoping for a different ending.

I slid the phone back into my bag and waited for the usher to tell me I could return to my seat. When the cameras cleared the aisle, he nodded and let me back through. Perry's seat was empty. He was still backstage finishing up interviews.

A few more of the nominated musicals performed scenes from their shows before the presenters of the final award of the evening, Best New Musical, took to the main podium. The presenters rattled off the list of nominees, ripped open the envelope, and in unison, shouted the word *Elizabeth* into the microphone. Forgone conclusion or not, the crowd went nuts. *Elizabeth* had just broken *The Producers* record, and the room was on their feet.

Perry and the other Tony winners from *Elizabeth* came out to the podium from behind the stage. The rest of the cast and the production and creative teams joined them from their seats in the audience. *Elizabeth's* producer accepted the award on behalf of the cast and crew, thanking the dozens of people instrumental in its development and mounting.

James Corden came back out to invite the Tony Award-winning company of *Elizabeth* to close out the show with their hit number "Brave New World." Perry and company took to the stage, singing and dancing their hearts out to the techno beat of the song. Normally, by this point, the audience would've started making their way out of the theater to get to the after parties, but everyone remained glued to their seats, watching, dancing, and celebrating along with the cast.

Different actors from the show started coming down into the audience and pulling people up onto the stage with them. Perry and I locked eyes, and a few seconds later he was at my chair, taking my hands and leading me up to the center platform. We danced our hearts out, and when the curtain fell for the final time, he swept me up into his arms for a long, passionate kiss.

The official *Elizabeth* after party was taking place at Tavern on the Green. Nestled deep within Central Park, the iconic Tavern on the Green was famous for its unique location and quintessentially New York clientele. Before heading over, we hit up a few of the other festivities around the city. We popped into parties at the Carlyle Hotel, the Baccarat, and The Plaza. Perry was unquestionably the toast of the town, and it seemed that everyone wanted to snap a picture with him or extend their congratulations.

We left The Plaza just after midnight, so we could finish off the celebrations with the cast of *Elizabeth* at Tavern on the Green. When we stepped outside the hotel, Perry's car was not in the loading zone. He shot off a few texts to the driver, who was nowhere to be found.

"It's only a few blocks through the park. What do you say we walk?" I suggested.

"That's perfect. I'm actually starving."

"We just left *three* different parties, all of which had a barrage food."

"I was too busy being pulled into selfies," he teased.

"You know what, I'm actually pretty hungry, too."

"What do you say? Two hot dogs and a park bench?"

"I'm in."

We walked into the park and stopped at the first food cart we saw. Perry bought two hot dogs with mustard and sauerkraut and two cans of soda.

"What you say we take these up to Belvedere Castle?" he suggested.

"You sure we have time for that?"

He nodded. "Yeah. I need a few minutes reprieve, anyway."

I nodded and followed him up to the observation deck. We settled down on an empty bench and devoured our snack.

"You have some mustard right here," he said, wiping a spot from under my bottom lip. "Thank you for coming with me tonight."

"Are you kidding, every time they called your name or mentioned *Elizabeth,* I felt like my heart was going to explode. I was—no, *am*—so proud of you." I pushed my hair behind my ears. "*Thank you* for what you said about me in your speech."

"Long overdue. There'd be no *Elizabeth* without you and, if I'm being honest, there'd be no me without you, either."

"That's not true."

"I was in such a dark place when we met at Chinooka. You brought me back."

"We brought each other back."

He smiled. "And now we get a second chance."

I moistened my lips and looked down to the ground.

He bent down and tilted up my chin. "What is it? What'd I say?"

"It can wait. I want this night to be filled with only celebration and joy. You've earned it. We don't need to talk about this now."

He furrowed his brow. "Just tell me."

"Well, Trini offered me an opportunity with *Top Designer.* They're doing a teen spin-off, and she wants me to be the contestant mentor. The salary and filming schedule would give me the flexibility to work on my line, while also keeping me in the public eye for when it launches."

"That's wonderful, isn't it?"

"The show films in New York. I can't go to London with you."

Perry stood up and walked to ledge of the overlook. I sidled up next to him and asked, "Do you remember the last time we were here? You asked me what I thought would've happened to us if you didn't write *Elizabeth* and I hadn't started G. Malone?"

"I remember," he said softly.

"You thought we could've been happy, but I don't. Perry, instead of composing, you would've been playing the piano at jazz clubs at night to keep G. Malone afloat. And instead of designing, I would have been spending my days doing research for *Elizabeth*. We wanted each other to succeed *so* badly that we would have sacrificed our own aspirations. We may have been happy for a while, but eventually, we would've resented one another."

"Are you saying we can't be together and be successful? Gigi, don't you see how we bring out the best in each other? We always have."

"I'm just being realistic. I know you. You'll give the movie your blood, sweat, and tears. And after that, you'll move on to something else, and you'll give that project the best of you. I'm just not sure where that'll leave us."

He turned to me and took my head into his hands, his big, brown eyes devouring every inch of my face. "Let's not jump into any decisions, okay? We don't have to have any of this figured out, not yet at least. Will you stay with me tonight?"

I nodded and buried my head in his chest.

We left Belvedere Castle and walked hand in hand to Tavern on the Green, where the *Elizabeth* party was well underway. We grabbed two drinks from the bar, hit the dance floor, and stayed there—no words, no promises, just the two of us letting the rest of the world fall away.

That night, I went home with him. It'd been over five years since we were last together, yet it felt like no time had passed at all. Afterward, I fell asleep in his arms and woke up in the morning to the sound of Perry's violin and the music of *Rhapsody in Blue.*

I sat up and tucked a pillow behind me. "Things must be pretty bad if you're playing Ravel this early in the morning."

"Gershwin, Gigi, always Gershwin."

"I know," I whispered.

Perry rested the violin on the table and climbed back into bed with me.

"I leave for London in a few weeks," he said.

"We still have a few weeks, then."

"And after that?" he asked.

"Semper Eadem, Ever the Same. No matter where they were, their two hearts beat as one."

The corners of his lips curved upward. "Semper Eadem."

CHAPTER THIRTY-EIGHT

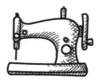

I peeked my head out from behind the stage. The tent was empty now, but in less than three hours, the space would be crammed full of buyers, socialites, celebrities, magazine editors, photographers, reporters, and the Queen Bee herself, Anna Wintour. I sucked in a breath and went back to the garment racks to do a final inventory of the pieces.

My haute couture collection, "Found Generation" was comprised of forty-five distinct looks. The separates, consisting of rich cream and gold silk shirts, lush velvet suits, skinny corduroy pants, and even skinnier ties, were meant to celebrate the more androgynous clothing that started to become popular among women after World War I.

The evening gowns were far more ornate and heavily influenced by the art deco and Egyptian-inspired fashions that came into vogue during that time. I incorporated beautifully textured, richly hand-dyed fabrics to add depth to the simple, angular lines. Because of the intricate beadwork and trim detail in every piece, even with the help of seamstresses and ateliers, the full collection had taken just over a year to complete.

Jordana was the first to arrive backstage and was surprised to find me already there. When I had told her about my plans to launch my own line, she immediately volunteered to come on board in whatever capacity I could use her. I encouraged her to move on to bigger, more established brands, even making introductions to the designers, but she insisted she was in it for the long haul. Since I couldn't pay her for her work on the new line just yet, I hired her as my personal assistant on *Top Designer Teen*. By day she handled all the aspects of scheduling and production related to the show, and at night and on the weekends, she helped me coordinate logistics for the new line.

"I was going stir-crazy in my apartment. I wanted to make sure everything came over from the workspace," I told her.

Jordana opened her laptop and checked the racks against her master list. "All here."

"And the final RSVP count?" I asked.

"There's not an empty seat in the house. All the major fashion press will be here, every top buyer, and all the hottest stylists." She scrolled down on the screen. "Wow, I didn't even realize how many A-list celebs said yes."

"Where are we with hair and makeup?"

"Frankie and his team will be here in the next hour to set up. We're in great shape, Gigi."

I blinked a few times and sat down. "This is really happening, then?"

She looked up from her laptop with a huge grin. "This is really happening."

An hour or so later, Frankie and his team of hair stylists and makeup artists arrived at the tent, and Jordana directed them to the staging area to unpack their equipment. After much debate, Frankie and I had agreed on glowy skin and intense eyebrows to focus on the models' natural beauty. For the hair, we settled on low ponytails with a deep side part, gathered at the nape, and textured bottom. As the successful owner of several top salons,

Frankie hadn't worked in the fashion show circuit in years. I was beyond touched when he offered to style the show at minimal cost.

Once the models started arriving, the tent quickly became a flurry of activity. Jordana hired a team of dressers and interns to help wrangle the girls from station to station. Even with their help, there were moments of what felt like organized chaos. A handful of top models showed up late, covered in glitter and hairspray from a previous show, and needed to be cleaned up and re-done. Jordana was completely in her element, shouting instructions to her team on how to expedite their makeover. She came to find me after she got them settled.

"There's a ton of press outside the tent. Do you have a few minutes to go out there?"

"Yeah, let's do it now. I want to be able to give the models a once-over before the show starts."

Jordana led me outside and to the press line, where there were over a dozen or so reporters and notable fashion bloggers waiting to talk to me about the collection.

The first reporter was from *Women's Wear Daily TV.* After a quick introduction, she nodded to her cameraman and guided the microphone toward me.

"Since you wore your own design to last year's Met Gala, there's been a lot of speculation about this collection, which we've been told you're calling 'The Found Generation.' Without giving too much away, what can you tell us?" she asked.

"After World War I, the Lost Generation came up with the social norms that gave rise to the Roaring Twenties and incredible fashions born in that era. Luxury fabrics were suddenly able to be mass produced, and the availability of the sewing machine meant women could easily make fashionable clothing at home. Couture was no longer restricted to the elite. This collection celebrates the idea that, while this generation has access to so much great fashion, women still want to feel chic and special. They want their look to be one of a kind. Each piece in the show was constructed using traditional haute couture techniques and practices."

"Word on the street was that you had offers to take the line in a ready-to-wear direction but decided to move forward with this more avant-garde showcase. Why?"

"I spent a very long time being known as the runner-up on Season One of *Top Designer*, then as the G. in G. Malone, and after that, the designer of Victoria Ellicott's wedding dress. It was important to me that this collection show the world what I was capable of on my own, and to do that, I needed to go big."

"Here we are at Lincoln Center for New York Fashion Week, surrounded by so many different designers and aesthetics. How would you describe the Georgica Goldstein woman? What sets her apart?" the same reporter asked.

"You know, if you had asked me that question even a year ago I'd have given a very different answer. Today, I'd say the Georgica woman is confident, capable, and willing to take chances."

I thanked the reporter for her time and continued making my way down the press line. After a half hour or so, Jordana came out to find me.

"The models are just about ready to line up. Trini's backstage. So are Thom and Jamie."

I turned back to the reporters and, with a wave, said, "Thank you all again for coming. It truly means the world to have you all here. I hope you enjoy the show." My heart was racing but was fuller than I could ever remember. I followed her back to the tent, where Jamie and Thom were waiting with a huge bottle of Crystal.

"I know G. Malone's a thing of the past, but some traditions, like our preshow toast, deserve to live on," Jamie said, passing around glasses of champagne. He lifted his in the air. "Here's to a fabulous runway show. May Anna Wintour crack a smile, and may no model fall on her ass."

I laughed, and we all took a sip. I noticed Trini in the corner, chatting with one of the models. "Excuse me for a second," I said, setting the flute on the table and walking over to her.

"Georgica, there you are." Trini placed her hand on my shoulder.

"I was outside, speaking to some reporters."

"You have a packed house out there. I haven't seen the fashion world this excited since the Fall '98 Louis Vuitton show."

"The year Marc Jacobs stepped in as Creative Director?"

"Ding, ding, ding," she teased. "Look, from what I've seen already, you're going to blow them all away. You've got this."

"Thank you, Trini. For everything. I couldn't have done this without you."

"Oh, that's a load of rubbish if I ever heard one. You were meant to do this. I knew it the moment you sent that marvelous glittery toilet paper wedding dress down the runway on *Top Designer.*" She pulled me in for a hug and whispered, "Knock 'em dead, kiddo."

Jordana tapped me on the shoulder. "The models are ready for your last look."

"See you on the runway," Trini said.

"See you on the runway."

The next eighteen minutes were the most exhilarating of my entire life. Standing backstage, eyes fixed on the monitor, I practically held my breath as each design went down the runway. After the final gown made its debut, the girls came out from behind the stage for one final walk. The last model on line grabbed my hand and pulled me out onto the stage, where I was met with thunderous applause and a standing ovation. I took a quick bow and waved to the crowd, while a million cameras and iPhones snapped in my direction.

The models walked backstage, looking happy and relieved that everything had gone so well, and were met by more applause from the stylists, makeup artists, dressers, and interns who'd been watching the show from backstage.

Practically blinded by the flashes, I didn't notice Perry standing backstage, holding a massive bouquet of flowers, until Jordana pointed to him. I ran over and threw my arms around his neck. "You told me you were stuck on location in Scotland this weekend."

A few weeks after the Tonys, Perry left to start pre-production on *Elizabeth* in London. The last time we tried long distance we practically imploded, and neither one of us wanted that again. After much heartache, we decided it would be better to leave our relationship in the past and try to move on.

Then, a few months later, I got a package in the mail from the UK. Inside was a box of matches and a note.

Distance does to love what wind does to fire. It extinguishes the weak and feeds the strong.

I can't stop loving you. Please, Gigi, let's be strong.

- Perry

After much soul-searching, I finally admitted I hadn't stopped loving Perry, either. He flew to New York the following weekend, and we vowed to make us work, no matter what. Over this last year, we talked as often as we could and flew back and forth as much as our schedules allowed. We finally figured out how to have our careers *and* each other.

He flashed a wide smile at me, his two dimples prominent on his cheeks. "I wanted to surprise you. Gigi, that was the most beautiful, incredible, magnificent, astonishing—I'm running out of adjectives that would even do the show justice."

"I second that," Trini said from behind him. "No question, you'll have your pick of investors now, and can take your brand in any direction you want *if* that's what you want? *Top Designer* would love to have you back, and I know Jan's been pursuing you all year to join his team at The Met. My dear, the world's your oyster."

I looked around the tent and the world I created. I had never felt more alive or more in my element. This is what I was born to do. I'd questioned and fought it long enough. Georgica Goldstein wasn't running or hiding anymore.

Perry and I were the last two people to leave the tent. We stepped out into Lincoln Center, which was surprisingly quiet since most of the press and crowds had moved on to other shows or after parties. We took a seat at our favorite people-watching bench across from the main fountain. It was uncharacteristically warm for February in New York, and Perry unwrapped his scarf and placed it between us. A few moments later, an ambulance, followed by several firetrucks and police cars, screamed down Columbus Avenue.

"The symphony of the city," Perry said.

"That's funny. My father always uses that expression."

"I know. You said it to me the first time we were here. Don't you remember? After all our campers were asleep, we took a walk and ended up right here in Lincoln Center. I think that was the first night I realized just how very much in love with you I was."

I put the scarf on my lap and slid nearer to him on the bench. He put his arm around me and pulled me even closer.

He continued, "The next time we were here, I got down on one knee and told you I wanted to spend the rest of my life with you." He turned to me. "Georgica, I learned *so* much writing *Elizabeth,* more than I ever imagined I could. And if there's one message threaded throughout that story, it's that personal glory is no substitute for love. Dudley and Elizabeth sacrificed true happiness in their pursuit of success, and I don't want that for me. I don't want that for us. We can have both. We can have everything, as long as we have each other."

I sat up. "Are you saying what I think you're saying?"

He slid a black velvet box out of his coat pocket and cracked it open. "Georgica Goldstein, will you do me the distinct honor and privilege of becoming my wife?"

I glanced down at the box. Inside was a gorgeous platinum Asscher-cut diamond with a pavé halo.

"Wait, that's a different—"

"Ring? I wanted something new, something that represented who we are now, not who we were then." He removed it from the box. "Besides, the paycheck from the *Elizabeth* movie wasn't small *po-tah-toes*, either," he said with his affected British accent and a twinkle in his eye.

"Po-tay-toes," I repeated in my American one.

"Tomato, *to-mah-to*, potato, *po-tah-to*, let's call the whole thing off."

I held out my left hand and let him slide the ring onto my finger. "Not a chance, Mr. Gillman, not a chance."

EPILOGUE

T he white votive candles up and down the aisles flickered in the wind coming off Lake Chinooka. The late summer sun was setting to create the most incredible red-orange glow through the trees and onto the wedding canopy in the center of the amphitheater. I turned to my mother, who kissed me on the cheek and then lowered the delicate lace veil down and over my face. My father straightened his tie and smoothed out his satin lapels.

"Ready, Georgie?" he asked.

I nodded as they took hold of each arm to begin our procession down the aisle. The conductor of the Milbank Orchestral Society tapped on his music stand, and moments later, "Sunrise Sunset" from *Fiddler on the Roof* soared out from behind the trees and settled into the space.

Halfway down the aisle, I locked eyes with Perry and felt every tinge of nervousness wash away. I was marrying the man I loved, in the place I loved most in the world. My mother, of course, had been hoping we'd get married at their house in South Hampton, or perhaps The Plaza Hotel, somewhere grander, but I couldn't think of a more perfect place than Camp Chinooka, or a more perfect person to marry us than Gordy.

When I finally joined him under the canopy, Perry stood back to admire every square inch of my gown. He leaned over and whispered in my ear, "You take my breath away."

Jamie and I had searched high and low for my perfect wedding dress. We hit every bridal boutique, every vintage shop, and after we came up empty, hit up every designer we knew, but no gown felt right. Then, one night, Jamie came by with a tea-colored French Chantilly sheath wedding dress with lace sleeves, and a point d'esprit underlay. The back, with its dramatic cathedral train, was as spectacular as the front, if not more so.

I swept my hand over the delicate lace. "Is this one of ours? Is this a G. Malone?" I asked, trying to recall if the dress was from one of our earliest collections.

"This dress predates G. Malone. Gigi, this is the wedding gown you created for *Fiddler on the Roof* the summer you worked at Camp Chinooka. This is the dress that started it all."

I blinked hard. Of course! The dress that had been inspired by my great-grandma Ruby's wedding gown, the dress that changed the course of my life.

Jamie helped me into the dress and zipped up the back. The moment it closed, I knew this was the one. Our search was over —it was perfect.

Perry took me by the hands, and we turned to face Gordy. Away from the white-hot spotlight that'd been in our lives for so long, and in front of our closest friends and family in the middle of the Pennsylvania woods, we exchanged our own vows and declared our commitment to one another. After Gordy declared us man and wife, Perry swept me into his arms for a long, deep kiss.

Following the ceremony, we made our way down to the lakefront, where waiters were serving hors d'oeuvres. Sloan, Clara, and Oliver were running up and down to the shoreline screeching with delight every time their little feet water touched the water while Alicia, Asher, Thom and Jamie kept watch from nearby. White couches and small Lucite tables had been placed all around to give the space the feel of an intimate lounge. Trini and my mother were deep in conversation on a settee while the staff finished setting up a makeshift dance floor on the Great Lawn.

Jordana and Archie brought over two glasses of champagne.

"To the happy couple," she said, lifting her flute to us.

"I should say the same," I said, toasting her back.

Jordana and Archie had quite the whirlwind romance. After the Met Ball exhibit closed, Archie decided not to go back to the UK, and instead, took a job with the museum's security team to be closer to Jordana. A few weeks later, they eloped to Vegas. It was the most impulsive and spontaneous decision I'd ever seen Jordana make, but she'd never been happier. They were a great couple, total opposites who brought out the absolute best in each other.

"I'm gonna go show Archie our old cabin," she said.

"Good old Bunk Fourteen."

She gave me a kiss on the cheek. "The place we became not just friends, but sisters."

A few hours later, after dinner and dancing, the guests made their way back down to the shore of Lake Chinooka for Gordy's fireworks show, while Perry and I stayed behind. The band was on a break, and we were the only two people left on the dance floor. Perry climbed onto the stage and sat down at the piano.

"They never did get around to playing our song." He sat down and started playing Gershwin's "They Can't Take That Away from Me." After a few bars, he stood up from the bench.

"May I have this dance?"

"I thought you'd never ask."

He took my hand and led me out to the dance floor. Moments later, fireworks lit up the starry sky. As colorful burning streaks of light danced all around us, I laid my head down on his shoulder, while he sang the rest of the song softly in my ear.

Hours later, after the rest of the wedding guests retreated to their cabins or hotel rooms at the Stanton Inn in town, Perry and I found ourselves alone by a campfire on the shores of Lake Chinooka. Perry wrapped the red plaid flannel blanket more tightly around us, as I snuggled even more firmly into his chest.

"Still cold?"

"No," I answered. "Not anymore."

"Now that *Elizabeth's* in the can, I think I've come up with an idea for my next musical."

I sat more upright. "Yeah? Tell me?"

"It's about this girl who goes to work at her childhood sleep-away camp to escape from her life and meets this counselor there. She doesn't know it, but he's trying to escape too. They think they hate each other."

"But they don't?"

"They get off to a rocky start, but they don't hate each other. They actually end up falling in love with each other over that summer."

My fingers strummed my chin. "Hmm, that's a good start. What else were you thinking?"

"The show will be peppered with old standards. Songs from the jazz age. The songs he thinks of when he thinks of the girl."

"Copeland? Stravinsky?"

"Gershwin, Gigi, always Gershwin."

"Of course," I said, smiling and leaning back into his chest.

Perry reached behind his back and pulled out a bag of marshmallows, a few bars of chocolate, a package of graham crackers, and two sticks.

"I think I have everything you asked for," he said.

"Remember what to do?" I asked.

"Remind me."

Perry watched as I loaded the stick with marshmallows and plunged them into the flame. When they were good and gooey, I pulled them off and fit them between the chocolate and graham crackers. I passed him the s'more and watched as he took a bite, the marshmallow squeezing out the sides of the sandwich and onto his chin.

"You have a little something on your face, Mr. Gillman."

He leaned in to kiss me. "Now so do you, Mrs. Gillman."

I looked down at my left hand and smiled. "Mrs. Gillman."

Perry wrapped his arms around me. "You've got goosebumps up and down your arms. Are you sure you don't want to go back to the cabin?"

"Tomorrow, on our honeymoon, we'll have all the warmth and sunshine of Bora Bora, but for now, would you mind if we stayed here, just like this, a little bit longer?"

"As long as you want, Princess."

Perry threw a few more pieces of wood onto the campfire, bringing the dying flame back to life.

WHAT'S NEXT FOR BETH MERLIN?

Beth Merlin's first novel after her hit <u>Campfire Series</u> - you won't want to miss it!

Break Up Boot Camp

After weeks of training to whip Joanna Kitt into shape for her big day, her picture-perfect relationship is torn in two and Joanna is left out on her perfectly toned rear end. In an effort to put the past and her heartache behind her, she gears up for a whole different kind of boot camp — but will 12 steps be enough to get her life back on track?

Or will her getaway to get over him prove healing the heart takes a whole lot more?

REVIEW REQUEST

Dear Reader,

Reviews are like currency to any author – actually, even better! As they help to get our books noticed by even more readers, we would be so grateful if you would take a moment to review this book on Amazon, Goodreads, iBooks - wherever - and feel free to share it on social media!

We're not asking for any special favors – honest reviews would be perfect. They also don't need to be long or in-depth, just a few of your thoughts would be so appreciated.

Thank you greatly from the bottom of our hearts. For your time, for your support, and for being a part of our reading community. We couldn't do it without you – nor would we want to!

~ Our Firefly Hill Press Family

The Campfire Series by Beth Merlin
    One S'more Summer
    S'more to Lose
    Love You S'more

ACKNOWLEDGMENTS

Thank you to my friend and editor, Danielle Modafferi, who has faithfully stood by this series. I value your insight and encouragement more than I can say.

To my momtrepreneur friends working on side hustles and passion projects. You inspire me daily.

For my husband, who never, ever wavers in his enthusiasm or support, I love you madly. And, finally, as always, my Hadley Alexandra.

ABOUT THE AUTHOR

Beth Merlin, a native New Yorker, loves anything Broadway, romantic comedies, and a good maxi dress. After earning her JD from New York Law School, she heard a voice calling her back to fiction writing, like it had during her undergrad study. Amidst her days in The George Washington University's School of Media and Public Affairs, where Beth majored in Political Communications, she found herself wandering into Creative Writing classes, and ended up earning a minor in the field. After 10 long years laboring over her first manuscript, her debut novel, *One S'more Summer*, released May 2017. International bestselling author Kristin Harmel called it "a fast paced, enjoyable read".

Love You S'more is the last book in the Campfire Series. While she's sad to say goodbye to the characters she's been working on for the last 10+ years, she hopes she's given readers (whether Team Gideon or Team Perry) a satisfying ending. And she is *so* grateful to all of the fans who have supported her and Gigi along the way.

When Beth isn't working on new novels, she's spending time with her husband, daughter, and Cavipoo, Sophie. Find Beth at on Twitter (@bethmerlin80), on Instagram (@bethfmerlin), or at The Firefly Hill Press website (fireflyhillpress.com)

And keep up to date on all of Beth's future releases, book bargains, sneak peeks, giveaways, special offers, & so much more by subscribing to our newsletter!

PUBLISHER ACKNOWLEDGEMENTS

We at FHP are so proud to represent Beth and the Campfire series. Every step of bringing this series to life has truly been a labor of love and we are so grateful for Beth's hard work and dedication to our press and to her fans. It was her diligence in writing to such strict and stringent deadlines (amidst her already busy home life) that has enabled us to release her books in such quick succession. Cheers, Beth - this series is truly a testament to your incredible creativity, fortitude, and passion for writing. We can't wait to see what's next for you!

We also want to thank all of the editors, proofreaders, and beta readers who have helped make this series the best it could be: Erin Bales, Lola Dodge, Laura Koons, Melissa Gray, and Ariel Raia - we are indebted to you. Thank you for your professionalism, your candor, and your time.

Thank you to our team at InScribe Digital, especially Kelly Peterson, Ana Szaky, and All Davis for helping us get this series out to as many people as possible!

To all of the reviewers and bloggers - we can't thank you enough for helping us spread the word about this series. Your opinion matters so greatly to us and we are grateful for your time and continued support.

And finally, last but certainly not least, thank you to all of the fans of the Campfire Series. Thank you for your kind words, your emails, your social media shares, and your ceaseless enthusiasm. You are the reason we work so hard and seeing your joy about something on which we have worked so hard could bring us no greater honor. We are humbled and encouraged to continue to bring you great fiction.

THE KEY WEST ESCAPE SERIES BY TRICIA LEEDOM

Looking for another series to dive into? The Key West Escape Series by Tricia Leedom has a little more steam, laugh out loud dialogue, and a whole lot of adventure. Do yourself a favor - take yourself on a book vacation and start the series with *Rum Runner* today!

CHAPTER ONE

London, England

A cold October rain pummeled the windshield as the wiper blades danced to the beat of the eighties synthpop classic on the radio. From the passenger seat, Sophie Davies-Stone reached over to turn the volume down. It was late and she felt a migraine coming on. Predictably, Andrew pressed a button on the steering wheel cranking the music back up. Annoyance bubbled inside of her, but she held her tongue and stared out the window at the rain-soaked night.

She was still disgusted with herself for having break-up sex with him. She'd insisted on separate hotel rooms in Paris, but then she'd stupidly accepted his invitation to go back to his suite for a nightcap. Of course, one thing led to another and—

Ugh!

She blamed the expensive French wine.

One would think having tepid break-up sex on an uncomfortable bed after imbibing a large bottle of vintage Bordeaux would be the most undignified way to end a four-and-a-half-year relationship. Not even close. Andrew had taken the regrettable situation to a whole other level when he waited until breakfast to break the news to her about the situation in Rome.

An invisible knife stabbed her just below the breastbone and twisted a little.

At least, it would make their breakup more definitive this time. She should be happy about that, but no woman wanted to hear the man she was supposed to marry was going to have a baby with somebody else.

The rain had slowed to a drizzle by the time they reached her West End neighborhood. The weather was more congruous with her mood than the upbeat Wham! song now blasting out of the car speakers several decibels too loud. Andrew tapped along on the steering wheel, oblivious to her discomfort.

The Aston Martin's headlights bounced off a thick patch of

fog as the car turned a corner. She lived in a flat on the fourth floor of a red brick Victorian mansion block building owned by her stepfather. Andrew parked illegally in the no parking zone by the front entrance and switched off the radio.

The soft patter of rain on the car's roof filled the sudden silence.

"Right then," Andrew said, turning toward her. "Shall I carry your suitcase up?"

"No, I've got it."

"Listen, Soph, just because we're no longer a couple doesn't mean we can't be friends. We're bound to chance upon each other at family events."

"I think that would be inappropriate considering the circumstances," she said stiffly. *Note to self: never get involved with anyone you're related to by marriage.*

"She's only six weeks pregnant. No one else has to know about it for some time yet. Look at me."

Raising her chin a notch, Sophie continued to stare straight ahead. Her voice was carefully devoid of emotion as she spelled out the problems with his logic. "I ended our engagement two months ago, but we never told anyone. Now people are going to think you cheated on me, or worse, that you dropped me for some Italian tart you met in Rome." The invisible knife blade twisted a little more and she bit her bottom lip to counter the pain.

"She's not a tart."

Sophie snorted derisively. "You knew her for, what, two weeks before she got knocked up? And you say she has two children from two previous relationships. She's a tart, and you're an idiot for not using protection."

"I did use protection."

"Then perhaps you're being duped. Did you ever think of that?" She finally looked at him. The street lamp they were parked beneath cast his handsome, aristocratic features in a golden glow.

The citrus and leather notes of his cologne drifted toward her in the confined space. Not his usual brand. It was probably Italian.

He shook his head firmly and insisted, "Gabriella isn't like that."

Sometimes absence made the heart grow fonder and sometimes it brought clarity. Andrew had wanted to give Sophie space to rethink her decision to end their engagement. He'd been the one to suggest they take a break rather than break up entirely while he was away on business. The only reason she'd agreed was because her mother had begged her not to end the relationship. Their reunion this weekend in Paris had been a complete waste of time. Sophie's feelings had not changed in the two months they were apart, and he'd made a reckless mistake that would humiliate both of them when word got out.

"Before this reaches the gossip pages," she said, "please be smart and insist on a paternity test."

Andrew slammed his hand against the steering wheel. "You are a snob and a hypocrite. You sit there on your high horse, judging others and worrying about protecting your precious image, while carefully hiding the salacious truth about your own paternity."

His angry words brought a new kind of pain that detracted from the other. It was centered around her heart and squeezed like a vice. She cleared her throat to remove the sudden thickness there. "Please don't bring my father into this," she said quietly resisting the urge to reach for the medallion hanging from the silver chain around her neck.

"What would you say if I told you I'm in love with Gabriella and plan to marry her?"

"I'd say you're a fool."

He nodded. "You would say that, wouldn't you? That's

because you don't know what love is. Or passion. Your heart is a block of ice. And you're even more frigid in the sack."

Sophie uncrossed her legs and reached for the door handle.

"You think the glitterati are your friends because you went to secondary school with most of them?" He sneered. "The only reason they accepted you was because of me."

She stepped out of the car and steeled herself against the bitingly cold gust of wind that met her. She pulled the belt on her jacket tighter and readjusted the purse strap on her shoulder before she turned around to close the door.

Andrew exploded again. "Damn it, aren't you going to say anything?"

Ignoring the puddle that was ruining her favorite Christian Louboutins, she said, "I think you've said enough for the both of us."

Her mobile phone buzzed in her purse, alerting her to an incoming text. It was probably her mother. She ignored it.

Andrew pressed a button on the steering wheel and the boot of the car opened on a motorized hinge.

"Goodbye, Andrew," she said and closed the car door. Mentally removing the knife blade from beneath her sternum, she dropped it like a hot mic before she fetched her suitcase from the back. The Aston Martin pulled away from the curb, splashed through a puddle, and honked at an oncoming car as it sped off, but she did not watch it go.

The smell of Indian takeaway greeted her when the lift doors parted on the fourth floor of her building. She suddenly had a fierce craving for The Curry Mart's chicken tikka masala and wished she had eaten something at dinner instead of just pushing the food around on her plate.

When her mobile buzzed two more times, she sighed and stopped in the hall. On her way up, she had stopped at the wall of postboxes in the lobby to retrieve the small stack of letters and junk mail that were waiting for her. She fumbled with them now as she righted her tipping suitcase and reached for her purse.

If it was her mother texting to find out how the reunion went, she was changing her number.

It wasn't. It was a number she didn't recognize, but the words in the preview window made her grow very still. A tiny ball of nervous excitement curled in the pit of her stomach and her entire body flushed with heat. Hands trembling, she scrolled up to the first of the three texts and began reading.

Ladybug, it's me. By now, you should have received the letter I sent you from Mexico City.

The second text: *I need you to send the medallion to me as soon as possible. The address is at the bottom of the letter.*

The third: *Be careful, sweetheart. And don't tell anyone I've been in contact with you. Delete these texts as soon as you read them. —M*

The texts were from her biological father. A man she knew only through a series of letters he'd sent to her sporadically over the past twenty years. They were always from a different postmark. Always with no return address. Her mother Lillian said Mitch Thompson had been an American Navy SEAL when she met him on the Caribbean island of Tortola while she was on an extended holiday with her parents. He'd charmed twenty-year-old Lillian, got her pregnant, and then left her to a family who disowned her the moment they discovered her condition. Mitch had long since retired from the military to become a full-time treasure hunter. He was as undependable and capricious as his chosen profession, but that had never prevented Sophie from being curious about him.

Three months ago, Sophie received a small package postmarked from a village in Northern Peru. It contained an ornate Spanish medallion on a silver chain and a note from her father apologizing for not having written in a while. He congratulated her on her engagement, which he said he'd read about on the internet, before asking her for a favor. He wanted Sophie to keep the medallion safe for him until he sent for it. He claimed it was a precious Thompson family heirloom and said it was very important she not tell anyone she had it in her possession or that she had heard from him recently.

By "anyone," she assumed he'd meant her mother, who would have likely told her to sell the thing on eBay. The only person she did tell was Andrew who seemed disinterested at first. However, later that night she'd found the medallion in the kitchen rubbish bin. When she confronted him about it, he feigned innocence, but she didn't believe him. She fastened the medallion around her neck that night and had worn it every day since.

Staring at the texts from her father, it suddenly occurred to her she had his number. She could phone him and speak to him for the first time in her life. The combination of excitement and apprehension brought on by that realization made her shake so hard she nearly dropped her mobile. Forcing herself to be still, she took a deep breath and pressed the number to ring him back.

A long silence met her on the other end of the line. Then three high-pitched tones, followed by an automated American voice that said, "We're sorry, you have reached a number that has been disconnected or is no longer in service. If you feel you have reached this recording in error, please check the number and try your call again."

Sophie pressed End. She stared blankly at the hall carpet and swallowed the thick lump in her throat. It settled heavily in her heart.

The silence in the hall was broken by a creaking door. The two doors to her right were still shut, as was the door on her left. The only door that remained was the door to her flat, which was around the corner and a few feet down the hall. The door to her flat, which should have been closed and locked.

She considered knocking on her neighbor's door, but it was nearly midnight and the people on her floor tended to keep to themselves. Sophie thought about calling the police but decided she should make sure her imagination wasn't playing tricks on her first.

She took a step toward the short hallway that led to her flat. Then another. She was nearly to the corner when the squeaky door groaned again, louder this time.

She froze and held her breath. Should she warn the intruder she was coming? Surprising whomever it was could get her knifed, or worse. She decided to take her chances. Raising her mobile above her head like a weapon, she turned the corner. Something screeched and lunged at her, and she screamed bloody murder.

Her neighbor's door flew open, and Hugh Oliver, a serious young barrister who worked long hours and was rarely at home, found her shrieking like a lunatic, holding her equally frightened cat in her arms.

"Are you all right?" he said.

"Yes. No!" Pointing to her door, which was gaping open, she said, "I think someone broke into my flat."

"Hang on." He disappeared inside his own flat and came back a moment later carrying a cricket bat. "Where's the light switch?"

"Just inside the door to the left."

"Okay, then. Stand back." He rushed into the apartment, flipping the switch as he went, and promptly tripped over an overturned end table.

Sophie peeked around the open door, and her breath caught in her throat. Her apartment was in shambles. Overturned furniture, gaping drawers, papers strewn all about. She hugged the orange and white spotted cat closer and said to him, "Oh, Romeo, what happened here?"

Hugh answered as he climbed to his feet. "I'm no expert, but it looks as if someone was searching for something."

"What could someone want so badly they would do this?"

He shrugged. "Money. Electronics. Jewelry. Anything of value really."

At the mention of "jewelry," she touched the medallion hanging from the chain around her neck. Realizing the barrister's gaze had followed the direction of her hand, she quickly lowered it.

"I'll check the rest of the flat to make certain the person who did this is gone," he said. "You should phone the police."

In a daze, Sophie nodded and dialed 999 on her mobile.

The police took their time getting there. She waited a good forty-five minutes for them, but they made short work of their investigation. After determining nothing of value had been taken, they blamed the break-in on "teenage pranksters" and advised Sophie to install a stronger lock on her door.

Now, she sat alone on a chair in the center of her ruined living room, cuddling her cat. "Why would someone do this, Romeo?" she muttered into the top of the feline's soft, furry head.

Hugh knocked lightly on the opened door making her jump. Romeo leaped out of her arms and dove under the still-upturned couch.

"Sorry for startling you," he said. "I fetched your things from the hall."

"Thank you." Sophie rose to take the stack of letters and the luggage from him. She gestured toward the chair. "You're welcome to sit."

"No, thanks. I have an early day tomorrow." "Oh, I'm sorry for keeping you up." "It's not your fault. I'm glad I could help. The police were

right, though. You should improve your locks. It appears someone managed to pick this one easily enough." He wiggled the knob. "Bolt it from the inside before you go to sleep."

Sophie wrapped her arms around herself and shivered at the thought of trying to sleep alone after all of this.

"Is there someone you could call to stay with you?"

She thought of Andrew and then immediately dismissed the idea. "No. I'll be fine. Thank you again, Hugh."

He grinned and nodded once. "Right. Good night, then."

"Good night." After bolting the door behind him, Sophie sat down to flip through the post. A big yawn stretched her mouth to its limits, but she didn't bother to cover it. One envelope caught her eye and she stopped on it. She knew her father's sloppy, slanted handwriting well. The letter was postmarked from Mexico City. In all the excitement, she had nearly forgotten about the texts.

The back flap of the letter was unsealed, as if it hadn't been fastened securely in the first place. Eager to read the letter, she dismissed the unusualness of this.

Hiya Ladybug,

I need you to send that family heirloom to me at the address below ASAP. I can't stress enough how important it is that you not tell anybody about this. In fact, destroy this letter as soon as you FedEx the medallion to me. Sorry for all of this cloak-and-dagger stuff, sweetheart, but the medallion is an extremely valuable artifact.

Hey, sorry to hear your engagement was called off. He wasn't good enough for you anyway. As your father, I might be biased, though.

Hugs and kisses, Mitch

The address listed at the bottom of the page was for a resort hotel in Miami, Florida. She was to mail the medallion to a guest at the hotel by the name of S. Davies.

As your father, I might be biased... That phrase raised her hackles. As her father? What did he know about being her father? Nothing. He certainly knew nothing about Andrew, who was more than good enough for her. His idiotic mistake notwithstanding. If anything, she wasn't good enough for him, but he'd wanted her anyway. Unlike her father, who'd wanted as little to do with her as possible.

And if the medallion was so precious, why on earth would he risk sending it to her?

Hugh said it looked as if someone had been searching for something. Possibly jewelry, and yet, they hadn't taken her diamond-studded earrings or emerald necklace. Could they have been searching for something much more valuable? Like the medallion? She pulled it out from beneath her navy blue blouse and studied it closely. Random letters were etched into an outer circle, while the inner circle displayed four images separated by a plus symbol: a sun, a moon, three little stars, and a crown. It might have been made of real silver as it was a bit heavy, but she couldn't see anything special about it other than the fact that it was very old.

If the people who wrecked her home were looking for the medallion, would they come back?

Her cat emerged from beneath the overturned couch and rubbed against her leg.

"How dare he put me in danger, Romeo?" she said to him. The cat froze, unsure if he needed to hide again. Sophie bent to pick him up and cuddled him on her lap though he was still uncertain if he wanted to be there. "Fool that I am, I was thrilled to have something that belonged to my father, even if it was only for a little while. I hadn't stopped to think he might be using me. Hugs and kisses my arse! He was just trying to emotionally manipulate me into helping him with whatever dangerous—and undoubtedly illegal—scheme he's involved in."

Her life was in turmoil because of her father. The discontent she'd felt in recent months. The longing for something unknown. It was all rooted in her past. She had so many unanswered questions. Questions she was afraid to ask her mother. Questions her mother would probably never answer even if Sophie was brave enough to ask them.

She grabbed the letter off the floor, where it had landed when she scooped up the cat. Romeo emitted an unhappy mewling sound and made his escape. Sophie stood up and started pacing the disaster zone that was her living room and reread the bottom of the letter.

"He's using my name as an alias, the bastard. He wants me to mail the medallion to a hotel in Miami, so he can retrieve it and be off on his merry way. Like hell, he is."

Sophie had twenty-six years of questions that needed answers. For the first time in her life, she had an address. She could write to him. She could reply to two decades' worth of letters, but why write when she could finally confront her father face-to-face?